HEGEMONY AT DALOU

FIRST CENTURION KOSNETT
BOOK 3

BLAZE WARD

KNOTTED ROAD PRESS

Hegemony at Dalou
First Centurion Kosnett, Book 3
Blaze Ward
Copyright © 2022 Blaze Ward
All rights reserved
Published by Knotted Road Press
www.KnottedRoadPress.com

ISBN: 978-1-64470-258-1

Cover art:
ID 71484287 © Luca Oleastri | Dreamstime.com

Cover and interior design copyright © 2022 Knotted Road Press

Reviews
It's true. Reviews help. Even a short one, such as, "Loved it!" So please consider reviewing this book (and all of the ones you've read) on your favorite retailer site.

Never miss a release!
If you'd like to be notified of new releases, sign up for my newsletter.

http://www.blazeward.com/newsletter/

Buy More!
Did you know that you can buy directly from my website?

https://www.blazeward.com/shop/

First Centurion Kosnett

Encounter at Vilahana

Consensus at Aditi

Hegemony at Dalou

Princes at Ewin

Empire at Gloran

Domain at Yaumgan

The Jessica Keller Chronicles

Auberon

Queen of the Pirates

Last of the Immortals

Goddess of War

Flight of the Blackbird

The Red Admiral

St. Legier

Winterhome

Petron

CS-405

Queen Anne's Revenge

Packmule

Persephone

Shadow of the Dominion

Longshot Hypothesis

Hard Bargain

Outermost

Dominion-427

Phoenix

Princess Rualoh

The Handsome Rob Gigs

Can't Shoot Straight Gang

Can't Shoot Straight Gang Returns

Hunting Handsome Rob

Handsome Rob, Assassin

Earth Force Sky Patrol

Birth of the Star Dragon

Flight of the Star Dragon

Call of the Star Dragon

Shadow of the Star Dragon

Trial of the Star Dragon

Hunter Bureau

Mirrors

Latency

Pleasure Model

Inhuman

PROLOGUE: KOSNETT

DATE OF THE REPUBLIC NOVEMBER 1, 411
RAN URUMCHI, MEERUT ORBIT

Phil studied the plot of nearby space from his comfortable seat in his office, just off the flag bridge. Harinder sat across the desk from him with a calm smile on her face and her own mug of coffee. Outside, the flag crew would be watching screens and talking quietly with ships of the squadron, as well as the former pirate fleet that had remained at *Meerut*. Some had tried to flee that day, six weeks ago, and been shattered as a result.

Phil hadn't been kidding when he ordered them to surrender or die. He wasn't kidding now. Anyone threatening this system got to deal with him directly, in one of his less-friendly moods.

The last six weeks had been a whirlwind, and he was working his ass off even more than before, constantly juggling balls to keep things from falling. Even his birthday party this year had been a political event, falling just two weeks after he'd conquered *Meerut* and captured or destroyed all the pirates who had needed killing.

Craziness, piled on craziness.

Jessica Keller might have gone deep enough—crazy enough—into her contingency planning to handle a situation like this. He'd seen her do things like that.

Phil hadn't, in his wildest imagination, come up with a scenario where he ended up Governor-General of a former pirate colony. But he was here, and he was damned well going to make the best of it.

Vilahana had come somewhat close, but he'd gone in there prepared to eventually negotiate a treaty allowing a forward *RAN* base from which freighters on that long sail to and from *Aquitaine* or *Fribourg* space could be protected. He might yet, too, depending on how things went in here, as *Vilahana* was as neutral as any former chop shop might get.

Meerut, on the other hand, was back in a pocket, closed off all the way around save for that long lateral sail through realspace to the edge of that bizarre gravity-well-lagoon effect the twin blue giants created.

"What's the latest news?" he finally asked, reaching for his coffee mug.

Harinder would outwait him. That was why he'd hired her.

"*Viking* is back," Harinder said with a cryptic smile on her face. "Popped up about an hour ago and is sailing sedately over, with a shuttle to follow. That's why I came in, but you looked like you needed a few more minutes of meditation before the next emergency."

"I do," Phil replied. "But the candle is always burning. We've been gone for just over thirteen months now, and there is still so much to do in the two years I have left before the next First Lord decides what to do with us."

"You think it will be anybody but Whughy?" she asked.

"Ninety-five percent sure he gets the job, based on regular updates that Pet Naoumov sends me," Phil said. "At the end of the day, however, the Senate still makes the final call, so stranger things might happen."

"Would they recall us?" Harinder asked.

"More concerned that they might decide to send a warfleet out here, considering some of our adventures," Phil grimaced. "Especially when they hear about *Meerut.*"

"Would that be bad?"

"It threatens the extremely delicate balance of powers and personalities that make up the Balhee Cluster," he said. "We're already big enough, but I've told everyone who would listen that we're a survey expedition, not a conquering fleet. Even if we are powerful enough to threaten anyone we want. If *RAN Kongō* shows up, with Raizō Tanaka in command and an Expeditionary-class battle fleet with him, we blow all that up and start from scratch, possibly unifying everyone in here against us in the process."

"Including *Aditi*?" Harinder pressed.

"They probably crystallize on *Aditi*," he laughed. "Like making rock candy in boiling water. Even *Yaumgan* would join them to keep the invaders out."

"You've told the First Lord all this?" she asked.

"Every message home suggests more merchants, more Fast Clippers to haul supplies, and more ambassadors, but no warships."

"What about *Meerut*?"

"That's the wildcard." Phil leaned back in his chair and drank more coffee. "They need forces in here to keep *Ewin* and *Dalou* at bay. If they were smart, they would take the five surviving platforms and drag them across realspace to sit on the inner edge of the lagoon as a defensive measure. Sacrifice that throat, since everybody understands now how to sail around such a thing, but those five platforms couldn't be easily surprised or taken now, unless someone puts an entire sector fleet on the task."

"And all the pirates?" Harinder asked. "Excuse me. Former pirates."

"By now, the smart ones realize that this is the only home they ever get to claim," Phil said. "They'll become a local fleet, but those are frigate and corvette-scale ships. Even *Tango* and *Blade of Kunke* are barely light cruisers as we would weigh them.

They will need us, at least until such time as *Dalou* and *Ewin* sign a treaty they intend to honor."

"Whether they like it or not?"

"That's why our next stop has to be *Ellariel*," Phil said. "I need to have a long, personal conversation with the Shogun of *Dalou* about the future. Makara Omarov and that Imperial Inspector, Samnang Sobol, will factor in, but everything starts there."

"What if he or the Dukes of *Ewin* don't listen to reason?" she asked.

"There's always *Kongō*," Phil said.

MEERUT

ONE

Heather watched Barnaby Silver, Command Centurion of *Viking*, as the man settled. He was not a poker player, so she could see the barely-contained excitement on his face. Next to him, his Science Officer, Sunan Bunnag, was much more calm and phlegmatic, but Heather wasn't fooled there, either.

They had *news*.

Phil had called them all down to a small conference room, not even his flag bridge. And limited the players. Him and Harinder. Barnaby and Sunan. Heather had brought both Iveta, her First Officer, and Leyla, her own Science Officer. Not even aides, past Markus, who went everywhere Phil did.

That was it.

"Spill, you pirate," Phil growled at the man in a friendly voice as everyone settled.

Interestingly, Barnaby turned to Sunan and gestured for her to talk.

She scowled at her commander then sighed. Heather suspected a barely-suppressed eyeroll.

"It can be done," Sunan announced.

Everyone made a sound, a grumble, a comment. It took Phil slamming his hand on the table to get them to shut up.

Dead silence. Phil smiled.

"So the whole Balhee Cluster, as near as anyone can guess, started as an enormous stellar nebula about a billion years ago, give or take," Sunan continued. "Maybe a part of one of the galactic arms that got pinched off at some point and twisted in on itself. We'd need different gear and a couple of years of exploring to really understand it, and that's not relevant to this."

She paused, but nobody interrupted. Phil nodded again.

"Early supernovae, almost mega-nova monsters, blasted big holes in the center of the cloud," Sunan said. "Shockwaves pushed materials outward like soap bubbles. That formed what we think of as the outer skin of the Cluster. Mostly solid."

"Mostly," Phil noted.

Sunan nodded now.

"*Meerut* was the sign, if anybody had been willing enough and maybe crazy enough to try what we did," she said, turning back to Barnaby.

He grinned.

"There is another reef out the back," the man said.

Again, the explosion of noise and disbelief.

"Has anybody else found it?" Phil asked. "My conversations with Captain Omarov, that first time, suggested that thin spots in the outer walls weren't common, but weren't impossible, either."

"I highly doubt that anybody other than us has ever had the patience," Barnaby replied. "Given time, we might drop down into realspace a few times, but I have concerns about our ability to get back out again, so we haven't, as yet."

"Get back out again?" Heather leaned in to ask.

"We're used to nice, clean edges of gravity wells," Sunan spoke up. "Planets and things dimple space/time. You can navigate by them, and they also force you out of JumpSpace when you get too close. Keller used to use that as a weapon."

"I remember," Heather reminded them.

She'd been there with *The Expedition.* Not many folks here could say that.

"That space out there is a complicated swirl of smaller dimples," Sunan said. "If your JumpDrives aren't as good and as powerful as ours, I'm not sure you could surf that mess. But yes, there is a pathway we found that allows someone to sail directly to the outside of the Cluster from here. Eventually, you'll want to put an outpost or base out there, but for now, I'm not worried about anybody else using it except us."

"Can we make the sailing easier?" Phil asked.

"Dunno, First Centurion," Sunan replied. "There are a few spots where we had to go inertial, because the scanners were just a white noise of ugliness. I suppose we could build something, but I'm not sure how."

"Markus," he said, gesturing the man close.

Heather watched Dunklin rise from the chair by the door, step close, and even come more or less to attention. More or less.

"This woman needs a redneck," Phil instructed him. "Assemble a team to build a detector, based on her scan logs. I need a ship to be able to turn it on, read all that craziness, and navigate it, preferably at high speed."

"I have some names," Dunklin replied, just like that.

But Dunklin was extremely competent as a redneck. He was just quiet most of the time.

At the same time, Heather had served with him during *The Pirate Raid.* She even remembered the grenade launcher he'd designed and built for attacking enemies during a boarding action, though they'd never ended up using it.

"I can get my own coffee for a couple of days," Phil told him. "You grab your folks and ride home with Barnaby and Sunan. Top Secret, this team only until I say otherwise."

"All ten, First Centurion," Markus grinned, holding up both hands.

As long as he had ten fingers, he was allowed to keep

working for Phil. If he blew one off doing something stupid, he got transferred back to engineering again.

No greater threat in the galaxy for that man, than to be left out of all the fun.

Phil took a deep breath and nodded. He scanned the room.

"Our next step is the *Dalou Hegemony*," he reminded them. "As that means *Urumchi* and most of the escorts, *Viking* will remain on station here while we're gone. *CM-507* can be put to use building mine fields wherever you want them. I've already made a few suggestions to Isabèl Pan, and she's busy supervising a local factory to build a whole bunch."

"Are we expecting an attack?" Heather asked.

Beside her, Iveta practically squirmed.

"*Dalou* already knows we're coming to talk, so I doubt that they would do something that stupid," Phil replied. "However, nobody has ever accused the *Ewin Principalities* of being bright or organized. There is a chance some Duke or Count tells the King to get stuffed and leads a squadron here to either earn some glory or maybe try to capture the system and extend their treaty boundaries."

"Do we allow that?" Iveta asked in a cold, hard voice.

People had taken to calling her *Junkyard*, like they occasionally called Heather *Ground Control*. *Junkyard Bitch* was the full title, like she'd called herself during the battle for *Meerut*, but it was a term of respect, not a curse or an insult. After that day, she'd earned it.

"If they try, I will expect all these little Pickets and Raiders to give good testimony," Phil replied. "*Viking* will as well, with *505* and *507*. If I have to, I will destroy *Ewin*'s ability to threaten their neighbors, just to make my point. However, I will remind everyone that they are a missile-happy bunch. That worked last year. Everyone is now furiously looking to rebuild their fleets. We have a few years before new warships come on line that they think will be good enough. I would rather not make enemies here. However, I have declared *Meerut* independent. You folks will enforce my will if it comes to that."

Heather nodded.

Don't throw the first punch. Always throw the last one.

About as simple as this kind of diplomacy got.

"Questions?" Phil asked.

"How soon do you want to depart?" Heather responded.

"With *Viking* back, I think we can give everyone twenty-four hours' notice from the end of this meeting," he said. "Are they all wanting to travel with us?"

"*Khandoba* and her Moat escorts have departed for *Aditi* proper, and I don't expect them back," Heather said. "*Aranyani* will represent Aditi for now. Similarly, the *Yaumgan* Battleship *Zhang Guolao* has headed home to brief their folks, leaving the Skycruiser *Li Jing* to travel with us. *Morninghawk* remained with us, so we sent word aboard a friendly Picket boat instead. *Shadowbolt* ran for home like demons were chasing them, but they are back, and didn't bring anybody else, so I think they've been somewhat cowed, at least for now."

"For now," Phil agreed. "I expect we'll have to deal with them after *Dalou*, but Captain Omarov on *Morninghawk* gives us an opening into the Shogunate that we need to exploit while we can. Heather, let everyone know we're departing tomorrow."

"You got it," she replied.

She found herself looking forward to the trip, after reading so much history of Japan's transition from feudal to industrial in a single generation, back on *Earth*. She doubted that history would repeat itself, mostly because those folks had to have read some of the old books.

Or had they? The Librarian at *Alexandria Station* had only been rescued by Doyle Iwakuma eleven hundred years ago. Trade and communication between *Aquitaine* and the Cluster happened, but rarely and in small amounts, due to the distances involved.

Maybe they didn't know about how the Shoguns had grown

ossified and inward-seeking. How many of the clans, that had been on the losing side centuries before, wanted to be eligible for power.

How corrupt and mismanaged the economy had grown.

How brittle.

Urumchi was one hell of a wind out of the east, if your feet weren't sure.

TWO

HEAVY ESCORT MORNINGHAWK

For once in his life, Captain Makara Omarov was not looking forward to returning home to Dalou.

Oh, some would treat him like a hero. That much was certain. Others, however, would wonder what the fourth son of a minor lord of a Komyo, one of the smaller clans, would do with his newfound notoriety.

Makara didn't figure that going back to where he'd been a year ago would ever be an option again.

More than once, he'd damned himself for a fool for not leaving *Vilahana* immediately when Kosnett had arrived and settled down. But he'd been too much a patriot. There had been no other *Dalou* ships in-system that day, so it had become Morninghawk's task—his duty—to learn as much as he could about the aliens for the Shogun.

Certainly, Makara had no doubt that his various reports had been read at the highest levels, parsed for every syllable and comma he had chosen to include, looking for some deeper meaning and the possibility of revolution.

It didn't help that revolution was the only thing likely to save the *Dalou Hegemony* from imploding, sometime in the next few years. New technology from the east practically demanded it. *Aquitaine* had beam weapons capable of eliminating firebirds as a viable threat. All of those weapons, even the biggest condors usually only found on battleships and major stations.

Dalou needed that tech. Worse, they needed the social and political upheaval that would come with designing and building an entirely new kind of star fleet.

Anything less and they risked becoming irrelevant. Watching helplessly as *Aditi* and *Yaumgan* leapt forward into a new future that didn't see *Dalou* as anything but a bit player, relegated to the fringes.

Much like *Ewin* frequently was already.

Today, he was on his bridge. Rinat Keo, his Second-in-Command, and Shamil Bulat, generally Third, were both aft, handling all the myriad tasks you need to check just before a flight.

The trip to *Ellariel* wouldn't take long, even stopping at *Ishiokoh*-jo in the *Serelye* Sector, where they would rendezvous with *Wraithruin* and his oldest brother Darra transporting Father, while his other brothers, along with their cruisers *Kestrel* and *Wraithhawk*, remained safely at a distance and didn't threaten anyone.

Even surrounded by the *Ellariel Home Fleet*, the Shogun would be nervous, with many overpowered *Aquitaine* ships moored nearby.

The main hatch opened beside him and Makara glanced over. It was like he could already smell her scent approaching.

Samnang Sobol. Imperial Inspector, representing the Shogun and authorized to speak in his name.

Wonder of all wonders, she hadn't ordered him imprisoned or executed yet.

He wondered if she would be sharing whatever fate awaited him when they got to the Shogun's court.

She entered, and came to rest. Not quite standing at attention, but obviously wanting him to notice her.

Makara looked around. Emar Tangan was handling navigation right now.

"Emar, you're in charge until Rinat or Shamil return," he announced. "If *Urumchi* sends orders, assume they came from me and do what they tell you. Then log it later. Understood?"

"Aye, sir," Emar replied.

Makara rose and turned to Inspector Sobol.

She had such a big personality that he was always surprised how much he towered over her as he stepped close. But then, Makara was even taller than Kosnett, though at the same time he somehow managed to be both broad-shouldered and lanky, like a sail being pushed by the wind, while the First Centurion gave the impression of an ancient oak tree.

Sobol was twenty-five centimeters shorter. Average height for a woman. Lean and muscular, but she trained with two swords at a fanatic's level. Black hair. Hard, black eyes.

She claimed to be an ally. To have been seduced by one Makara Omarov and his commitment to honor and patriotism. They had even kissed, exactly three times.

For the last six weeks, he'd kept a polite distance from the woman, uncertain what it meant and unwilling to get physically or emotionally engaged with her.

At some point, he would have to stand alone before the Shogun and explain himself. Sobol had sworn that she would stand beside him. Makara had his doubts that she would be allowed.

"My office?" he asked as he loomed over the woman.

She looked up without any trepidation. Nothing intimidated this woman.

Sobol nodded and stepped back. He followed her out the hatch and down the main corridor, allowing her to enter first before joining.

Previously, he had gone to sit in the far chair on this side of the desk, where they had sat too close together and spoken of things normally forbidden.

That was one more thing than he felt he could handle today. As she took that far seat, he sat on the side of his desk, not even in the nearer chair. Out of reach, as it were.

Her knowing smile didn't help.

"We will depart in eleven hours?" Sobol asked.

"According to the schedule from *Urumchi*," he agreed, unwilling to cede any ground.

She might be madly in love with him, or at least his ideals. And she might be waiting to get him home to denounce him in a complicated betrayal.

Dalou politics rarely made sense to an outsider. Some vendettas were centuries in playing out, though he had not been able to research any allies or relatives of the woman that his Omarov family or the Sugawara clan he belonged to had previously insulted or harmed.

Which just meant that it might not have been written down in the right places.

She studied his face.

"What do you expect when we return home?" she asked.

"First Centurion Kosnett, with your approval, intends to award me the Republic Cross of the *Republic of Aquitaine* Navy," Makara replied.

"And?" she prompted.

Makara stared at her hard for a long moment.

"And that I will make many friends and enemies when I tell those people that our way of life must change, and do so quickly, if we wish to survive as a free nation," he continued. "What no one can tell me—including you—is what position the Shogun will take. By now, they have read my reports up to and including the battle, as well as the evolving social outcomes of allowing the pirates to survive."

She nodded, as if expecting those words. This was not the first time they had chewed on this particular bone.

"As we do not even colonize all the worlds we claim, I do not imagine that *Meerut* will cause that much consternation on our side of the border," she said. "*Ewin* is a different matter. They will eventually try something."

"Should we ally ourselves with the former pirates?" Makara asked. "I am but a lowly ship captain of a mere Heavy Escort, but *you* might be able to negotiate such a treaty."

"There have been discussions," she replied.

Makara nearly fell off his perch. That had been a throwaway line on his part. She had been quietly in communication? With whom?

Something of his surprise obviously showed on his face, because her smile became knowing and almost predatory now.

"Yes," she agreed. "It is not a treaty. At the same time, it is more than a mere understanding. We will carry a letter from Governor Dexter to the Shogun, laying out his hopes for increased trade and friendship, while they make promises to behave, and possibly to request sales of military goods at a later date."

"*Dalou* yards already turn out warships that show up on the secondary market in remarkably good shape," he breathed now.

"Almost new, as it were, Makara," she agreed. "I have heard that you went to *Vilahana* in the first place looking for old hulls that might be reconditioned and returned to service, amongst all the detritus of those orbital junk yards."

"*Gloran* has a significant portion of their fleet that seem to follow *Dalou* design lines," he offered obliquely. "I had always assumed that they stole our plans and built them. Or that some pirate yard somewhere was doing the same. Is there something more ominous?"

She scowled, as if taking his measure. They were far past fellow-travelers at this point. She might hang with him.

"The Shogun has been quietly selling *Gloran* and various of the pirate syndicates new or old hulls for some time," she admitted. "That includes at least a half-dozen such vessels within hailing distance, having done my research."

Again, he nearly fell off the edge of his desk in his surprise.

Makara thought he had always understood politics. A man in his position had to. At the same time, he was playing in a whole new arena now.

That she was willing to say these things to him damned him irrevocably.

Or rescued him.

"Why?" Makara forced himself to ask.

"*Aditi* would like to think of themselves as the most powerful nation in the Cluster," she replied. "Certainly, their central location means that they can play off all the other players. The pirates are best thought of as a leech, sucking blood from the *Consensus* on a regular and on-going basis, bleeding them of the strength that might have allowed them to expand militarily."

"Because they already do so with trade stations and agreements," Makara nodded. "Deals with some of the pirates to help, while fighting with others."

"A grand, sloppy mess, politically," she agreed.

"What happens without the pirates?" he asked.

"The *Aditi Consensus* just might be able to grow large enough, powerful enough, to become a threat to the rest of us," she nodded. "Especially as they will have no compunctions about using *Aquitaine* technology to do so. That is why the Shogun needs you. And why I need you."

"You?" he asked, still surprised whenever this hard, cold woman suddenly shifted over from the *professional* to the *personal.*

"There will be changes in the power structure of *Dalou*, Makara," she said. "Have no doubts about that. I want more power than a mere Imperial Inspector might achieve. More wealth. More glory. Our culture rarely allows women into positions of authority, except as they might marry or inherit it. That needs to change also."

"You've been speaking to Heather and Iveta," he realized. "Their First Lord of the Fleet is also a woman."

"The greatest hero in the history of *Aquitaine* civilization, after Henri Baudin himself, is a woman," Sobol nodded. "Jessica Keller. Almost a Goddess of War, to hear them speak of her. If you and I are to remake *Dalou* culture into a new thing, we need to be dreaming far beyond merely building a few new ships and hoping it will be enough to save us."

"We?"

"We," she said.

He considered it. Considered her. An attractive woman. Brilliant and merciless as well, but also an exceptional dinner conversationalist.

She held out a hand for him to take in the customary manner. Makara grasped it instead and pulled her to her feet, even as he did the same.

They ended up dancing, as it were, pressed against one another, in ways highly improper for two officers. Samnang Sobol seemed to be inviting a fourth kiss.

He took advantage of it.

What better way to seal a conspiracy?

THREE

YAUMGAN SKYCRUISER LI JING

Stunt Dude considered the scene theatrically. Occupational hazard, even two decades later.

Where he would have put the cameras. Which shots. Which zooms. This time, however, it would be a close, cozy scene.

Previously, there had been big dinner parties, including any number of folks from the *RAN* and even a few from the planet below. Tonight, it was just him, Sam, and Captain Xue Dao Zhiou, down in the officers' wardroom of *Li Jing*, in a side room that had been reserved.

Dao Zhiou sat closest to the door. *Stunt Dude* was across from her. His wife Sam was on the woman's left. Dinner had been fantastic, as the chefs had gone all out. The dessert plates were empty of the little pastry tarts that had capped a perfect meal.

Everyone was having tea of some sort. The *Yaumgan* Domain didn't grow coffee on any of their worlds. At least not yet. Surely, there were places somewhere that you could, with six primary planets to work with.

Tea was a cultural thing.

"So you don't mind much if I steal him for a little longer?" Dao Zhiou asked Sam. The two women were holding hands like old friends, even though they'd only been introduced a few months ago.

"I'm only a little jealous that he gets to go off and have adventures, and I'd be aboard *Urumchi* instead," Sam grinned back at the woman.

"I could ask the First Centurion to let me borrow you, too," Dao said with a grin. "At least for the flight to *Ellariel*. Would he go for it?"

Both of them looked at *Stunt Dude* now. He'd served with Phil in the old days, as his Dragoon aboard *CS-405* in the third greatest adventure of all time. This expedition only came in second.

Finding Sam was still bestest.

"I will ask, if you would like me to," he said to Sam. "Your staff are good enough. And you've got all the escorts if they need more medical staff for something."

"I'd swap one of my junior medical staff," Dao offered. "They won't know your technology at all, but people are people when it comes to illness and healing."

"That would probably make it palatable," he said. "Phil is all about cultural exchanges, whenever he can arrange it."

"You folks are weird that way," Dao nodded.

"Says the woman whose entire culture hides behind mystique and vague threats of doom to keep outsiders from bothering them," he teased now.

Stunt Dude had spent enough time with this crew to have almost become one of them. All his experiences behind enemy lines—both times, even—helped him slip comfortably into any social situation quickly. That included serving as a liaison/ambassador to a *Yaumgan* warship attached to Phil's squadron for his war on the pirates.

Dao laughed. *Yaumgan* were outsiders in the Cluster, having arrived from farther galactic west on a standard map. Much closer to *Earth*, but not directly. They had arrived centuries ago, conquered one planet, expanded to six, and drawn a hard line in the sand there, only allowing a handful of independent merchants to trade on their worlds. On *Yaumgan's* terms.

"True," Dao agreed. "But it has worked, to date. At least until the First Centurion arrived and got the philosopher-kings back home all a-lather with excitement and maybe a touch of dread."

"I would really like to be aboard the first Skycruiser you send to *Ladaux*," *Stunt Dude* laughed back. "Just to watch folk's faces when they realize that it really is a giant fighting robot, like some child's cartoon. Or worse, when the whole thing lands on the surface and stands there."

"We might do that for a reason, you know," Dao grinned.

"Why, though?" Sam asked now. "I understand the secrecy, but in the *Holding of Man*, everything was radically different. What cultural inferiority complex drives you to build such ships?"

Stunt Dude blinked hard. Dao did as well.

Had nobody ever asked that question? *Yaumgan* was taken as a given. What really made them tick?

What did they fear?

Dao opened her mouth to speak, then closed it.

"I'm sorry," Sam said, squeezing her hand. "That's not a question for outsiders to ask."

"No, it's okay," Dao spoke, her voice suddenly rough with various emotions. "I've never heard it phrased that way, but it makes perfect sense. I don't know the answer."

"Fear of those you left behind finally tracking you down?" *Stunt Dude* asked. "I have a lot of experience behind enemy lines, as it were, looking over my shoulder."

"That may play a role," Dao replied. "Certainly, the mystique element cannot be overlooked as well. Nor the single great hero who rides into town at the beginning of the story. That is an *Aquitaine* thing, and *Dalou* to a lesser degree. *Yaumgan*—and the *Aditi Consensus*—are more keyed in on a small band of adventurers. A team of heroes, if you will, righting wrongs."

"But to most outsiders, your ships would immediately bring to mind the samurai cowboy archetype," he pointed out. "Even if it is not truly representative. We've spoken of this."

"We have, Trinidad," Dao nodded. "It was the other part of Sam's question. What do we fear that drives us to behave this way? I don't know. Our culture simply is. Now, I need to reach out to some true philosophers to ask."

"Find a historian," Sam urged. "The culture will have already absorbed it by the time a philosopher speaks. The historian will be able to tell you when it happened."

"Yes, you are entirely correct," Dao agreed. "All the more reason why you, Sam, should travel with us to *Ellariel*. *Stunt Dude*, go convince Kosnett."

He grinned at her order. He could ask Phil for a favor and probably get it, especially if Dao offered a trade.

But he found himself intrigued in ways he hadn't felt since his first days aboard *Li Jing*.

What did *Yaumgan* fear?

FOUR

DATE OF THE REPUBLIC NOVEMBER 2, 411
RAN VIKING, MEERUT ORBIT

Markus stared at all the faces around the small auditorium, gathered here to listen to his speech. He had spent enough time around folks like *Fribourg*, or even back in *Buran*, to understand just how weird it would be for most places to find a mere Yeoman giving orders to Chiefs, to say nothing of Centurions and Senior Centurions.

That was the *Aquitaine* way. Someone was put in charge. In this case, by Phil. That came with responsibility, and everyone else fell in until such time as they evolved patterns. That was another *Aquitaine* thing.

Always learning. Always moving forward. Keller had taught the entire galaxy that.

Markus had actually met the woman once. Been awarded a medal by her along with the other pirates. Physically small. Culturally so big that she cast a shadow clear the hell over here.

The Queen of the Pirates would have been right at home with all these folk. And all their neighbors. Until she needed to kick all their asses.

"So that's where we're at," he concluded, nodding over to Senior Centurion Bunnag. "*Viking's* Science Officer needs us to build her a better control system for her arrays. I haven't been

25

inside a Baudin Detector in years, so I can't tell you what it needs to do, but we're all familiar with his original concept of a tuning fork that harmonizes with nearby space. How do we make it better?"

Viking's Chief Engineer, Kealoha Nogueira, sat next to Bunnag, scowling with concentration. Across from her, Machinist Chief Claire Steele was actually smiling, but she was another crazy-ass redneck like Markus. Ten fingers just meant you were lucky in this game.

Markus had disqualified a couple of folks without ten from this team, purely on those standards. They might have argued that they'd used up all their bad luck, but Markus was convinced that it was a contagion kind of thing.

Better not to have it in the room at all.

"What are our limits?" Steele asked now.

"Materials in squadron," Markus nodded back. "If we end up asking the locals for any kind of parts, they might figure out what we're up to, and the First Centurion wants to keep this a secret for as long as possible."

"Timeline?" Nogueira pursued.

"I'm detached from *Urumchi* for now and staying on *Viking,*" Markus reminded them. "I'd like to get back before someone else figures out exactly how Phil likes his coffee, so nobody ends up stealing my job when I'm not looking."

That got a round of laughs. *Stunt Dude* had taught Markus the way to put people at ease in situations like this. *The importance of not being important,* he'd called it.

"Sunan, would you like to start us off?" Markus asked the Science Officer now.

She rose and he sat. There were a dozen folks in here. Most of them had only now gotten his take on things, plus whatever rumors and tidbits had floated about previously.

"We were tasked with finding a back door into *Meerut* from outside the Cluster," she began. "In that, we were mostly successful, but getting there is pretty much limited to somebody with Survey-quality sensors right now. *Viking* and *Urumchi*. None of the corvettes. The problem is that all those various gravity wells are pulsing off each other constantly, because those big stars are so close together. At night, it never actually gets dark on the surface of the planet, like summer at extreme latitudes."

"How much deadsailing are we allowed?" someone asked from the back.

"Preferably none," Markus spoke up. "From what I understand, none of the cluster walls are actually impenetrable in realspace, but crossing that way can take months or years, even at high speed. We need to do as much of this in Jump as possible. *Viking* has a way, just not an easy one."

"I've got a silly question," Steele smiled. "We're in the wall of the cluster here, which is why we think it's thinner. Is there a backdoor in and out of neighboring space, getting you inside the cluster?"

Markus blinked in surprise. Turned to Sunan, who was just as off keel with that question.

"I'll put some of my folks onto reviewing the charts," she said.

"Is there a way to predict them?" Markus asked the room, even as he was staring at her. "Astronomy and mathematics and whatever else to know where they should be?"

Mic drop. The whole room went silent. Mouths opened in his direction.

On the one hand, that was probably why Phil had put him in charge here. On the other, that meant that he probably didn't have the right team. Or maybe he needed to start a second team of pure scientists?

"You know, we've never been in a situation like this," Sunan replied. "Maybe we need some folks off *CM-507*?"

"I'll ask when we're done here, but somebody needs to spell out what skillsets they think that would be. I weld shit."

The two Senior Centurions nodded and put their heads

together quietly while he watched. At least all that Academy training would come in handy.

"Chief," he said now, turning to Steele, "you're in charge of rednecking me some thoughts on new or better sensors that we can test now and install on other ships later. Anybody else got any questions before we break up and start to work?"

Markus looked around. He could already see the teams starting to break into theoretical folks and mechanical folks. That was fine. He'd ride herd over all of them for a while, then get the hell out of their way when they had an idea to test.

Then he could get back to the First Centurion and turn into the coffee boy again.

ISHIOKOH

FIVE

Phil studied the ships presented on the big holographic projector. Sugawara had a small fleet here, mostly just to say hello, as this was an Omarov world. *Wraithruin*, *Kestrel*, and *Wraithhawk* were closest to the station, with others generally a quarter of the way around the planet.

Everyone was behaving themselves today, which was good. If they wanted to get aggressive, he didn't have enough firepower to do more than defend himself while fleeing to the safety of JumpSpace.

At which point he might bring *Kongō* back later, along with a few dozen of his friends.

Phil still remembered a day spent facing down an Imperial Grand Fleet with nothing but a handful of desperately outclassed older ships. Arlo could have stomped him and his into the mud so quickly that they might not have worked up a sweat.

Dalou was still something of a stranger, but Phil was certain that the Imperial Inspector on *Morninghawk* had enough authority to make the locals behave. Even had they been less friendly.

"Where's the shuttle?" he asked Harinder.

"About thirty minutes out," she replied. "Last note said that they had a last minute hiccup in protocol."

"Oh?"

"Lord Sugawara decided to join Lingyi Omarov after all," she smiled. "Highly unusual for them, as Omarov is something of a planetary governor as they rate such things, so technically he would be your peer. Sugawara himself would be an overlord as head of the extended clan, and thus would not normally deign to call upon foreign barbarians."

She was grinning. Phil grinned back at her.

Barbarism was in the eye of the beholder. Still, if the man was coming here, perhaps he saw the need to make a personal connection with Phil, rather than the formal audience that would be arranged when everyone got to *Ellariel*.

Makara Omarov had, after all, displayed such courage and valor that Phil had no qualms awarding him a Republic Cross. Whether or not the Senate later decided to upgrade it to the Legion of Valor would be a political thing. Probably contingent on what happened at the Shogun's Court.

"Let's take it up a notch, then," Phil decided. "You, me, and Heather in full dress uniforms for this. Have the wardroom scale themselves up a notch as well, for a visiting head of state. String quartet and all that, forward in the arboretum."

"You're cruel, Phil," she laughed.

"We are being honored by a powerful nobleman of the *Dalou Hegemony*," he reminded her. "And we need all the friends we can get."

SIX

DATE OF THE REPUBLIC NOVEMBER 6, 411
RAN URUMCHI, ISHIOKOH ORBIT

Heather didn't really like her dress uniform. Only wore it sparingly, on those occasions when protocol called for it. Too many of those in the Cluster, but every obscure planetary governor saw themselves as big-shots to be toadied to, rather than the other way around.

They were surrounded by trees now. Morninghawk's father and Lord Sugawara had been piped aboard with full honors, speeches of welcome and friendship got exchanged, and folks got to walk forward from the landing bay to the forest.

As usual, it worked on people. Trees, ponds, and birds on a starship was an exotic, rare thing.

Except that the elder Omarov apparently had something just like it aboard his station. Not as big or complex, but the man was currently deep in the weeds with Sergey Cummins, *Urumchi's* Master Gardener in charge here. Heather was just close enough to listen, and swoop in if necessary, as Sergey could be a bit of a curmudgeon.

Instead, the two were discussing cross-breeding flowers and making plans to swap seeds and cuttings.

She hated it when Phil was right. He'd get a whole other round of *I told you so* about this place before he shut up.

33

A shadow approached on her right flank. Samurai, which was just bloody weird in deep space. At least he wasn't armed. The decorative, lacquered armor was statement enough.

The man came to rest scowling at her. Probably upset when she turned and had a centimeter or so on him. Some men couldn't deal with tall women. Especially not in a culture that relegated women to wives, mothers, and mistresses.

His armor was green, laced with black. Exactly the opposite of what Makara Omarov wore today. Sugawara then, rather than Omarov.

A second figure emerged from the underbrush now. Lord Sugawara himself.

Heather smiled and bowed her head deeply and politely.

"Captain Lau," he murmured as he stepped to a friendly distance.

She didn't correct the man. Command Centurion was an *Aquitaine* thing nobody else in the modern age used.

"Lord Sugawara," she replied. "Has the reception been to your liking?"

Always the politics with the strangers. Always trying to put them at ease, with music, food, and friendliness.

Phil's repeated reminders about bulls in china shops had taken root with everyone.

"It has been," he nodded. "I sought you out to ask a question."

Heather turned more fully to face the man, ignoring the two bodyguards standing far enough away to be statues.

"I have heard the stories of *Vilahana*," he began. "Did this vessel truly push a small moon out of an impact path?"

"It did," she replied.

"How?"

Heather smiled and gestured sideways with both hands, indicating *Urumchi*.

"Power and need, Lord Sugawara," she said simply. "Had we not, *Vilahana* might have been ended as an inhabitable world, and nobody else had the technological capabilities necessary. So we did it. I presume you have seen the scan log footage?"

It was his turn to nod. She noted that the man was wearing some layer of white makeup on his face by the way he had paled beneath it, leaving his neck a darker color.

"I have not yet seen a *Dalou* Battleship," she continued. "*Urumchi* has roughly two orders of magnitude available engine power over *Morninghawk*, which I understand you classify as a heavy escort rather than a light cruiser?"

"That is correct," the man replied in a soft, hollow voice.

Heather kept her face perfectly neutral. *Wraithruin*, nearby in orbit, was supposedly a famous vessel in Sugawara history. Heavy cruiser, though they didn't classify it that way. Comparable to her old-style battlecruiser *Jellicoe*, before she'd stepped up to *Urumchi*.

Heather was willing to bet anyone a Lev that *Urumchi* was two to three times more powerful than a *Dalou* Battleship, based on *Wraithruin*'s scan this morning. *Kongō* would be five to eight times.

"At that point," she said carefully. "It was just a case of physics. One gravity well slowly falling into a second, but still susceptible to a large enough nudge, if delivered in time. The moon was instead fired out into deep space via a gravity slingshot, where it will become nothing more than a navigational hazard in the future."

Heather wondered if the man had swallowed his tongue. He certainly gulped.

"And your terrible Type-4 beams?" he followed up now, quieter than he had been. "Those would have been insufficient?"

"In the time allowed, yes," she said. "My tactical officer has since confirmed that we could have successfully carved it into smaller pieces that would have only done localized damage, rather than catastrophic, if we had been given two to three days to bombard it."

She watched the man do math in his head, in his eyes. They

had beams like that around here, but only mounted on larger stations, not even the small ones where a condor might be sufficient to chase off pirates.

Until recently, the firebird had been considered the peak of their military culture. *Buran* would have laughed themselves silly to be facing such weapons.

Right before annihilating the local forces without mercy and conquering the entire cluster in a matter of weeks. Just about as fast as those sharks could have sailed to every world with defenses, in order to destroy them.

"And you are here to trade?" he breathed.

"We are here to explore, Lord Sugawara," she corrected him carefully. "To blaze the trails that merchants and scholars might later travel in safety. Both coming as well as going. Such is the First Centurion's mission."

He fell silent. She did the same, wondering if Lord Sugawara might ever recover from the multiple, systemic shocks Phil had delivered. The elder Omarov had taken to things around here in a manner much like a duck to water, to watch him and Sergey squatting down now and pointing at various plants off the meadow where the reception was being held, one bodyguard standing painfully uncomfortably nearby.

"Thank you," Lord Sugawara finally managed.

He bowed to her and Heather returned it, deeply and formally. Hopefully, she'd just made Phil another ally, instead of frightening the man so badly that he went all in on whatever plan someone might come up with to hold on to the old days.

She watched him go and noted the concern on the faces of the nearer bodyguard.

Samurai, in the era after the Black Ships, fighting a doomed, rear-guard action against the Emperor Meiji's vision of the future.

And that future was coming, because Kosnett was far better at this than Perry ever had been.

SEVEN

AQUITAINE VESSEL URUMCHI

Makara wandered through the crowd, accepting nods and congratulations from old friends and foes alike. Deflected questions about what he would do with his future.

Morninghawk had always been all he ever wanted or expected to command.

Fourth son. Unlucky, when all sailors were superstitious to some degree.

He had kept a low profile over the last two months. First, standing patiently to one side as all the other vessels got priority on repair, then remaining behind when all those messengers went forth to the capitals, letting them know that Kosnett intended to further upset their delicate sensibilities.

Makara wondered if the man understood that having a sixth, independent star nation wouldn't last long. Either it would collapse down to five again, or it would embolden others to do the same.

Was the man using *Meerut* as a test case to break the entire cluster? Get all those thinly-aligned worlds to simply demand their freedom from whatever overlords there might be?

Vilahana didn't count, as they were just a junk yard and

chop shop, mostly dealing with pirates and other criminal elements. There were others, however, who might take notice.

More revolution in the offing.

Makara found it terribly amusing that all the important people today, including his oldest brother Darra, had bodyguards with them, Kosnett included. At the same time, Makara understood that even as small as she was, Centurion Xochitl Dar was at least the equal of the most dangerous of the visitors, so Kosnett was safe.

Makara himself had come alone, leaving Keo in charge back home, because the man was too much a practical joker for this situation. Solid other times. Deadly in combat. Goofball when confronted by the pompous. And much of what this room contained bordered on pomposity. All such receptions tended that way. Kosnett's were actually better than most.

Makara spotted Beridze standing off to one side, mug of juice in one hand and listening to the musicians play softly. She glanced at him and smiled, so he stepped close enough to speak to the woman, under the music.

"We have not really had a chance to speak," he said, referring to another such reception in the aftermath of *Meerut*.

Makara had been too emotionally fried to deal with this woman that night. Doubly so now that people had begun to whisper the name *Junkyard* in the same hushed tones they did *Ground Control*.

Beridze smiled at him without speaking, an invitation to continue.

"Before the battle, Lau suggested that nobody would have nightmares about *Morninghawk*," he continued. "You demurred."

She smiled like a predator now. It was chilling to see. She was not an unattractive woman. Dark hair worn short. Heart-shaped face and sharp eyes, if a little plain. Skin paler and more golden than common around here.

Lethal.

"Why?" he asked, when she didn't speak. "What caused you to think that *Morninghawk* would be an existential threat to the pirates of *Meerut*?"

"You intended to ram the Salvager *Wulfa*, Omarov," she spoke now. "When it became clear that they were going to try to same thing to *Urumchi*. *Morninghawk* would have been destroyed and most of your crew killed instantly. You did not hesitate."

He shrugged. The life of an Escort Captain, when such sacrifices might be called upon to protect more valuable ships or cargoes. He would have done the same had it been *Wraithruin* behind him.

"Those other captains are all good sailors," Beridze continued. "Competent. Capable. Deadly enough when the situation warrants. None of them are killers."

The way she emphasized the word seemed to rate him in a different category. A stratospheric one, perhaps, with the others on the ground below.

Makara had heard rumors and stories about this woman. How, of all the ones who styled themselves students or clones of the famous Jessica Keller, Iveta Beridze had been the one that both Lau and Kosnett selected as Tactical Officer.

Killer.

She was elevating him to stand with her on a small perch, a hawk watching rabbits feed in the grass below.

But then, *Aquitaine* didn't hold that fourth sons were unlucky, nor that eighth were luck itself. They rated you on your deeds.

And Samnang had called him the *Harbinger of Doom*.

"Sometimes killers are necessary," he offered as a deflection, uncertain if he should cede the battleground to this woman and withdraw to lick his wounds.

"Indeed, Morninghawk," she agreed. "If your elders had any sense at all, you would be commanding one of the big cruisers after this, if not a battleship. *Dalou* is ill-served with you in a

Heavy Escort, save that it put you at *Vilahana* on the right day."

Truth. He had tried to serve the Hegemony well, from his minor post. Distant cousin, quite removed, from a minor lord.

"What future do you see now?" he asked, tossing that out there to see if the woman would bite.

She might be a seer, finding things in him that he had never adequately expressed.

Until it came time to give the order to ram.

"Does *Dalou* wish to join *Aditi* and *Yaumgan* in the future?" she fired right back at him. "Or stay with *Ewin* and *Gloran* in the past?"

Well, he had asked. Damned for a fool, too, not to expect an oracle to occasionally cut you to the quick with her words.

"And the *Zen-Mekyo Syndicates?*" he asked.

In for a pfennig, in for a mark.

"Phil ended their civil war with a sledgehammer," Beridze smiled. "The rest, the ones outside, were always going to be the ones to either retire or cut a deal with someone. Assuming that all of you up-gun your fleets faster than the pirates can steal the tech, their era is over."

"Can we?" he pressed.

"*Aditi* is already in the process of designing new hulls, assuming they can buy or trade for Type-3-Pulse and Pulse-Two," the woman nodded. "I presume *Yaumgan* will as well, though they have new things supposedly never brought out of the lab and mounted on warships. *Dalou* might. *Gloran* will lag. *Ewin* is doomed to fight a civil war over those who see the future and those who refuse."

Makara found his mouth dry with implications. This woman had a reputation as a warrior, not a scholar and philosopher. And yet, she had a remarkable grasp on things for a stranger that had been here for nine months or so.

Were all *Aquitaine* officers like this? Previously, he had dealt primarily with Kosnett and Lau. Beridze was the rough peer of

Rinat Keo on *Morninghawk*, though you would never get such an analysis out of that man.

The future was about to arrive. Iveta Beridze just reinforced that in her second role as Oracle.

"Would *Aquitaine* support us in such an endeavor?" Makara asked. "Assist *Dalou* in making that transition to the future that you talk about?"

"That's why we're going to *Ellariel* next, Captain Omarov," she said with deadly intent. "*Yaumgan* invited us, as did all the others. Phil wants to talk to the Shogun, because he thinks you people have the most upside available."

It took him a moment to translate that culturally.

She meant social potential. *Aditi* was advanced, and could continue. The *Ewin Principalities* were backwards in their own way, as was the *Gloran Empire*. Nobody understood the *Yaumgan Domain*, and the *Zen-Mekyo Syndicates* were broken.

That left the *Dalou Hegemony*.

And whatever revolution he needed to ignite.

Maybe *Aquitaine* would support him, after all.

ELLARIEL-JO

EIGHT

ELLARIEL-JO ORBITAL PALACE

Jirou, Shogun of Dalou, paused in his forms as the hatch to the dojo opened and his various bodyguards moved from alertness to poised for violence. He himself stood alone on the floor, armored and bearing a dull, two-handed greatsword, sweat dripping off his body inside the shell and a cloth tied above his eyes to keep his vision clear.

Kohahu. Middle daughter. Fourteen and the most like him of the three, with elder Kokoro more of a scholar at sixteen, and the youngest, Ema, an artist at eleven. Yoshi had never given him sons, but she had given him nearly two decades of support, love, and sanctuary. Not many men could say that.

Kohahu was not armed. Nor armored. She wore simple black pants tucked into boots, with a gold half-kimono tunic over a crimson shirt. Kugosu colors, associated with the Shogunate for four generations now. Her black hair was shoulder length, but drawn up in a quick braid to keep it out of her eyes.

"Is there news?" he asked, still paused with a bared blade in his hands.

Always move with steel until you are sparring, then use bamboo that lets you strike with full power and little risk.

Kohahu bowed at the waist, centered by four bodyguards

who each outweighed her by perhaps double. He had no doubt that she could take any one of them in close combat. Jirou had seen her train.

"None, Father," she said. "I have arrived unfortunately early and disturbed your training. I would seek enlightenment when you are complete."

Formal, as a daughter should be, when facing her lord and shogun. Bold, verging on impetuous, which was why he could see her being the power behind a throne, one of these days.

He regretted that *Dalou* culture would not be able to take orders from a woman. Otherwise, she would have been able to hold the shogunate at least as well as any man he knew in the current Court.

And it wasn't like Jirou, *Second Son*, hadn't maneuvered Ichiro, *First Son*, out of contention for the Shogunate, a decade ago when their father, Kenzou, had chosen to retire to a monastery.

Jirou nodded to the girl—the young woman, as she was nearly as tall as her mother now—and centered himself again, tracking by sound as Kohahu withdrew and knelt outside the ring of his guardians.

Perhaps he moved a shade faster through the rest of the form today, but he had been doing these moves for much of his forty years now. The bones knew them, to say nothing of the muscles.

Jirou bowed to the space where his teacher had once watched patiently and sheathed the blade on his hip. Kohahu remained kneeling on her shins, *seiza*, so he moved directly in front of her and did the same.

"Daughter," he prompted, wondering if they would play the game of Socratic Dialogues today.

It was one of her favorites.

"Father," she bowed her head. "I have been reading the reports from *Morninghawk* and Inspector Sobol."

Jirou nodded. Of course she would. Kokoro would be studying the politics of power as a previously-secret star system on their flank was cast first into sunlight and thence into Cluster politics. Ema had already produced oil paintings of a night sky that never fell dark.

He nodded to prompt her.

"At the Battle of the Mouth, the six ringships had condors," she continued. "Other weapons, including missiles and beams, but it is obvious to me that condors and cranes made up the bulk of their preparation to defend the corridor into *Meerut*."

"As was my assumption as well," Jirou said. "I am expecting spies to eventually get me the full schematics of the remaining stations, as well as their final disposition."

"First Centurion Kosnett's escorts were able to annihilate condors with their new, rapid-fire beam weapons," Kohahu noted now. "Cranes as well, as they did at *Vilahana* against *Tango* and others."

"That is correct," Jirou noted with some concern.

Dalou naval culture venerated the firebird, as much for the psychological implications of the weapon as the military. If Kosnett could destroy them so easily, much of *Dalou* was at risk.

Worse, he had no doubts that *Aditi* and others were wheeling and dealing to acquire such weapons, or the secrets of their manufacture. Jirou wondered how many capitals had dispatched merchant ambassadors to *Aquitaine* space with instructions to return so armed.

"*Ewin*'s missile swarms are even more at risk than firebirds," Kohahu continued. "At least until they start manufacturing better missiles. And equipping border fleets with them."

Jirou nodded. She indeed took after him far more than either of her sisters. Warfare, as a field of in-depth study, over and above the politics and history that drove it.

It was important to understand how everyone came to this place, but never lose sight of what you must do to escape any trap as it thinks to close on you.

Jirou watched his impetuous daughter work up the will to

challenge her lord, even a little. Perhaps that was why she had chosen the dojo for this confrontation, mild though it might be.

"What can we do to survive?" she asked with a grimace that marred the pretty lines of her face.

She had a rectangular face, long with a square jaw. Only her cheekbones kept her from looking masculine, even as she grew into a woman's body from the lankiness of youth.

"Survive, child?" he challenged, hearing the words of that ancient, Hellenic scholar in the back of his mind, demanding to know *What is Justice?*

"*Yaumgan* has emerged from their slumbers," Kohahu nodded. "That means the philosophers see a time of great upheaval ahead, or great threat to the *Domain* itself. *Aditi* appears to be turning itself inside out in an attempt to woo the strangers, perhaps finally giving them the leg up on their neighbors that they needed to extend the Consensus to the walls of the Cluster, as has always been their goal. That suggests…"

She paused there, frowning as she sought the words to convey the image in her head. Jirou waited patiently.

Fourteen, and already at least as good as many of his seasoned advisors. She would have made a formidable Shogun, would the clans allow it.

Or would they?

If Kosnett's future represented revolution, what were the limits of dreams? Could he find her a wise and learned scholar for a husband, capable of allowing her to rule while he remained in the shadows?

"That suggests an image, Father," Kohahu continued. "The long, empty beach as all the water has withdrawn into the harbor. Moments before the terrible waves come ashore and destroy entire villages."

Tsunami. That was the thing she envisioned? What did this bright, impetuous child—no, young woman—see?

"And how do we get our people to high ground safely?" he asked.

Tidal waves were a terrestrial thing, unknown in space. At the same time, he could see the shape of the thing in her mind. Kosnett's squadron, headed this way with many others hanging from his coat tails for a chance to visit fabled *Ellariel*-jo and perhaps meet the Shogun himself.

Few could claim such a privilege, as mystique aided his own legend.

If the villagers were safely moved to high ground, the buildings could be rebuilt. Perhaps improved, as all old assumptions would be destroyed in the process.

Was it time to destroy all the old assumptions?

"I do not know, Father," she said now. "I have studied many old books and inquired with my teachers, but this is a unique thing, as far as any of them could dream."

"Black swan," Jirou spoke.

"Father?"

"A bird so rare as to be unique, like the fabled phoenix," he said. "A thing which cannot be predicted. One can establish various contingencies, but none will be sufficient, so one must adapt while in motion. Our martial forms are structures to teach movement. Only the masters can seamlessly flow out of one and into another."

"Are you enough of a master?" she asked.

It was an impious question, even from a beloved daughter in the privacy of the dojo.

Still, she was not wrong to ask. He had found himself doing the same many times since that first audience with Morninghawk.

Jirou made a snap decision. Dithering would compound any errors of his logic. Better to move now when there might be time to recover, than to wait for the perfect moment that might never arrive.

"You will join my staff as an advisor," Jirou announced.

"Father?" she asked, horrified perhaps at the sudden change of emotions in the room.

"None of the others were wise enough to ask such an impertinent question," he grinned at her. "They know the old ways of power that have served the Hegemony for many generations. But as you have said, the water has suddenly withdrawn, exposing all those things normally hidden. No sudden visions compel them. None has looked at the line of darkness on the horizon, rapidly approaching, to seek to understand what is coming."

Kohahu blinked at him for a moment. He doubted that she had come in here looking for new responsibilities. Instead, she had sought wisdom. And done so by questioning.

That made her useful. And powerful in his eyes.

She bowed fully in understanding, bent forward to touch her head to the floor without moving from her knees. Jirou wasn't sure he was still that flexible, as he had not had to bow to any man in many years.

Hopefully, that wasn't about to change.

NINE

Heather was watching Leyla, so she saw her Science Officer stiffen with surprise. As with every harbor, Heather had ordered a hard ping of all nearby space. With *Viking* back at *Meerut*, along with *CG-505* and *CM-507*, they wouldn't get as good of results as they might have.

She still commanded a Survey Dreadnought. Nobody in the Balhee Cluster built proper scouts, as far as she'd been able to tell. No need, when you weren't engaged in an all-out war, nor surveying new places.

Everywhere around here had already been scouted. Or so folks had thought. *Meerut* would ruffle a lot of feathers and maybe cause folks to rethink their smug complacency.

"What have you got, Leyla?" Heather asked.

"They build serious when they want to," the woman replied. "I'm picking up local transponder codes for three different *Dalou* battleships. *Colossus*, *Behemoth*, and *Goliath*. If we assume *Morninghawk* scaled up, each ship has a pair of condor mounts, one over each engine pylon. Presumably a couple of cranes forward, then falcons and shrikes on the wings and flanks as protection against envelopment. Main guns and Point guns, but nothing like Power Taps or titan bolts."

"As expected," Heather nodded. "How close are the smaller ships to *Wraithruin* or *Morninghawk?*"

They'd spent enough time around those two vessels to get a feel for naval architecture as the *Dalou Hegemony* did it. Weird, compared to everyone else, but the sort of thing you got when dealing with a slightly introverted culture like this.

"So *Morninghawk* is a Heavy Escort, according to them," Leyla said. "What we might have rated as a destroyer, if we built those instead of the smaller corvettes. About the size of Keller's famous *BrightOak*. Most of the small ships here are either a little lighter than *Morninghawk*, or one of those tiny Patroller ships they build like our old revenue cutters. Nothing in the range of frigates or corvettes."

"And the big ones?" Heather pressed.

"I might call *Wraithruin* a command cruiser," Leyla said. "Not like your old battlecruiser *Jellicoe*, but bigger than a *Founder-class*. *Kestrel* and *Wraithhawk* are both smaller than *Wraithruin*, and run about par with most of what's sharing orbital space with us in that class."

Heather nodded. *Aranyani* and Kaur Singh had produced a pretty detailed encyclopedia of warships in the Cluster, once they'd decided to become allies and friends. Everyone was constantly adjusting when building new classes, but nothing out of the ordinary here.

Just three, enormous *Dalou* battleships. One hell of a statement of purpose. Without *Viking*, she'd give the locals the edge, if it got stupid. Granted, she still had *Aranyani*, *Li Jing*, *Shadowbolt*, and *Juvayni*, but not the other two big ships that had sailed home after the last mission: *Zhang Guolao* and *Khandoba*.

With those two and *Viking*, the *Dalou* Home Fleet could have gotten its teeth kicked in.

Not that Heather was expecting combat, but *Dalou* was the least flexible of the six major cultures in the Cluster, and would be a bit riled by everything Phil had done. Especially as so much of it happened right on the edge of their treaty space.

"Standing rules still apply," Heather announced, looking around to make sure everyone was listening. "Anybody maneuvers to get above us in orbital space and the squadron automatically comes to alert. That includes allied vessels, so convey that to them. *Aranyani* and *Li Jing* I'm not worried about, but *Juvayni* and *Shadowbolt* haven't always impressed me with their professional alertness. No mistakes here, people. The First Centurion is going to be pushing the envelope in a number of places and expecting us to have his back."

She got nods back, thought about it for a moment, and rose.

"Iveta, you have the bridge," she announced. "I'm going to go chat with Phil."

TEN

Phil looked up as his door chimed, then opened a moment later, admitting Heather. He hadn't bothered to replace Markus as a door guard, so Harinder mostly ran interference today.

She must not be feeling the need. Nothing drastic had happened, or Heather would have called directly.

"What's up?" he asked, putting aside the tablet where he'd been reviewing paperwork.

"Have you looked out the window?" she asked as she sat.

He hadn't, so he called up a quick image of nearby space.

"That's impressive," he noted. "Three of them?"

"I don't have spies, but rumors suggest that they only have five in their whole fleet," Heather said. "Are they trying to impress us or intimidate us?"

"By now, they have read the notes about the force that went with us to *Meerut*," he replied. "At the same time, they might not have believed that *Zhang Guolao* and *Khandoba* really left, so maybe they felt threatened enough to put on a show of force. You've warned everyone to be on their toes?"

"And their best behavior," Heather nodded. "What happens next?"

"According to the folks tasked with organizing it, we'll hang out for a day or three while final arrangements are made," Phil said. He leaned back to visualize things. "At some point, there will be a formal ceremony on the station to recognize Omarov, followed by a State Dinner sort of event. Formal and stuffy. I'm hoping that we can engage in a number of side conversations with folks, though their cultural protocol is much more stiff about such things than us or *Aditi*."

"Do we know if the Emperor will be present?" Heather asked.

"I doubt it," Phil grimaced. "The Shogunate has ultimate power, and the Imperial Household is more of a symbol than anything. They might rule in his name, but that's about it. Even the President of *Aquitaine* has more authority and visibility. No, I expect a medium-to-high level representative. Enough to be present, but not enough to honor us, as it were."

"How many of these things will you need me at?" Heather asked.

Phil shrugged.

"Technically, none of them, if you believe various rumors," he said with a slight grin. "A mere captain, such as they might see you. Plus a woman. And an outsider. You'll be there for the big thing with the award ceremony, because every one of the captains will be. You, Kaur, and Captain Xue of *Li Jing* will stand out for your gender among the *Dalou* retainers. I'm hoping that it makes them a little uncomfortable. Past that, we're going to have to play it by ear. If you and Kaur Singh had any ulterior plans, I'd make them now and then be a burr under someone's saddle. Polite, but not taking any shit from anybody who might want to grieve you. Captain Xue might help, and she might not."

"Oh, I have that in hand," Heather laughed. "And yes, Kaur and I have been chatting. If I thought it wouldn't push a few people too far, I'd put Nam in one of our uniforms with *Aranyani's* patch on her shoulder and bring her to the party."

Phil paused and considered that image.

"Do that," he said firmly. "Specifically that. Put her in black. All the right tags, but *Aranyani's* flag on her shoulder. I'll get you the paperwork for a temporary commission as a Senior Centurion. She can decide later if she wants to keep it."

"Why?" Heather asked, obviously intrigued by the way she leaned forward now to study him.

"You've met Casey *zu* Weigand," he said. "Back when she was a mere Centurion of the *RAN*, before she turned into something a bit bigger."

"Bigger, yes," Heather laughed.

Her Majesty Karl VIII, Emperor of Fribourg by Grace of God and King of St. Legier, among her many other titles.

Back then, she had merely been a princess, and the youngest child of Karl VII. Until the famous *Flight of the Blackbird* and the subsequent orbital bombardment of her homeworld had forced her to grow up too fast.

She hadn't done too bad for herself. Having Vo *zu* Arlo handy as an advisor helped. Phil had stood across a battlefield from that man.

"So what does it do to the entire Hegemony if we can do the same thing to them that Jessica did to *Fribourg*?" he smiled. "If daughters start asking *Why not me?* to their fathers."

"I seem to remember that the current Shogun is rumored to only have daughters," Heather noted. "None of them could rise to power, could they?"

"Neither could Casey, Heather," he said in a hard voice. "And yet, she did."

"She did. How hard are we going to push *Dalou*?"

"I had a personal chat with Iveta after we left *Ishiokoh*," Phil said. "Following up on her report of a conversation she had with Omarov at that big reception. She told the man to his face that *Dalou* had a singular chance to move into the future with *Aditi* and *Yaumgan*. If they didn't, they'd fall into second place with the *Gloran Empire* and the *Ewin Principalities*."

"Ouch," Heather flinched. "A bit brutal. Even for Iveta."

"Indeed," he agreed. "However, accurate, and perhaps necessary. I've talked with Samnang Sobol more than once, and I am convinced that she is going to try her own kind of social revolution, using us as a wedge. We're not dealing with stupid people here, Heather. Extremely hidebound, yes, but not dumb. We need to press softly, allowing them to push us back when they will, but also, maybe getting them to a place where they embrace that future."

"Do we want them undergoing a full Meiji Restoration here, Phil?" she asked now, leaning forward to stare hard at him.

Phil understood her concerns. He himself had seen to it that everyone studied the late era of the Tokugawa in preparation for coming here. The locals might not have known it that well, but it did form a template against which he could draw.

"When we arrived, *Aditi* was the most powerful, by virtue of being slightly in advance of everyone else in terms of trade and politics," he said. "*Yaumgan* had withdrawn two generations ago and was content to let everyone else go to hell without them."

"And they were on their way," Heather reminded him.

Phil nodded and considered his words carefully. He could trust her to keep any secret. At the same time, it needed to be framed just right, so that when she issued orders to her people, she would know what he was up to.

"We just destroyed the pirates as a viable economic and military entity, Heather," he said. "They maybe don't know it yet, but the end has already happened, and they have only a few years to retire, cut a deal to go straight, or be destroyed. Without the Syndicates bleeding *Aditi*'s strength, what happens?"

"They become expansionist, at least for a while," she replied. "If for no other reason than nobody is pushing back and they aren't paying as much for bribes to criminal organizations."

"Exactly," Phil said. "They expand. There is nowhere to expand around here. Every star is claimed at least on paper. *Aditi* thus risks coming into conflict with someone. They are smart enough to leave *Yaumgan* alone. *Ewin* is likely to implode at some point. *Gloran* sees themselves much the same way as the ancient Spartans did, which makes *Aditi* something of Athens in this story. Only *Dalou* has a large number of claimed systems that are not currently occupied. At least officially. *Viking* has made me a list of current and presumably soon-to-be former pirate outposts. I don't intend to do anything about them. At the same time, I will happily provide that list to the Shogun if he asks. Great trade value there."

"I'm not sure I see where you are going, Phil," Heather said.

He nodded to her. It was an obscure point to make. And well in the future, as you measured such things. The next generation would confront it, whatever the outcome today. And if it wasn't handled adroitly here, that confrontation would likely be ugly.

"I need *Dalou* intact, Heather," he said. "I need them coherent. I need them powerful enough to tell *Aditi* no. Anything less risks *Aditi* waking up one morning and deciding that they could conquer most of the rest of the cluster if they cut a deal with *Yaumgan*. *Gloran* and *Ewin* will be bystanders. Victims in the middle of the road that get run over. Only *Dalou* might be able to hold a détente in place that keeps a broader peace."

"Prepare for war, if you would have peace, Phil?" she asked sardonically.

"Threading a needle, Heather," he replied. "Keep everyone intact while they simultaneously undergo a cultural transformation as all this new technology comes along. Yan Bedrov so radically destabilized *Aquitaine* that I have my own fears for the next generation there, especially with what Nils Kasum did, early in Jessica's days back on the first *Auberon*."

"What was that?"

"When he cleared out and retired most of the old Noble

Lords from the fleet, leaving only the Fighting Lords," Phil replied. "The result was a much more combat-oriented, professional force. We needed that, in order to stop *Fribourg* from overwhelming us. And to go after *Buran*. There are consequences only now becoming evident, even as Kasum and Keller are retired and off the stage. Whughy will be dealing with it when he becomes First Lord."

"What do you see, Phil?" she asked, leaning in enough to put her elbows on his desk now.

"Denis Jež calls it *Imperial Aquitaine*, from his perch advising Karl VIII, Heather," Phil said. "He and I have exchanged rather detailed letters on the topic. Graduate and Command level classwork on the potential for Republican Rome to migrate into Imperial Rome, and what that means for *Aquitaine* in our lifetimes."

"And the Balhee Cluster?" she asked.

"Can you think of a better place to go conquer, if they were already engaged in their own petty wars, and unable to stop the *RAN* from sailing in and stomping everything they encounter?" he asked.

"Are we talking treason here, Phil?" she asked in a hard voice.

He understood her concern. Aiding and Abetting enemies of the Republic was a capital offense.

"No. Pet Naoumov tasked me with exploring the Balhee Cluster, Heather," he turned hard and cold now. "Nothing more, even when I asked her about Jež's fears. She agrees with the possibilities, but doesn't see it happening. I think she is wrong. We are here to establish trade and communication. To make new friends. In the process, I might have to start several petite revolutions, but my end goal is to strengthen the Cluster, for the same reason I want to insure that *Dalou* survives. If the Cluster is modern and stable, the *Republic*, or *Empire* if that's what we become in a generation, might just have to look elsewhere. My mission is to protect future generations out here. You will not share those details with your crew, but communicate to them that we're uplifting, not tearing down. Whenever possible."

"Who knows?" she asked.

"Harinder. First Lord Naoumov. Denis Jež. Casey *zu* Weigand. Me," Phil smiled at her. "And now you."

ELEVEN

SUNFLOWER IMPERIAL PALACE, MIDDAY

His Imperial Majesty, Osamu of *Dalou*, fifty-fourth *Dalou* Emperor, studied his coffee and glanced up through the trees of his garden, as if he would be somehow gifted with the sudden ability to see the many new warships overhead.

No outside fleet had been allowed into *Ellariel's* orbit in hundreds of years. And yet, Osamu's spies reported the arrival with breathlessness.

As if it mattered here on the ground. In the distance, Osamu could see a wall cutting across his view, well in the distance, at the bottom of the hill upon which his palace and garden were perched. It demarcated his kennel from the rest of the planet.

Oh, others might see the Imperial Palace as the pinnacle of *Dalou* culture, but Osamu was not fooled. He was allowed to reign supreme, but only within these walls. Outside, others would bow and defer, before confirming any order he might give with that damnable Kugosu in orbit.

The Emperor had been a paper tiger for nearly half a millennium now. Pretty. Fashionable. Scholarly.

Irrelevant.

The Shoguns had kept the barbarians at bay.

What did it mean that they had failed?

Others might call it something else, but no enemy fleet had been allowed into orbit in centuries. Worse, according to his spies, the outsiders might be powerful enough to stay, if they chose, regardless of the Shogun's opinion.

How had they gotten thus?

Osamu grumbled and reached for the coffee pot. Elsewhere, he might be forced to sit patiently and watch as servants poured his coffee, delivered his snacks, or waited on him hand and foot. Carving out an hour in the afternoon where none were allowed closer than his bodyguards had taken a decade.

He could pour his own damned coffee, thank you. *I am an emperor, not an invalid.*

He didn't grumble that out loud, though. Osamu knew the limits of his power. Even within these walls, his writ was barely law. And only until it annoyed someone enough to complain to the true power in this system.

That same power that was sharing orbital space with aliens and unwelcome neighbors.

He found it too much to handle today.

Osamu rose with a mug of coffee in one hand and watched his bodyguards all nearly fall over in their haste to come to attention. Had he grown so predictable in his dotage?

Was fifty-one really old? His father yet lived, retired and living a monastic life of peace, without any retainers interrupting or attempting to do things rather than letting important hands grow sullied.

Days like this, Osamu understood what had driven the man off the stage at a younger age than he might have chosen.

Prince Shingo, however, was only nineteen, and far too young to ascend, even if he had been finally broken of his teenage rebellion by being allowed to study for perhaps joining the navy at some point.

Discipline could be invited, but not imposed, at least not on that youngster. Still, the threat of withdrawing an invitation to a military academy if his grades or behavior ever became scandalous, had transformed Shingo, almost overnight.

He would make a good emperor. Assuming Osamu's pique didn't get the better of him first.

An irritated emperor stomped through the garden to the rear door of his palace, watching ripples of panic take hold of his various courtiers.

Mice, suddenly realizing that the cat's nap was over and fleeing madly. Scurrying away through the corridors ahead of him as if he might bite.

Maybe. Perhaps he should destabilize his standard schedule, just because so many people around him appeared to have grown lazy.

Empress Aimi and Princess Sota has been sitting in a library, quietly discussing something. Osamu had waved their own guards to silence as he approached, so both looked up in surprise. Only Sota had any panic in her eyes.

"Perhaps we should continue this conversation another time, daughter," Aimi said soothingly as she realized who had interrupted.

His middle child, the older daughter, exploded out of her seat, bowed, and made to slide around her dread lord's temper without turning her back.

How bad was the scowl on his face? Apparently sufficient. He watched her go.

"Close the door behind you," he announced. "Remain in the hall."

Let the various bodyguards sort out how to protect a closed room from the outside.

The space was comfortable. Large enough for a half-dozen people to sit in the various chairs and talk companionably. Dark-stained walls and built-in bookcases, with light blue on the ceiling and colorful rugs on the floor in a variety of geometric patterns.

Empress Aimi wore a tunic and baggy pants, almost harem-style, both in a rich, royal blue that contrasted well with her gray hair that he still remembered being black in their youth. Sota and Moriko both took after their mother in looks, which was good.

Aimi made to stand, but he waved her down and took the warm seat Sota had just abandoned. There was even a table for his coffee at hand.

"It appears to be infectious," Aimi noted. "Our daughter was similarly distracted this afternoon. What brings my lord to abandon his quiet time early?"

It wasn't a love match. Marriages at this level hardly ever were. At the same time, he had come to treasure the woman's calm demeanor and intellect. Many of the potential, eligible young women his parents had considered had been great beauties. Tall and elegant. Distracting of form.

And generally about as intelligent as a cat.

He had been lucky. Aimi might be short and perhaps squishier than was considered fashionable. She was also smarter than he was. And cagier. That had saved his ass a few times.

"*Aquitaine*," Osamu replied, sipping his coffee then setting it down.

Aimi nodded sagely.

"As with Sota," she replied. "Is it anything in particular, or their mere arrival?"

Osamu considered his words. Even with his wife, they needed to be chosen with care. Others might grow offended. She would pick apart his sloppiness with a knife.

He smiled at the image.

"What?" she asked.

"I have been exceptionally lucky," Osamu announced. "You."

"Me?"

"Indeed," he continued. "*Aquitaine* arrives and disturbs all protocol and precedent. I find myself restless and annoyed, but to explain it to you, my closest advisor, I must delve deep within and find the heart of the truth, because any loose thinking will cause you to savage me with your wit. Thus, I must be prepared to think."

She grinned. It was an old conversation. And a good one.

That was a better form of love than mere lust for a particularly nice bottom, after all. And hers still was, underneath whatever she wore to hide herself.

"So what about the aliens has discombobulated you to the point that the entire palace is probably currently atwitter?" she asked with a knowing smile.

"What did Sota ask?" he countered.

"She wondered if they would visit us on the ground," Aimi replied. "Specifically, if one of the female captains would do so."

"Female captains?" Osamu asked, a bit lost.

He had been aware of such things. Conversations with his Premier, Anil Gadhavi, who had learned them from the Court of the Shogun overhead. He had been slightly insulted that such things were allowed, but *Aditi* and the others were barbarians, at the end of the day. Even *Yaumgan*. The Sunflower Throne remembered *Yaumgan*'s arrival.

Philosophical they might be. Outsiders still. *Aquitaine* was merely the newest arrival.

"Three of the five major ships to arrive have female commanding officers," Aimi reminded him. "*Aquitaine*, *Aditi*, and *Yaumgan*. It almost gives one pause to wonder if *Gloran* or *Ewin* have such."

"They do not," he said.

He had caused Gadhavi to check when he first learned.

Aimi nodded, bowing to his knowledge, if not particularly much. She was like that. It was good.

"Why would our daughter wish to meet the outsiders?" Osamu asked, already deflected from his original disgruntlement, but allowing it. Aimi was an expert at his moods.

"She is a woman," Aimi replied, as if that covered it.

"And?" he asked, confused now.

"And as the daughter of an emperor, she has little to look forward to as an adult, Sire," Aimi said with a bit of iron in her voice. "A marriage to one of the powerful clans to help bind them as allies. Hopefully a good one, but that is not guaranteed. Raising a family on some estate, where she will be mistress of her domain, as long as it does not extend past the walls of the estate itself."

"That is a feeling I know well," Osamu replied grumpily.

"Oh?"

"Today, I looked at the walls of my palace grounds and saw only limits on my power," he admitted. He could do that with this woman. "I am Emperor of an estate, and irrelevant beyond it. My symbolism is sufficient for my people, as they draw whatever strength and guidance they require from another."

Even here, he rarely mentioned the Kugosu name out loud. Generations ago, they and their allies had merely been clans that made up the Kingdom of *Dalou*. Until two sides came to disagreement, eventually erupting into a proper civil war.

Osamu's ancestors had chosen the wrong side. However, instead of being displaced, they had been exiled to the surface of *Ellariel*, where they were retired into genteel civility while the Shogunate had ruled in his name ever since.

"Should you make use of that symbolism?" she asked now.

"How so?" he replied, knocked further off-center by her words.

"If he rules in your name, perhaps you should take the opportunity to inspect the job he does," Aimi said primly now, eyes practically glowing.

"It is outside of protocol," he snapped.

"So?"

"What?"

"What is the purpose of the protocol that binds you to your palace and forces you to do nothing with your life but study the ancient ways and perhaps write poetry, dread Emperor of *Dalou*?" she asked with a wicked grin. "If the strangers have come, are we at another one of those historical junctions when all of *Dalou* is to be overturned? Should you overturn it yourself, lest any of the other houses seek to take away what little power you might have?"

"How could they?" he demanded.

"*Aquitaine* is not an empire," Aimi pointed out. "Nor is *Aditi*. If the strangers bring a new kind of future, does it require an emperor?"

"*Gloran* has an Emperor," Osamu noted. "*Ewin* has a king."

"And how relevant are either in the current discussion of power politics in the Cluster, my husband?"

He bit his tongue at her tone. Sarcastic. Biting, even.

One hundred percent correct. How well she knew him.

"Shit, or get off the pot?" he asked.

"Crude, but essentially accurate," she nodded with a sly smile. "I fear that the future is knocking at our hall. If we do not answer it, will it come a second time?"

Osamu felt a chill overtake his soul at her words.

He had never been one to gamble. That had made him better than average as emperors went. Not rocking the boat in the face of what little power he did have.

He could squander it all on one roll of the dice, or watch it slowly bleed away, having been unwilling to assume any risk.

He rose and stepped close to her now, bending down to kiss the woman. She knew him better than any, and still liked him.

How many men could say that?

Osamu, Emperor of *Dalou* and fifty-fourth of that string, picked up his coffee and took a sip, fearing that it had grown cold. Instead, it was just right.

He took that as a sign, walking to the door of the library and throwing it open. Many retainers had gathered in the hallway, reminding him of vultures now in a manner he did not find attractive.

If nothing else, this had shown him just how much he

needed to take a machete to the entropy around here and turn this place back from a museum into…something.

What, he wasn't entirely sure. Different.

More or less depended on things he could not yet see.

He picked out one of the senior pages and speared the man with a glower.

"Summon my Premier," he announced.

TWELVE

ADCON CRUISER ARANYANI

Kaur Singh, Commander of the *Aditi* Cruiser *Aranyani*, sat in her front room as Arya stood at attention. She considered the message that Nam had sent. The one Arya had just delivered and closed the door to Kaur's quarters before handing to her. What did it mean that Phil Kosnett had offered Nam a full, if temporary, commission in the *Republic of Aquitaine* Navy as a Senior Centurion?

It had the equivalence of a lateral transfer, though she doubted that Nam would be in line to ever command one of their ships. Unless Kosnett intended to carry through his earlier threat to buy or repair a local vessel and crew it by thinning out his own ships some.

According to Heather, they had carried about ten percent more crew than normal on all ships for this mission. Heather had mentioned how thinly stretched things had been when *CS-405* had been trapped behind enemy lines and forced to make do by stealing *Buran* civilian vessels.

Could they put Nam in charge here and give her an *RAN* crew?

What would that mean to the *Consensus*? Or the Cluster?

She looked up at Arya.

"Sit," Kaur ordered her Second-In-Command. "Let's talk."

"I'm not getting her back, am I?" Arya asked.

"That's the least of your worries, woman," Kaur said with a laugh. "Eventually, all this will be yours anyway, including the headaches. You will be wading through applications for filling senior slots, with all the publicity and notoriety we've achieved this year."

Arya laughed as well. Strange luck to have arrived at *Vilahana* on the right day, and to still be there when Phil and his squadron arrived. It would put Kaur in the command chair of a ship like *Khandoba* at some point.

They just had to navigate the fussiness of *Dalou* to get home.

"Has anybody from home ever been here like this?" Arya asked. "Visited *Ellariel* or *Ellariel*-jo?"

"Not as part of a fleet," Kaur nodded. "Nothing larger than a Moat-style ship, as far as I am aware, and few of those. Usually, messengers traveling on small hulls at high speed between capitals carrying diplomatic news."

"Was *Khandoba* sent home so as to not present a threat?" Arya asked.

Kaur considered her response.

"You are not to mention this," she said. Arya nodded. "I had a conversation with senior officials before we departed to *Meerut*."

"How senior?"

"*That* senior," Kaur confirmed. "*Khandoba* was sent out originally because *Yaumgan* did the same and we couldn't be outshone. After *Meerut*, they were withdrawn, where it is my understanding that they will undertake a number of anti-piracy patrols."

"Going to go destroy all those people we use to wink and nod at in passing?" Arya asked with a sly grin.

"Your words, but essentially correct," Kaur said. "This mission is us. With Nam accompanying Phil and Heather, you're stuck here going forward. It's not that I don't trust my other officers, but they don't have the seasoning to handle an emergency in *Dalou* space. Not like you do."

"Are we expecting trouble?" she asked. "We were invited."

"They made a point of having three-fifths of their Line of Battle present when Phil arrived, Arya," Kaur reminded her. "Whether that is a statement of intimidation or not depends on how Phil decides to take it. He's made no bones about his ability to go back and bring in a fleet large enough to annihilate every navy in the Cluster at once if anyone attacks him. Imagine what a Heavy Dreadnought might be like. Or an Expeditionary cruiser, when *Viking* is *merely* the undergunned Survey version. It is not a hollow threat. *Dalou* might get lucky and ambush Phil here, but if anybody got away, the *Republic of Aquitaine* Navy might end *Dalou* as an entity in response."

Arya cringed at the image. *Aditi* wasn't that much more powerful than *Dalou*, fleet-wise.

"What's to keep them from pressing their advantage at that point?" Arya asked.

"Nothing at all," Kaur said. "Save for you and I being friends, with Nam serving on his flagship and wearing his uniform."

"What do we do?"

"We keep our eyes open, and our heads down," Kaur said. "Phil would have to be provoked, and we've come to his aid before. We'll do it again if we have to, even against overwhelming odds."

"Does High Command understand all this?" her Second-in-Command asked now.

"No," Kaur admitted. "But their bosses do."

THIRTEEN

Phil looked at Harinder, feeling his mouth want to drop open and his eyes bug out, like this was all a cartoon. They were doing the usual daily briefing on his flag bridge, where he could see his staff and they could see him. Some of them would cycle around to mix with Heather's usual crew, so he wasn't entirely sure who all got to see him like this.

Stories would get around by dinner, he had no doubt.

"Repeat that?" he asked, certain he'd heard it wrong the first time.

"We received a message from the ground a few minutes ago, Phil," she said with a sly smile, drawing all this out in case anybody hadn't been looking the first time. "The Imperial Palace has announced that they intend to be present when First Centurion Kosnett awards Sugawara retainer Omarov the Republic Cross for Conspicuous Gallantry in battle. Unquote."

"Shit, that's what I thought you said," Phil grumbled.

He leaned back, utterly gobsmacked. None of his plans had ever included that sort of an outcome or option. He wasn't Jessica Keller, but today he felt like maybe he needed someone like her.

He did.

Phil opened a comm line to the bridge.

"Bridge. Beridze here," she said.

"I need you back at my flag bridge right now, Iveta," Phil said simply. "Find Heather and send her back, too. Then track down Nam Nagarkar and bring her as well."

"On it."

He cut the line, watching the concern etch itself slowly into Harinder's face.

"I'll explain it, but only once," he said.

She sat back and watched.

Iveta arrived first, but she was the closest of the three. Heather was next, not even wearing shoes, but her socks were good enough, and Phil might have intended to light a fire under Heather's ass. Nam was breathing heavy, having apparently run from wherever she had been.

They got settled. Phil turned to the orderly whose job it was to get coffee for everyone and signaled the woman closer. Unless Markus blew up his hands, it was still his job, so Phil had just instructed the closest wardroom to handle things with whoever happened to be on duty, rather than assigning someone long term.

He did note that half the staff in here, as well as everyone else at the table with him right now, was female. A good sign in *Aditi* space. Possibly concerning in *Dalou*. Those folks would just have to deal with it.

"We have received confirmation of the event tomorrow night, local time," he said to the newcomers. "Everything as originally planned, considering that my protocol people and theirs are all experts. However, we have a potential issue, and I wanted you three to be involved."

Heather nodded. She was used to him dragging her into strange conversations for her perspective. The other two would learn.

"We have just been notified that a party from the Imperial Palace will be in attendance," Phil continued. "There was already such a group on the docket, so I take it to mean that we might be dealing with the Emperor himself, or at least a personal representative, instead of just another flunky."

It was telling that Iveta was confused, Heather phlegmatic, and Nam's mouth had dropped open, just like his had done. He nodded.

"Harinder handles protocol," Phil said. "That's always been her job as my Command Flag Centurion. I heard the news and realized I had other issues. Nam, how far out of normal would it be, for the Emperor of *Dalou* to be present at such festivities?"

"Unique, I think," she said in a small, gasping voice. "Certainly so rare as to rate discussion in history books. The Shogun handles everything. *Everything*. And it all goes through the Shogun. I'm not even aware of another *Aditi* warship calling on *Ellariel*, any time in the recent past. Usually, courier vessels make the run directly. Sometimes, our diplomats will travel via cruiser to a *Dalou* world closer to the border and then be carried, if they aren't just picked up at *Aditi* itself by a *Dalou* vessel. Nobody meets the Emperor."

"Exactly my point," Phil said, turning to look at everyone around the table with him. "I know we've talked about how revolutionary this whole business might be. I was talking socially and culturally. However, someone has gone and raised the stakes precipitously on me and *I don't like it*. Not one bit."

"We back to solving the Tunnel into *Meerut*, Phil?" Heather asked. "Blue team/gold team exercise?"

"Of a sorts," he turned to Iveta now. "The thought that I had at that very moment Harinder told me was that I'd never go too deep, or so utterly complicated in my planning. Keller used to do things like that routinely. This is three times now, when someone has come at me from a blind side. I spent years planning all this, so that my planning has fallen so short irritates me greatly. I think I need my own, personal Keller, dreaming up various outlandish scenarios, and how she might solve them. That way, I don't have ten minutes of flailing panic while I try to trim my sails to bizarre new realities. That's your job, Iveta."

Iveta had frozen. Now she nodded, hard and sober. Deadly.

He turned to Nam next.

"You have two jobs, and they will be significant enough to pull you off whatever it was you were previously doing, Senior Centurion," he continued, waiting for her to nod. "One, you need to sit down with Harinder as soon as we're done here and brain dump anything you can remember about *Dalou* culture, history, and protocol that hasn't previously come up. Specifically, the Emperor and imperial protocol. Normally, I'd call Kaur or Omarov, but this feels like it suddenly got to Plenipotentiary-level stakes, so we're playing in the biggest leagues, and I don't want to compromise them. Second, in your spare time, you will make yourself available to Iveta as her assistant, reviewing her ideas, adding your own, and bringing in anybody you think should contribute. I'd give you Markus, but he's back at *Meerut*. Similarly, *Stunt Dude* is with *Li Jing*. Work around those gaps as long as you can. You have longer than tomorrow to out-think the rest of the cluster, so focus on the Imperial and Shogunate Courts with Harinder for now. Questions?"

Nam shook her head, eyes still big.

"We expecting trouble during the reception?" Heather asked.

"Not with what I currently know," he replied, looking at each of the four women equally now. "However, the Emperor has just opened up a new fault line in *Dalou* politics and I'm not sure how the Shogun will respond. I expect their Home Fleet to be completely loyal to the Shogun, so nothing happens this week. What about next week, *Junkyard?*"

That last, asked directly to Iveta. His personal Jessica Keller clone. She had earned her own pirate nickname now. Best to turn her loose to be the thing she had always dreamed of being.

"Correct on both assessments, I think," Iveta replied carefully, already deep into the weeds of analysis from the gleam in her eyes.

"Other questions?" he asked. The rest shook their heads.

"Then route things to Harinder as you think of them, and let her decide what to do with it," Phil said. "I'm going to focus on being charming and friendly, especially if something ugly just happened around here. Everyone will be on their best behavior during the reception. Iveta, you will have Tactical and the bridge. Possibly the flag if I am out of contact, but listen to Command Centurion Galia Abbasi on *CC-501*, because I chose her specifically as my escort squadron commander."

"Yes, sir," Iveta replied.

"The rest of you will be with me on the station," Phil continued. "Plan for *weird*."

FOURTEEN

ELLARIEL-JO ORBITAL PALACE

J irou studied the faces around him. Men he had promoted to his staff after long experience, either in command of starships, or handling the myriad political tasks that went with running a Shogunate. Men who had been with him for years, plus a few he had inherited when he took the job.

Plus one newcomer who had the men around her a little on edge.

Jirou decided that she had already proven her worth, just from that alone.

"Who failed?" Jirou demanded, tapping an angry finger on the conference room table. He had to sit, so he didn't pace. "Which one of my spies should face reprobation for not informing me of this in time to stop it?"

He scowled at them, daring them to put their careers on the line right now. Jirou's own brother had learned the penalty for failure. One of these days, Jirou's other spies would even locate the man, but he had vanished a decade ago, and was hiding well.

Tane Eiton stirred now. Minister at Large. A much older man, who had served Jirou's father previously. A trusted advisor, almost a *consigliere*, to use the ancient term, because the man could argue with Jirou in the public space of the Private Council.

"Tane?" Jirou asked, withdrawing his fire a little, no doubt as the man expected.

He might look a little hunched and mostly harmless. Many fools had fallen for such an act over the decades.

"I have heard a rumor," he said in a quiet voice. A wheezy shadow of what it had been in Jirou's youth, but enough to remind him. To remind everyone.

"Go on."

A rumor would allow the man to speak truths right now without necessarily casting blame. Useful, Jirou supposed, when the Shogun was verging on a killing rage. And he was.

"It is said that the Emperor emerged from a meeting with the Empress in a private room," Tane said. "He immediately demanded the Premier be brought before him. The message to the ships in orbit went out within the hour after that, so it was perhaps decided and immediately acted upon."

"Has that man ever acted decisively?" Mota Shibu asked derisively.

Mota Shibu held the official title of First Minister.

First among equals, generally. When Tane Eiton chose to allow it.

"Not that I can remember," Tane said in a careful tone, reminding everyone here that they were generally not more than a decade older than Jirou, while Tane was older than Jirou's retired father, Kenzou. "Nor his father before him."

As that probably spanned roughly sixty of Tane's seventy-five years, it was enough to quell the murmuring around the table.

"How do we use this situation to our advantage?" a bright voice broke in now.

Most of Jirou's advisors recoiled as if he had dropped a poisonous serpent on the table. Only Tane Eiton did not flinch.

Kohahu glowered at all the older men around her, daring them to speak down to her right now. Like them, she wore the crimson and gold. In her case, a gold doublet over a crimson shirt, with red lacing down the center and a red ribbon tying her braid.

Daughter of a Shogun.

"Mistress?" Tsuma Toshei asked in a somewhat snotty voice. Minister of the Treasury.

Jirou had always considered his personal accountant old fashioned and a bit sexist. Toshei had chosen today to be seated diagonally from Kohahu. Not across from her. Not next to her. Far enough away that her cooties might not reach him.

Jirou smiled rudely at the image. He extended that to the others.

"She asks a valid question, gentlemen," he stated. "Kohahu?"

"It is a done deal," she said, placing her sword hand firmly on the table before her. "To force the Emperor to give way at this late of a moment disturbs the Shogun's power. Threatens to expose him to ridicule by the general public. Or allows whispers that he cannot control the imperial household. This cannot be allowed. Thus, *fait accompli*. Then what?"

Already, adding his daughter had changed dynamics in this room for the better. Old minds, worn into ruts and unable to see future challenges? More and more, that seemed to describe most of these men in ways Jirou had not really internalized until this moment. Only Tane Eiton stood aloof from that opinion, which truly indicted the rest.

Had he grown stodgy in his own thinking?

"We've never faced such a situation," First Minister Shibu replied nervously.

"Obviously," Kohahu said with such disdain that Jirou was surprised not to find the old man bleeding. Then she turned her face to Hida Taro, Minister of Protocol, which usually meant law enforcement and related administration of justice and government tasks, rather than dealing with unruly emperors. "Where would an Emperor be seated, with the Shogun hosting the party, First Centurion Kosnett awarding a medal, and Morninghawk given prize of place as the honoree?"

Jirou watched the man's glacial thought processes grind. Normally beneficial, as law and justice were best handled with the steady deliberation of a grain mill. Inadequate to the task today. That much was obvious. Jirou chose to rescue the man.

"Where would you place the Emperor's party?" Jirou countered to his daughter, watching her fall automatically into the Socratic methods he himself had instilled in her. Not quite the dojo floor, but her expertise there was growing daily as well. Socrates with a blade.

Cut and cut again, until you find the truth at the core of that most ancient question: *What is Justice?*

"The Emperor is attending as an honored guest," she answered immediately, flowing into a perfect state similar to what you got when practicing martial forms. "Kosnett is also such a guest of the Shogun. That suggests a triangle. Isosceles but not equilateral in shape, as it keeps the Shogun distinct and aloof from both, in power over everyone as host. Kosnett on the left, facing in, the Emperor on the right. Place a trusted clan between them to keep the two separate. The visitors can form the leg on Kosnett's side. *Dalou* guests on the Emperor's side, declining in importance to the center, then rising again until your second friendliest clan is on your immediate left."

Jirou saw the structure as she had laid it out and nodded. He turned to Hida Taro.

"Have your people inspect such a design and confirm that it can be done without offering insult to anyone," he ordered the man. "That allows allies of the Emperor who might not be friendly to the Shogunate to be present and honored, without letting them rise above themselves."

"Why are we even allowing this?" Akin Toko interjected now.

Second Minister. First Admiral. Commandant of the Fleet, at least from a bureaucratic standpoint. Jirou still *commanded.*

"What would you suggest as an alternative, Admiral?" Jirou asked, scowling at the interruption. "Kosnett asked for permission to bestow upon Morninghawk one of their highest awards for bravery, as a result of the man's actions at *Meerut*. My own Imperial Inspector checked with the Court before allowing it. *Under my approval.* Now, they are here. Should we suddenly withdraw such approval and insult the visitors?"

"They are outsiders," Admiral Toko wheezed squeakily, perhaps too overcome by his emotions. Or too old and hidebound. There was always that. "Why should we honor aliens? Especially as this Kosnett has made it clear that he will fight us if we attempt to claim that pirate stronghold. It sends all the wrong messages!"

Jirou bit back the first words that came to mind. They would be crude and cutting. But then, maybe it was time to unsettle this Private Council. Bring in some more fresh blood, because just adding his daughter had uncovered how badly things had settled into a predictable routine.

Routine had been fine, until last year. Until the *Republic of Aquitaine* had arrived. It might be lethal now

"Your fleet, *Admiral,* never located *Meerut*," Jirou stated, cold and lethal. "Even as it has been apparently colonized long enough that the pirate warlord Utkin was reputedly born there. What other unknown and perhaps illegal colonies might we find on our borders, if we were to really start looking, I wonder?"

The man had gone so pale that Jirou suddenly wondered how many different pirate syndicates had been paying him under the table to remain *undiscovered*. It was one thing for unofficial official policy to fund the pirates to prey on the shipping of other nations. *Dalou* didn't necessarily manufacture all the goods they needed, so they would buy some from *Aditi* and steal others.

But if his staff were cutting deals on the side, that presented a much deeper problem. It suggested disloyalty at the highest levels.

Akin Toko might not be in a position to ascend to the Shogunate himself, as it had remained in one of five clans since the beginning. At the same time, Kugosu had only held it for four generations now.

Was the man maneuvering to displace the Kugosu?

Jirou pounced now.

"When this meeting is done, Admiral Toko," he said coldly. "I suggest that you go to your staff and produce an updated sailing gazette of all *Dalou* systems, including the last time they were officially surveyed. That will let us know what systems and sectors need to be revisited in the immediate future. As I noted, *Meerut* was overlooked. We shouldn't allow other places to escape our gaze."

Toko nodded, face frozen with fear it seemed. Jirou wondered if the man might just pack his bags in the dead of night and flee into the wilderness ahead of the vengeance of his lord and master.

How bad had things gotten around here?

FIFTEEN

YAUMGAN SKYCRUISER LI JING

Sam Au always found it odd to her original way of thinking, looking around the bridge of *Li Jing*. Back in her birthplace, the *Holding of Man*, having women in command or on the bridge was common. The Eldest found the spot where you could best serve and promoted you as far as your competence allowed.

Yaumgan and the *Aditi Consensus* were similar in that way, as was *Aquitaine*. *Fribourg* had been a conservative nation, but having a woman emperor trained by that dangerous woman Keller was undoing centuries of tradition. *Dalou* apparently ran a male-only culture. The *Gloran Empire* and the *Ewin Principalities* were a close second, but less well organized, for lack of a better way to explain it.

"You have a far-away look in your eyes," her husband leaned over from next to her and whispered. "*Buran?*"

Like her, he didn't call it her home, as she had a new home at *Ladaux*. Just as he had traveled many places looking for her, unwilling to let her go.

"I understand why Harinder and Phil request my presence," she replied quietly, watching everyone at work. "At the same time, I'm not sure if I actually help or hinder."

"How so?"

"You are already aliens, to many of them," Sam grinned. "Weirdos with impossible cultural traits come to ruin everything that has worked for centuries."

He grinned back. That described another place they knew. Several, actually, as *Fribourg* was undergoing a slow revolution as well.

"And you?" he asked.

"I can talk about being captured by pirates," Sam smiled wider now. "And forced to confront the nature of evil, once the blinders were pulled from my eyes by Phil. And this irresistible Dragoon from *CS-405* who kissed me once before sending me off, only to then show up on my doorstep one day, two years later, with roses."

"You like roses," he reminded her.

One comment she had made over dinner, one night. And it had stuck with him through everything. She leaned over and kissed him on the cheek.

"I wonder if we might not be better off asking *Fribourg* to send a representative to assist," Sam said now. "Someone who can talk to *Dalou* about life under a new way of thinking, just as Phil expects me to do with anyone and everyone we meet here."

"You should tell him that," Trinidad said. "Or Harinder. Someone. We can send a message back to Fleet with a Fast Clipper, so it might get to *St. Legier* quickly enough for some ambassador to arrive in about a year."

"You're assuming that they don't have one coming now," Sam said.

"I'm reasonably confident," Trinidad replied. "Phil is on good terms with the Emperor and her Consort. They've blessed this mission, specifically because Phil's an explorer, not a conqueror. Still, she'd probably send someone. Not herself, though that might be the most interesting. And now that she has a family, doubly so."

"So I should just be even more exotic than you?" she asked. "Is that possible?"

He laughed.

"What are you two lovebirds up to?" Dao muttered from her nearby command station.

"Talking about how exotic *Buran* might be, over and above *Aquitaine*," Sam said. "And whether Phil should invite the Emperor of *Fribourg* to send folks."

"We would love to meet them," Dao said. "The same standing invite to *Yaumgan*, though we understand that they might not be as open-minded."

"Hidebound is the term I would have used," Trinidad said. "Not sure who Casey might send. Denis Jež would be an interesting choice, but he might be too important."

"Keller's former right hand, yes?" Dao asked. "The one who is an advisor to *Fribourg* now? Why does *Aquitaine* allow it?"

"The price of peace," Trinidad replied. "After the *Aquitaine* government nearly caused a general war to break out again, Keller broke them, even as she withdrew to *Petron*. Her senior commanders from the Expedition, the so-called Merry Men, all retired and largely vanished from history. Some teach. Some travel. Jež accepted an appointment at *St. Legier*, similar to the one the former First Lord of the Fleet took."

"Friends made across the battlefield," Dao said with sudden understanding. "Is Keller really that much larger than life?"

"And then some," Sam said. "Physically, a small woman. Dark skinned. Hispanic. Curvy because she works out constantly to stay in shape. Simply the smartest human I have ever met or heard of. Her Merry Men were all exceptional commanders themselves, and together they drove the *Holding of Man* back, when it had seemed an impossible task."

"Would she ever visit?" Dao asked.

Trinidad laughed.

"Last I heard, she had decided to circumnavigate the galaxy

as her delayed honeymoon, aboard a vessel similar to *Urumchi*," he said.

"Similar?" Dao asked.

"Both were designed by Yan Bedrov, who did so much to create the new generations of warships," Trinidad replied. "*Urumchi* was his original design, then he had another breakthrough and that became her flagship *Terra*."

"Does anyone know where she is?" Dao asked.

Trinidad gestured to the heavens.

"Out there," he said. "But she was never a diplomat. Not like Phil Kosnett. She was a destroyer, come out of the night to ravage your systems and your fleets until you chose to surrender or withdraw and behave."

"And Phil will just talk?" Dao asked.

"As long as he sees a reason," Sam said. "Even Phil can be pushed far enough. Look at *Meerut* and the *Ingham Syndicate*."

Dao shuddered. Sam understood how she felt.

How much of the Balhee Cluster might Phil disrupt before he was done?

SIXTEEN

SUNFLOWER IMPERIAL PALACE, MORNING

Osamu checked his attire in the mirror and smiled. His glorious imperial robes would be transported up in a case designed to keep them clean and sharp, so he was free to simply travel in as much comfort as he could while retaining the imperial dignity.

How many decades had it been since an Emperor had actually traveled to the Shogun's station/palace *Ellariel*-jo? He had palaces on other worlds, but even travel to them was infrequent. The entire Household had fallen into a pattern of predictability that had grown…prosaic.

Today, he wore comfortable boots with baggy pants tucked in, both in a rich emerald green that had originally been merely the color of House Yosan, before they had become emperors. A long tunic, also emerald, trimmed and laced in white, with a white shirt underneath. He kept his hair short and his face clean, such that many might mistake him for a younger man than his fifty-one years.

"You look fine," Aimi said from her chair in the corner watching. "I'm just sorry I cannot join you."

"We are already likely to make Kugosu nervous," he said with a wry grin. "If the entire family attended, it might look like we were intending to flee into the unknown wastes. Perhaps claim sanctuary with the aliens as a way to be free. That would never do."

A knock at the door interrupted before she could reply. Probably for the best, because even he wasn't ready to consider such a course of action. He was the Emperor of *Dalou*.

And yet, he was also generally a prisoner in his own home.

Did he wish to change that?

Maybe. Not today.

"Come," he called, turning to the door.

His bodyguards would have already passed whoever it was, so he had no worries. Unless the entire Household had conspired to assassinate him.

Then none of this would be his problem anymore.

When did you grow so morbid, old man?

The door opened and Prince Shingo stood there, a hint of nervousness underneath the obvious pride the young man had in the uniform he wore.

Dalou Navy. Black uniform such as they all wore, trimmed with green in Shingo's case. Not necessarily immediately identifiable, but there were few clans who wore a green that bold. It would mark him as a Prince.

Today, he was just a nineteen-year-old boy, verging on adulthood yet edgy, because Osamu had ordered his son and heir to accompany him to orbit. Let the strangers meet the man that they would deal with in another few decades, when Osamu tired of the weight of his crown.

Kugosu might plan a long game, but they were upstarts in grand politics. The current Shogun was only the fourth of his line to command, having displaced Sunyu four generations ago to ascend to ultimate power.

Osamu didn't know the current Shogun on a personal basis. They met twice yearly when the Shogun attended the traditional ceremonies here, where a grateful emperor bestowed supreme authority on the man. Whether he wished to or not.

"Come," Osamu instructed. "Close the door."

Shingo came to attention in the center of the room.

"Your Majesty," he said.

"I am your father when we are alone like this," Osamu instructed him. "Relax and kiss your mother before we depart."

Shingo had his height, so he towered over the woman and bent down to kiss her on the cheek awkwardly. The family was not particularly tactile. *Dalou* culture did not foster hugging.

There were times when Osamu wondered if he might have to change other parts of their heritage, now that the outsiders had forced everyone's hands.

"Should we be traveling on a single shuttle, Father?" Shingo said as he turned now. "Does that not place the Imperial Line at risk?"

Osamu laughed.

"Let them assassinate us both then," he countered. "That means our dread Shogun has to deal with finding worthy husbands for Sota and Moriko himself, and possibly deal with either a ruling Empress, or the headaches of a regency."

Shingo shuddered. Both had happened historically. Neither situation had ever boded well for the *Hegemony*. In that, Osamu could prey on the fears of his Shogun and those retainers.

Touch me, and chaos might descend on all your houses.

He suppressed a grin, wondering if all this might be the expression of some bizarre mid-life crisis he had not expected nor encountered previously. A rogue emperor probably factored high in the nightmares of many aboard *Ellariel*-jo right now.

Let those fools on the station deal with it. We have grown too self-absorbed.

Self-absorbed? Is that really it?

Osamu nodded to his son and kissed Aimi again for luck as he considered what futures he might be creating for his son. And his people.

"Come," he said, moving to the door and opening it.

Shingo's lone bodyguard he needed around the palace fell in

with Osamu's group as they walked. The front door was down several flights of stairs and forward. Gadhavi had obviously cleared all the hallways of retainers that might be scandalized to see their emperor engaged in even sartorial revolution, let alone political or social. Because that was what this was, at the end of the day.

He saw one chance, today, to seize some control of his destiny, at the moment when the aliens had already disrupted everything. He would take it, or be damned.

"Your Majesty," Gadhavi said nervously as they emerged into the noontime sun of the front porch and the vehicle that would take them to the starport. "May I register my resistance to your actions one final time?"

Osamu stopped cold and scowled at the man. Premier was a fancy name for an advisor who didn't do much except spy on him for the Shogun and occasionally run errands. There had been no power in the position for many, many generations now. Just the wealth and glory of serving in the Imperial Palace.

"If you feel so strongly, I suggest you resign," Osamu said flatly, hearing even his bodyguards gasp in surprise at his words and tone. "Tell your true master that I am uncontrollable and get out of my hair for good. Is that sufficient understanding between us, Gadhavi?"

In the back of his mind, some idle function wondered if he'd been drugged at some point, to engage in such outrageous behavior. Doubly so in public.

In the end, though, he knew the truth. The weight of history and protocol was heavy on his shoulders, rounding them and hunching his back and mind, however metaphorically, with each passing day. Osamu's own father, Shōhei, had withdrawn entirely from the life after it got to be too much, leaving his son to deal with it.

And deal with it he would.

Aliens had come to the Cluster and already done the impossible. Twice.

What more would Kosnett do to disrupt centuries of tradition?

Osamu watched his Premier bow deeply at the waist. No doubt to hide the fury on his face, lest Osamu simply fire him in disgrace.

The dread Emperor of *Dalou* chose to accept that retreat for what it was and stepped right past the man as everyone was paralyzed by indecision, going so far as to open the rear door of the transport himself and getting in, even as others around him squawked in barely-disguised outrage.

Where have we gotten to, that a man opening his own door is unacceptable?

At the same time, didn't that describe much of modern Dalou culture?

Shingo took a seat next to him and bodyguards entered up front. Gadhavi made to join them and Osamu stopped him.

"No," he said abruptly. "You will remain at the palace until I return to deal with you. Driver, move out."

Someone outside the vehicle pulled the Premier back and shut the door, with that old man standing open-mouthed on the gravel roadway.

Freedom felt good.

Osamu hoped that the price he had to pay later wasn't too great.

SEVENTEEN

I veta felt her face want to fall into its natural scowl but stopped it. The creases would turn into wrinkles at far too young an age if she did that. Already, the first gray hairs were visible in places and she felt the touch of middle age creeping up on her.

They were in a conference room with a holographic projector. Her, Command Machinist El-Amin, Gunner Hào Boyadjiev, and Pilot Bozhidar Virág. Nam was busy with Harinder for now.

Urumchi's top people for this. The big guns.

"Thoughts?" she asked of the Command Machinist sitting across from her.

Rais Hosni El-Amin. Technically, he outranked her, but Phil had assigned her a gold team/blue team exercise, and he'd volunteered to assist. It was that or let one of his engineers have all the fun.

Can't have that.

"Those three monsters can throw six condors at us at once," he replied, gesturing to the readout. "*Wraithruin* could add another one, so I assume the same from these other two cruisers as well. Plus a shitstorm of cranes from all directions."

"Everything weakens with distance traveled," Virág said. "Presumably we would have to maintain our distance and snipe with the Fours."

"If we did that, we lose everything else and end up ceding them the initiative," Iveta reminded everyone. "We don't have the full squadron, either, so they could launch some firebirds at us and then charge in behind them, like happened at *Meerut* with *Wulfa*."

Wulfa had chosen to die gloriously in battle, but Phil had also had two extra battleships on his side to annihilate the ship when it tried.

"Has anybody tried using those Shield Projectors that the locals use like snowplows?" Hào asked now.

"Explain," El-Amin ordered brusquely.

"They have close shields like we do, and that projector," Hào spoke. "It works like a curved piece of glass. Is that the only shape it could take? Could we change the pitch of it somehow and drive a firebird off to one side as it charged? Maybe force it to stop completely, pivot, and come back to us?"

"Can they even do that?" Iveta asked. "I've only ever seen them take the most direct route to a target, tracking as the ship evades."

"They have some level of guidance systems aboard," Hào said. "At least according to *Aranyani*'s notes. Whether that's good enough to let them hold a lock on us, I can't tell you."

"Lock," Iveta said quietly. "How do we break a lock?"

Every head turned towards her now.

"*Aditi* has a technique where they shut down all their active sensors and launch a shuttle broadcasting as much electronic snow and noise as they can," Iveta said. "Most of the time that succeeds, because the firebird accepts the new target. The tradeoff is that they are blind for a while and have to come to rest, so again they also lose initiative. The other guy gets away, or has the chance to get to knife-fighting range."

"What would you suggest?" El-Amin asked tersely.

Iveta considered it. She had studied every battle Jessica Keller had ever fought, beginning to end. Others had done the same, but they had been intent on learning how to fight like the woman.

Iveta wanted to *think* like her.

A lightbulb came on over her head, however metaphorically.

"*Thuringwell,*" she said suddenly to the others. "Warspite Four."

Blank faces greeted her. No surprise. Only a complete nerd like her would even know that reference.

"Keller's flight wing included a scout fighter, even as her force had the original Survey Cruiser *Ballard,*" Iveta said. "*da Vinci,* when she was a pilot, rather than a pirate. She and *Ballard* turned everything to max, and were able to convince the Imperials that a light missile cruiser had just *appeared* out of nowhere. Think our friend *Shadowbolt,* the light missile bombard. The imperials fell for it and wasted a lot of ammunition there, which the flight wing had been specifically prepped to destroy. That and *Shivaji* might have broken *Fribourg* for good."

"How?" El-Amin asked.

Fourteen years ago, he would have been a simple Engineering Centurion somewhere, while Keller was invading imperial space and forcing them into the peace that might have eventually saved the galaxy.

"They called it Ghost Mode," Iveta said. "Can we maybe do something like a shield projector, but instead of trying to create a forcefield that is strong enough to hold off firebirds, can we create an image of us forward and off to one side? If the firebird gets there, it should explode when it thinks it is about to damage *Urumchi.* What if we cause it to sail into a ghost and detonate?"

"Why has nobody ever tried it before?" El-Amin demanded.

"They don't have the spare power that we do," Iveta replied, reminding the man what Heavy Dreadnoughts were like, compared to the old days. "And they've never fought a serious war in their lives. Not one for survival. We're a century or more ahead of them on warships because we spent all that time losing to *Fribourg* before Jessica beat them. Then Bedrov designed the Expeditionary-classes. Then he improved them. Three generations head start? Maybe five? They don't even use the Primaries here, which still surprises me, but they have Power Taps and titan bolts and firebirds instead. Again, most of these ships are designed for anti-piracy patrols, rather than fleet actions. What can we do with this much of an edge?"

El-Amin fell silent when she did, but Iveta could see the wheels churning furiously. Best way to get an engineer to think outside the box was still to tell him something was impossible, then watch him move heaven and earth to prove you wrong.

Like moving a planetoid out of the way, instead of letting it slam into *Vilahana*.

She checked the others, but they were all a little green around the gills with shock at her words. That was fine. Heather had hired her as the best of the so-called Keller-clones on the market.

Junkyard.

She had finally earned a pirate nickname from Heather and Phil. Now, she needed to prove to the rest of the *RAN* that she was more than just another killer. After all, hadn't future First Lord Arott Whughy originally invented the Pulse-Two that formed the backbone of this squadron?

What could Iveta Beridze contribute to the Art of War?

EIGHTEEN

Heather physically rotated her upper body to look at Leyla. "Repeat that," she said in disbelief.

"The shuttle that's coming up broadcasts a transponder signal identifying it as containing both the Emperor and the Crown Prince," Leyla said again. "It appears to be unarmed and without escort."

"Yes, that's what I thought you said," Heather breathed heavily.

She thought about it for a long moment then keyed the flag bridge.

"Harinder," the woman said.

"You and Phil need to take the flag, right now," Heather said ominously. "We might have a situation on our hands."

"Stand by."

Phil was there in conference mode a second later.

"Talk to me," he said earnestly.

"The Emperor of *Dalou* is flying up to the station in an unarmed shuttle without anyone around him, Phil," Heather said simply.

The profanity that escaped his mouth was one she'd been

considering for several seconds, so it was good to know that they were on the same page here.

"Is anybody reacting?" he asked.

"Not currently," Heather said. "However, all of the Shogun's warships are sitting at the top of the column of sky that the shuttle is circling up into. If anybody wanted to do anything, it's likely to be over so fast that there will be no warning."

He fell silent for a long moment.

"Bring the squadron up to a soft alert," he ordered. "All guns locked down, but engines and shields ready for anything, including running like hell if we have to."

"Running?" she asked.

"If this turns into an assassination, that's the prelude to a civil war," Phil said. "Remember the ancient events, and the order to expel all foreigners. I can hold *Meerut* just fine against *Dalou* while I send home for help, if the absolute worst case scenario happens today. At the same time, I do not wish to contribute anything to it, so maybe let the squadron drift back and away some while we're at it."

"Understood," Heather said, turning to Bozhidar and nodding for her Pilot to start plotting something that looked innocent.

She had the kind of team that could almost read her mind, these days. *Ground Control* owned all their souls now.

"Anything else?" she asked.

"Go full defensive at the slightest hint of trouble," Phil said. "I'm going to make some calls."

He cut the line and Heather looked around.

"Leyla, communicate to everyone quietly," she ordered. "QUIETLY. Bozhidar, find me a soft spot in the perimeter. Everyone else have some coffee and amp it up a notch for a few hours, until we know what happens."

"We expecting anything?" Leyla asked.

"Even Phil doesn't travel that wide open home at *Ladaux*,"

Heather said. "Man has balls of steel, or he's being set up. Either way, nothing we can do but watch."

NINETEEN

ADCON CRUISER ARANYANI

"I'll take it in my office," Kaur said, rising and moving aft.

Phil calling right now, even as the squadron was being told to come to a low alert status, told her what it was about. It wasn't that Kaur didn't trust her crew to remain quiet. They had nobody to gossip to.

However, that changed the moment the ship got home. She needed to cover her own ass, as well as her posterity. She closed the hatch and locked it before sitting at her desk and opening the line. She even confirmed that the scramble was active.

This was an *RAN* code that hadn't even been shared with the rest of the force. Just *Aranyani*.

"Hello, Phil," she said in a grim voice.

"You've seen the Emperor's message?" he asked.

"I have," she replied. "Are there orders?"

"Be ready for anything, until he docks with the station," the man said. "And I do mean anything. For now, we watch, and hope we aren't witnesses to history."

"History?" she asked, confused now.

"What would happen if someone assassinated the man?" Phil asked. "With the Crown Prince aboard at that? As I understand it, he has two younger daughters, but *Dalou* would be even less interested in a female emperor than *Fribourg* was."

"I agree," Kaur said, feeling that cold weight of history land on her back.

Already, she would go down as a witness to great things, as well as a participant. What more evil might the gods throw at them before it was all done?

"Could we somehow interrupt anything?" she asked.

"No," Phil said definitively. "Heather and her team tell me that it would be over too quickly, even if we were in the middle of it. That's why I want us over on a flank, in case we have to run."

"Run?" she repeated, just to make sure she understood the man.

"That's right," he said. "If something stupid happens in *Ellariel* orbit and the squadron is running for our lives, I need you to split off, *Aranyani*. We'll be heading to *Meerut*, and hopefully outrunning any ambush. You will proceed directly to *Aditi* itself and communicate with the *Consensus*. They'll need to know."

"We don't know anything, Phil," she offered.

"The stakes have just gone up to a level that makes me extremely uncomfortable, Kaur," he said. "One fool. One fanatic. One mistake. All hell might break loose."

"What would you expect the *Aditi Consensus* to do, First Centurion?" she asked, feeling her voice grow serious and distant.

"Watch from a safe distance, Captain." He fell into the same didactic tone, every syllable a separate thing. "Such an event, such a situation, would be an internal situation for *Dalou*. One that outsiders should not allow ourselves to be drawn into. At any cost."

Kaur blinked. Why wouldn't Phil want the *Dalou Hegemony* in a state of utter chaos? The *Consensus* might take the opportunity to move in and establish a new wall of forward bases in that instance. Armed trade stations, but the kind where the fleet could call.

Or defend.

It wasn't like the *Consensus* didn't do that occasionally now. Probes, to see if they could slip in and hold some otherwise empty system. Or one that had illegal colonies on the ground somewhere and maybe needed trade.

Not all of them had been pushed back out later, either. The *Consensus* had successfully claimed at least a dozen stars from *Dalou* that way over the last century or so. Patience.

Phil had to know that. Was this a threat not to engage, if the *Dalou Hegemony* broke down into a civil war? Would there ever be a better time to do so?

"You would expect the *Consensus* to remain entirely aloof from any such situation?" she asked, just to confirm.

"I might *require* it, Captain," he said ominously. "Nobody is served, in the event such a thing comes to bear. Not over the long term."

Kaur bit back her sarcastic response, wondering what the man was about. The *Consensus* was always pushing their existing borders, mostly because most of their neighboring nations weren't usually organized enough to push back. With the pirates broken, that might even get easier, as the Syndicates had generally preyed on *Aditi* shipping.

Spies back home presumed that the others had been paying the Syndicates to do so. Without that, nobody could stand against the *Consensus*, with the presumed exception of *Yaumgan*.

Kaur felt a chill descend on her very soul.

Phil had to know that. Had broken the Syndicates intentionally, and declared open war on them to get them to behave. *Aditi* would automatically flow into that vacuum. Doubly so without anybody pushing back.

Except that Phil had just intimated that he might push back.

By himself, a laughable proposition.

But the entire *RAN* could run roughshod over the Cluster if they wanted. If they had any reason to.

Would Phil defend *Dalou* from *Aditi* in a confrontation between nations? And *Gloran* and *Ewin*, the two flanking neighbors?

She felt like something important had just happened. Like someone had forced Phil into a situation that wasn't supposed to come up, or at least be publicly acknowledged, until much, *much* later. Like she had a window into his secret plans, that somehow involved *Dalou* remaining a close second to *Aditi* in strength.

Except that made no sense whatsoever. Wouldn't *Aquitaine* want the Cluster to descend into the chaos of a general war if they could arrange it? That opened an entire flank for *Aquitaine* to expand into, much like *Aditi* would fill, given the chance.

And Phil didn't want that? Wanted her to convey a deep and dangerous message to her superiors if it came to that? Stay out or count me as an enemy? That sort of thing?

Kaur released the deep breath she had been holding. She studied the man's face on the screen.

"Next week, we should probably sit down for a frank discussion, First Centurion," she said curtly.

Phil nodded, like he wasn't surprised by her response. That almost frightened her more, that he might be counting on that from her.

"If we can make it safely to next week, Kaur, I will tell you more," Phil promise. "Not everything, but perhaps enough."

Then he cut the line from his end, leaving her almost gasping with released pressure.

Was Phil negotiating some secret pact with *Dalou*? Something that might aid the Emperor? At whose expense, though? The only other power center in *Dalou* was the Shogun himself.

Unless Phil was planning on overthrowing the Shogun at some point.

Kaur leaned back, cold dread like a cloak on her shoulders.

TWENTY

ELLARIEL-JO ORBITAL PALACE

J irou did not scream in rage. Barely. How he held it in, he wasn't entirely certain, other than a lifetime of training on the dojo floor to keep all emotions contained.

Was that stupid son of a bitch *trying* to get himself killed? To destroy the entire imperial house? To bring down the *Dalou Hegemony*?

He was in his office. The door was closed. Only Kohahu was present now to see the flash of emotions roil in his eyes. Even she had flinched as she sat across from him, perhaps expecting a blow. Or a shattered desk.

Jirou focused everything into the chair beneath him, as if he could draw a breath heavy enough to cause it to collapse under his weight. That image calmed him.

"No escorts?" He finally looked up again to take in the slightly frazzled nerves of his warrior daughter.

No doubt, someone had sent her in to save themselves from being screamed at. He wasn't sure if he should inquire as to who might deserve punishment for such an action, or assume that she might have just volunteered, because he would refrain with her.

"None, Shogun," she said carefully. "They lifted off from the starport without any formal notice except an automated flight

"

plan. It was when they were challenged at the edge of the atmosphere that it became obvious who was aboard the craft. And the type of craft."

Jirou nodded, still grinding his teeth hard enough that she might hear it. He took a second breath. Focused himself on what he could control of the situation.

There wasn't much. Any orders he might issue this late would make him look feeble and reactive, rather than in control of the situation.

Was the Emperor intending to try his patience? Obviously. But to what end?

Or had the man finally snapped under the pressures of the imperial palace? Jirou did not spend any more time down there than was necessary, though he had his spies, all of who had failed to foresee any of this.

Jirou could see firing the lot of them and starting over. Assuming that nothing happened to the Emperor and the Crown Prince in the next hour that caused all of *Dalou* to implode.

He reached out a hand and tapped the intercom. The motion seemed to calm suddenly-ragged nerves.

"Shogun?" the man outside answered immediately.

"Find the Minister of Protocol and have him in my office," Jirou said. "Now."

"At once, sir."

Jirou closed the line and considered the scene that would play out.

"Shift over to the other seat," he told Kohahu.

The office had two, for those times when he needed to talk with someone privately. It was only the grand audience chamber with all the guards when something needed to be public.

Hida Taro had—*probably*—not risen to the level of a public execution for his recent failures.

The day was young.

Kohahu moved silently, out of the line of his rage, as it were.

Perhaps grateful to only be a witness. She needed to learn the hard parts of the job, as well as the easy ones, though he doubted that she could take his place. Doubted that she would be allowed to.

Jirou would burn that bridge when he got there. She was too young to begin arranging a marriage that might eventually see the Shogunate merge to a second clan. Even sixteen-year-old Kokoro, the more scholarly of his daughters, wasn't in line for a few years.

There was time, assuming that idiot of an emperor wasn't trying to get himself killed today.

A knock preceded the door opening and Hida Taro stood there, slightly out of breath for an old man, in the manner of one who has just run from wherever he was when the message arrived.

"Sit," Jirou ordered.

Taro was flushed and his clothing was slightly disarrayed, to the extent that Jirou wondered if the man had been with a mistress five minutes ago. If so, then it would absolutely be time to retire and be replaced by someone with…different priorities.

"What can you tell me about the Emperor's impending arrival?" Jirou asked in a calm, professional voice.

Taro froze. His face went white, which had the unfortunate effect of showing the white roots in his hair that hadn't been dyed recently and the layer of pancake makeup that only went to the edges of his jaw. Jirou had always wondered if the man's black hair was natural. Now, he was certain that it was not.

Just another false presentation to the public, just as he was perhaps keeping a mistress on the station. Jirou could smell a perfume that Kohahu hadn't brought in with her. She smelled of leather and steel and the dojo floor.

Like her father.

"Shogun?" Taro asked.

"The Emperor will arrive shortly," Jirou said. "Aboard a

common shuttle, flying from a public starport, without any escorts. How did that come to happen, *Minister of Protocol?*"

Taro started to stammer some bullshit response, but Jirou cut him off like the great blade.

"I begin to doubt your efficacy, Minister," Jirou growled, perhaps pronouncing the worst possible doom on a man of power and privilege like one of his ministers.

That they had all grown old and stale. That they had fucked up one time too many.

Taro grew so white that Jirou wondered if he might have a medical event.

That might just cap the day, all things considered, if one of his senior ministers died of a heart attack, right here in his office, in the middle of everything else.

When had it all gone so wrong? Jirou wasn't certain, but the recent arrival of Kohahu had provided him a new stick against which to measure things, when he himself had perhaps grown comfortable with the old ways.

Shit. *Comfortable kills.*

"Hida Taro, I am sorry to see you go, but I agree with you that perhaps retirement now lets you go out with nothing but glorious accomplishments on your ledger," Jirou said, rising.

Kohahu exploded silently to her feet. Taro took a moment to process that he had just been fired. He blinked rapidly, several times, before his ossified brain caught up with the situation. He still wasn't breathing.

The fool rose on uncertain feet, almost tottering for a man who was yet only fifty-five. But used up. Grown *comfortable.* Had stopped challenging his environment. Mastering it. Dominating it.

Because comfortable kills.

Jirou keyed the intercom.

"Shogun?"

"The Minister of Protocol has offered his resignation and is taking retirement, starting immediately," Jirou said sternly. "You will arrange a shuttle to transport him to the surface without delay, that he can most easily return to his estates in comfort.”

The Taro estates were grand, picturesque things, almost rivaling the Imperial Gardens themselves in many ways. Jirou wondered if that attention to beauty and pleasure had caused the man to lose sight of his duty. Allowed him to grow *comfortable.*

Sloppy. Lazy.

Old.

“Immediately, Shogun,” the aide said.

The door opened a moment later and two guards stepped in, perhaps a bit surprised that Hida Taro wasn’t bleeding to death, from the tone Jirou had used. Quickly, they escorted the old man from the room and closed the door again.

Jirou sat. Kohahu remained up, so he gestured her down. He studied his middle daughter. Fourteen, going on forty, perhaps. No longer a child. Not yet a woman. Better than many of his bodyguards on the dojo floor. Smarter than all of them, as well. Maybe his best ally right now, because she was not *comfortable.*

“In an hour, the Emperor of *Dalou* will set foot on this station,” Jirou said in a suddenly-tired voice.

He could do that with this child. She was the most like him. She nodded her understanding.

“Kugosu did not hold the Shogunate, the last time such a thing happened,” Jirou said carefully, reminding her that all things were eventually just sand on a beach to be swept away by storms. Even mountains. “We are largely without precedent.”

“How my I serve?” she asked, chin up and eyes glittering in way almost exactly the opposite of the now-departed old man Taro.

Because comfortable kills, and she had not yet learned to seek comfort for herself. Jirou wondered if he had. Certainly the last few years he had been safely keeping all waters calm in *Dalou.*

Was that his mistake? Circumstances had utterly forced his

hand. Doubly so, with no Minister of Protocol to greet the Emperor of *Dalou* as the man arrived.

Dare he just chuck everything out the airlock? Assuming that nobody opened fire on the shuttle right now and started a civil war, how else might this day turn completely insane? He hadn't even gotten around to the aliens yet.

But if comfortable kills, then just uncomfortable might keep you alive, assuming it didn't become a permanent thing. Chaos might grind down the edge of your blade over time, until it wasn't there when you needed it.

Jirou felt the need to walk into the forest for a week with a canteen, a knife, a bow, and a compass. Break the bonds that *comfortable* had twined around his limbs in the guise of power.

Before they pulled him under the surface of the water.

"You will take charge of the Imperial party when it arrives, Kohahu," he decided. She blinked, but gave no other outward response. "You will be my personal representative. If the Emperor can take a shit on centuries of protocol with such a stunt as he has pulled on us, we can do no less than to match him."

"Is this wise, Shogun?" she asked in a carefully neutral voice.

He shrugged. Smiled, even. He could do that in the privacy of his personal office, attended only by his warrior daughter.

"I have learned a valuable lesson today, daughter," he said so quietly that she had to lean forward to hear him. "Comfortable kills."

She blinked again, but was too young to understand. Certainly, Jirou didn't think such a thing would have made sense to him until he was at least a decade older. But she was his daughter. The most like him of the three, at that.

"And if everyone is uncomfortable, we might all yet survive, Father?" she asked, cutting him to the quick with the depth of her understanding of ancient Socrates.

He nodded, unwilling to trust his voice at the utter pride that might erupt.

She rose. Bowed deeply.

"Then I will cause all your friends and foes discomfort in your name, Shogun," she said simply.

He nodded again. They shared a secret smile that would mean nothing to most of humanity, as she withdrew.

Jirou studied the closed door and wondered if she had just pronounced his salvation, or his doom.

TWENTY-ONE
ELLARIEL-JO ORBITAL PALACE

Makara had spent most of today in his assigned quarters aboard the Shogun's palace station, meditating alone as a way of dealing with everything being out of his control.

Smallest of fish, largest of oceans. Still, he represented any number of folks who were counting on him, so it was necessary to sit calmly and smile productively with the performance that would begin in a few hours. He'd had his hair cut by a palace barber, as well as a formal shave better than he normally did to himself in the morning. All his clothing had been laid out, perfectly cleaned again by the locals, obviously uncertain that a Sugawara retainer could manage to dress himself properly.

In an hour or so, he would dress. Suit up for war, as it were, on an entirely different battlefield.

Weirdly, he might still be escorting Phil and the others into the fray, just as he and *Morninghawk* had done twice at *Meerut*. As with the second battle, hopefully it would not be necessary for him to die today to prove his loyalty to the Shogun.

A rap at the door intruded. Disrupted his calmness, what little he had been able to assemble over the last hour. Maybe for the best, then.

He rose to his full height and let everything loosen and

stretch as he walked across the room. For now, casual slacks, layers of shirts, and socks, as he had no intention of going out in public until it became necessary.

Makara Omarov understood necessity.

He opened the door, somehow not surprised to find Samnang standing there. Unlike him, she was dressed to the nines in the House colors of Kugosu, gold trimmed in blood red. At least she was alone, as the look of disapproval she gave him was almost withering.

"Dress now," she instructed, putting a hand in the middle of his chest and literally pushing him backwards into the chamber unresisting as she followed.

It made him a bit uncomfortable, having her in his personal space. Aboard *Morninghawk*, she had been a powerful and influential guest, a few stolen kisses notwithstanding. They had progressed no further in their relationship, leaving everything by unspoken agreement until after this evening's charade of silliness was complete.

The Shogun might yet find a reason to fault him for something. Makara could not help but flash back to that interview in the man's grand chamber, alone and surrounded by danger.

"Now?" Makara asked, letting her force him backwards, in spite of her smaller size.

"There have been developments in the last few hours, while you have been removed," she said, gesturing to the clothing on the end of his bed. "The Emperor will arrive shortly."

Makara nodded. He'd seen and heard the message yesterday that had caused such a ruckus and whirlwind about the station.

"I thought I was to meet him during the formal reception tonight?" Makara asked, uncertain whose pawn he was these days.

The Shogun's, by definition and the presence of Samnang Sobol. Kosnett's, by right of conquest at *Meerut*, perhaps? Omarov and by extension Sugawara. The Emperor had so rarely factored into things that it took Makara a moment to remember the man's name. Osamu, of Yosan. Emerald and white, to Sobol's crimson and gold.

He considered the uniform on the bed, and realized that Sugawara's clan colors, dark forest green and black, might automatically make him appear an ally of the Emperor when people noted colors. That had been the case centuries ago when the Shogunate came into being.

It was also why Sugawara was a minor clan today. They had been on the losing side of that ancient civil war, and had worked assiduously ever since to be loyal to the Shogun.

And, he supposed, the Emperor.

He turned back to the woman, standing before him.

"What happened?" he asked.

"The palace is in something of a turmoil," she replied in a dark, foreboding voice. "The Minister of Protocol abruptly resigned half an hour ago, with no explanation given."

Makara grimaced. Palace politics was one of the reasons he preferred the purity of starship command. Far less people working against you that way.

"What is the Assistant Minister doing?" Makara asked. He went ahead and stripped his outer shirt, certain that he would get no peace from the woman unless he complied.

Imperial Inspector. Not that many steps below a Minister, at the end of the day.

"Nothing," Samnang replied simply.

"Nothing?"

"The Shogun has charged his own daughter to take over the situation," she said. "The young woman reached out to me and ordered you to be present."

"He has a daughter?" Makara asked.

Up until a month ago, Makara had hardly known anything about the man. Shoguns were aloof, terrible dragons in their orbital fortresses, never seen by little people.

At least until Phil Kosnett had invited a lesser retainer of a smaller house to accompany him on a grand adventure.

Shit.

"He has three daughters," Samnang informed him. "I've never met the oldest or youngest. This one is named Kohahu, and she is handling everything."

"How old is she?" he asked, pulling the second shirt up now to reveal his spare build. The current Shogun was younger than Makara, if he remembered correctly.

Samnang's grimace contained more information than some encyclopedias. None of it warmed him.

"Fourteen Standard," she said.

Fourteen. FOURTEEN? And in charge of a reception for the Emperor on short notice?

Shit.

He sat on the edge of the bed and finished stripping. She handed him the nice pants and he dressed as quickly as he could, uncaring that she had seen him thus. It was the Inspector's reputation that would be ruined, coming to his chamber, rather than the other way around.

Assuming he survived. All of this felt like that battle plan Heather had laid out before going into *Meerut* orbit for the *Twilight of the Pirates*. Do your best. Assume that the other side is about to panic and throw everything they have at you like rats in a trap. Try to survive, understanding that the *only* irreplaceable ship in the entire formation was *Urumchi*.

Including when that involved issuing an order to lay in a ramming course and charge.

"Fourteen?" he finally managed, after thirty seconds of pregnant silence as he dressed.

"And more dangerous than almost anyone you will meet today, Morninghawk," she reminded him. "Barring only her father, from what I remember of the Ministers that remain."

Remain? Yes, one down. How many other heads would roll

because the Emperor had surprised everyone at the last minute, and given them no option but to grit their teeth and play along?

What terrible game was the Shogun trapped into playing now, that he had to place an untested teenager between the Shogunate itself, and the Imperial Household?

And how did Morninghawk survive this one?

TWENTY-TWO

ELLARIEL-JO ORBITAL PALACE

Kohahu studied the bay reception area like it would become a battlefield shortly. It would, but hopefully only on the social and emotional scale. Nothing requiring any of them to bare steel.

As the Shogun's daughter and aide—Minister herself?—she of course had two blades at her hip, though she had not added a holster nor a pistol, unlike the dozen Kugosu bodyguards and station troopers surrounding the outer edges of the space.

Nobody else was armed. Nobody else was *allowed* weapons on the Shogun's station.

And yet, protocol that she had checked an hour ago said that the Imperial Party was to be escorted by their own armed troops at all times. Yet another reason it had been so long since any of them had come to orbit. According to the book she had consulted, the last such event had required nearly two years of delicate negotiations and planning that had involved more than one hundred people on the various sides.

She had herself, an hour, and instructions from her Lord to cause everyone some level of discomfort.

Morninghawk entered now, escorted by the Inspector that

had been sent with him to *Aditi* originally, to insure the man's loyalty. Kohahu had read some of the reports Sobol had filed.

Something was off about them, but she decided that she wasn't old enough to understand some elements of adult behavior, for all that she presented as such.

Sobol stood too close to the man, and didn't scowl enough, for all her face was rigidly controlled.

Kohahu nodded to the man and gestured him to a particular spot on her right. A favored location for a retainer, indicating honor. It would place him on the Emperor's left when that man entered, causing him to react backwards. To twist against himself if he chose to greet the man who was technically the entire reason for this thing.

But wasn't that exactly what Father had instructed her to achieve?

Discomfort.

Morninghawk was taller than she had been prepared for. Perhaps one hundred and ninety centimeters, though not as broad-shouldered as her Father. Kohahu was tall for a woman at one hundred and seventy-five. Morninghawk still made her feel tiny. At least Sobol was more normal in height, perhaps ten centimeters shorter. The Inspector wore a blade, as was her right as a personal representative of the Shogun.

Much like a middle daughter.

Morninghawk came to rest and bowed his upper body to her.

"How may I serve?" he asked in a voice lacking any emotional content whatsoever.

Not even boredom or *ennui*. Just…nothing.

She had read the reports on the man compiled after the First Centurion's initial message arrived. Read the interview that had been conducted.

Studied the battle of *Meerut* and listened as Morninghawk gave the order to sacrifice himself to protect the alien flagship.

A duty every Heavy Escort, every retainer, must be prepared to make.

Many of Father's Ministers had expressed doubts about the man. She saw something now that they had all missed, intent on their little scams and mistresses.

None of them would have rammed *Wulfa*.

"Continue being Morninghawk," she instructed the man simply, watching the impact of her words on the set of his eyes.

Father had taught her that eyes lie on the dojo floor, but not across the negotiating table. And that was exactly what this chamber represented.

All of them were going to be accidentally establishing new protocol for the *Hegemony* itself, in some cases from whole cloth.

Morninghawk shivered once, as if he was back at *Meerut* facing down a charging *Wulfa*. Then he nodded succinctly and moved to face the grand airlock doors that would open to admit an Emperor shortly.

"This is station control," a calm, certain voice filled the room now. "We are opening the outer bay doors."

Kohahu turned in place once to confirm the rest of the chamber. She held the center, as Father had instructed, with Morninghawk to her right and Sobol between them and back a step, as befit an Inspector. Guards around the perimeter. Bureaucrats and clerks inside that, providing a welcoming party that would be assigned to the imperial suite for the length of their stay.

Hopefully, she could stand here again tomorrow and bid this stupid asshole *adieu* before he did any more damage to things, beyond what a rogue emperor had already done.

Kohahu breathed once to calm herself. It was inappropriate to think of the Emperor of *Dalou* as an asshole, regardless of the accuracy of the term. There were other ways that this situation could have been handled. Polite. Protocol-driven, even.

She was facing a rabid animal, uncertain if it was a vole or a boar.

"This is station control," the man's voice continued laconically. "Outer bay doors are closing and the shuttle has landed. Stand by for pressurization."

She watched it all through a grand window beside the airlock itself. Commercial shuttle, hired at the last minute, almost literally. The port aft corner revealed shininess, as though several panels had been removed recently and replaced. Perhaps as a result of age or damage?

And they had trusted themselves to transport an emperor in that hunk of junk? The rest of the craft showed signs of aging and entropy. But then, the Imperial Household had no need of a fleet of private, armed shuttlecraft. Not like the Shogun.

They never went anywhere, again without long planning and negotiations with their true master.

Was that it? Kohahu found her breathing suddenly shallow as some emotion broke through the cast-steel frame that was her shell. Had the Emperor come to resent being a mere trophy that the Shogun kept around?

Of course he would, but was all this a way of expressing his pique at being a servant? Suddenly, many pieces fell into place in her mind. She supposed that an adult would have already had the range of personal and emotional experiences to grasp such things immediately, so she reminded herself that it was okay for a fourteen-year-old to need a step to catch up.

They were all servants, because the *Hegemony* could only have one master. One *Hegemon*. One man holding all the reins in his hands.

Not even an emperor could change that, but this one seemed intent on pushing back, and allowing the excuse of the aliens to cover his resistance.

Kohahu smiled. That gave her an idea.

TWENTY-THREE
THE SHOGUN'S PALACE

Osamu watched out the porthole as the shuttle landed. He'd never flown in such a mundane craft. Emperors didn't do that. Shingo, seated beside him and wound tightly, had at least traveled on military shuttles, which were supposedly more ruggedly constructed.

This thing was an eggshell with a strange smell emanating from the life support vents. Sour, in a strange way and unpleasant.

Of course, he could have stayed home in luxury and perhaps invited the barbarians to visit him there for tea, rather than thrusting himself upon them with no notice.

Better this way, as they would find it harder to control him.

Through the distant window, Osamu studied the party waiting in the lounge, even as the shuttle pinged and settled. Kugosu crimson and gold dominated, as he had expected. Only a figure in black trimmed with green stood out. Taller than almost everyone else, so that must be Omarov, the guest of honor who had opened the door for this small revolution.

Hida Taro was not visible, which caused a small jolt of anger to pass through Osamu's frame. Not to be greeted by the

Minister of Protocol? How greatly did this Kugosu punk wish to insult his Emperor?

Osamu might not have much power, but he was still a figurehead with some level of authority. He just so rarely invoked it that many people, sometimes including himself, forgot that he had it.

How painful could he make the Shogun's next visit to the Sunflower Palace? A man with almost no power might have to use it, just so nobody overlooked him again.

As he rose, Osamu knew his to be the thoughts of a petty man. He also knew that he had been reduced to pettiness. What else better described this entire performance that he was subjecting everyone to?

Four bodyguards rose, as did Shingo and a pair of Gadhavi's men who were nearly frantic without their own master to guide them, the Premier having been left entirely behind, along with most of his people. They were only here to handle the costuming trunks, else he'd have abandoned them as well.

Osamu felt his jaw just out.

Petty could still be meaningful. If Kugosu demanded that the Emperor be a songbird in a golden cage, then he could deal with the accumulation of shit on the papers at the bottom.

Osamu gestured the others out of his way and brusquely opened the hatch, just as he had done the vehicle door at the palace, now that the lights were all green. Imperial protocol had volumes of text dedicated to the arrival of an emperor at a station, with each of his underlings emerging in a carefully calculated and orchestrated pattern of ascending wealth, power, and prestige.

Osamu, Emperor of *Dalou*, had already chucked most of it out the airlock with this stunt, so he didn't figure he could make things much worse. And if he did, Kugosu would probably demand that he *retire*, like his father had, and Shingo could be promoted to deal with all the bullshit instead.

Because forcing Crown Prince Shingo to give up his dream

of becoming a naval officer over something so petty as this was a *grand* way to insure that you didn't get another night's pleasant sleep.

Osamu paused just inside the door and smiled serenely back at everyone in the rear of the shuttle. Shingo looked like he had a touch of food poisoning. Most likely just a metaphorical queasiness, as the young man had not yet learned the sorts of subtle guile that emperors had to practice. The bodyguards were stern. Unarmed because he had ordered it, which just increased their edginess. The two others were clerks, mostly along because they handled the imperial robes and could be trusted more than other clerks with such ancient cloth.

Or did he need to have new ones made? Chuck protocol. Chuck subtle. Chuck fashion?

Shit, he was turning into exactly the sort of revolutionary his father had warned him might come with the job, though Retired Emperor Shōhei had never once moved on his juvenile delinquency tendencies. Merely mentioned them occasionally in recent letters the two living emperors exchanged.

Had Father ever wanted to do something this crazy and withheld? Food for thought.

"Follow my lead," the dread Emperor of *Dalou* instructed his much-reduced Court with a terrible smile.

He emerged first and watched the ripple of surprise pass through the bodies on the other side of the window. Marching directly across, he moved just fast enough that Shingo was on his wing and the bodyguards behind that, unwilling to act without firmer orders. The clerks would be along, as they had no business in this reception.

The airlock was huge. Exactly the sort of thing that would hold a party of forty, had Osamu brought the full embassy with him, instead of abandoning them below. It was even remarkably clean, though he didn't know if it was always like that, or his arrival had triggered something.

There was no smell of cleaning solvents in the air.

Osamu came to rest near the inner door, Shingo on his right. Two bodyguards appeared on the forward corners of his vision. The other two presumably were closing the outer door, as it began to beep loudly.

Shingo stirred, then refrained. The mass of the airlock door meant that they were invisible from the lounge, unless someone had cameras on them. The young man settled.

"Speak," Osamu ordered quietly.

"I would ask if this is wise, but we already know the answer to that," Shingo murmured. "What do we hope to gain from… all this?"

"I live in a prison of golden walls," Osamu replied. "One day, it became too much."

"Will the Shogun allow you freedom?" he asked cogently, understanding where the real power lie.

"More, I hope," Osamu answered his only son and heir honestly. "I will never be free while I wear the robes. You will lose all yours when you assume them, in case you were in some hurry."

Shingo's shudder told him everything he needed to know. The man Omarov was more of a polestar for his son, a captain of a warship in Hegemony service, though Osamu doubted that his son would ever make it that far.

Still, no emperor had served as a naval officer in centuries prior, so already they had made some headway in changing the future.

Osamu turned his mind for a moment to the aliens now. The barbarians, though that was a poor term to describe a people at least as powerful and advanced as *Yaumgan*, and well beyond anything *Dalou* could even aspire to today. He did not yet understand why they here. Why they had carried this charade so far as to invade *Ellariel* with a squadron of outsider ships? More than had ever been allowed in orbit.

Or was this just another revolution? Had this Kosnett somehow heard his mental cries for freedom and decided to assist? Could an emperor even be free, as long as the Shogunate existed?

If so, what did that imply?

Or was that why the barbarians had come? Was his freedom going to have to come at the price of bringing down Kugosu? Would all of *Dalou* fall with it?

Osamu found himself teetering at the edge of a great fall, wondering if he had stepped into an exquisite trap none of them had seen, because they were all bound up in their own petty conflicts.

Was *Aquitaine* friend or foe? They could be both. Friend to Yosan. Foe to Kugosu. Friendly to *Dalou*, and yet the doom of them, all at once. Possibly without ever doing anything except presenting a thwarted emperor an option to misbehave in public.

Osamu suddenly wondered if he had miscalculated everything, because he was intent on fighting the wrong war. He drew a heavy breath as the inner door began to open, and nearly cursed out loud as he realized that the Shogun had sent a child to meet him. Worse, a girl, though she wore the Shogun's colors and carried a blade.

He drew his chin up and scowled at the room as only an Emperor of *Dalou* might achieve, striding forward and wondering what shape his doom was going to take.

TWENTY-FOUR

ELLARIEL-JO ORBITAL PALACE

Makara came to a more rigid attention as the two bodyguards preceded the Emperor himself into the chamber. He bowed at the waist. Felt Samnang do the same. And the Kugosu daughter.

She had not given him permission to use any name, so Makara understood that he was just a pawn here. A pretty bauble intended to distract everyone from whatever grander scheming Kosnett had invoked by setting this stage.

He could not say he was surprised by anything at this point, as Kosnett was at least the equal of any other player on the field. Unpredictability seemed to be one of the man's hallmarks, wielded like a razor.

Motion at the top of his vision, looking at the expensive carpeting beneath his feet. Makara held for another breath and rose.

The Emperor was a smaller man, but most were shorter than Makara, even Kosnett, however barely. Emperor Osamu was still tall and thin. Just not as tall as Makara, and even thinner. The man was studying him now. Makara had the chance to see the Crown Prince, a smaller, younger version, though broader across the shoulders. Perhaps merely normal that way. It was hard to tell.

Makara had been unconsciously expecting imperial finery, when instead the two were dressed in a manner similar to senior naval officers.

"Omarov," the man acknowledged him now.

"My Lord Emperor," Makara replied, bowing his head again slowly and respectfully.

"Your companions?" the man asked.

Makara froze.

Shit. Nobody briefed the Emperor on what was coming? What idiot needed to be tossed out an airlock for this scale of a fuckup?

But Makara already knew that, as well. The Minister of Protocol had *suddenly resigned* an hour ago. Absolutely the worst possible time you could manage, even with weeks to plan ahead.

Makara Omarov, unlucky son to a minor lord of a Komyo house, found himself in the bizarre role of host for this debacle.

Harbinger of Doom, indeed.

He pivoted to his left, shifting the center of gravity in the room a little. Maybe enough to escape.

"The Imperial Inspector Samnang Sobol," he introduced his as yet unindicted co-conspirator, watching her bow deeply at the waist with a courtier's smile on her face. "She accompanied me originally to *Aditi* when the First Centurion asked the Five Nations for help suppressing piracy, then on to *Meerut* when Kosnett smashed the pirate kingdom on your border."

Technically, the Emperor of *Dalou* owned everything, including their souls. At least on paper.

Makara took a deep breath and a desperate gamble now. He stepped back and around Samnang, until he was between the two woman.

"And this is Kohahu Kugosu, Lord," Makara indicated the young woman with his hand. "Daughter of the Shogun and standing in for the former Minister of Protocol, who has been called away from his duty suddenly."

He was looking over enough to see the double jolt of surprise on both men's faces. Ministers of Protocol didn't do that. Ever. Hopefully, the Kugosu Daughter would not draw her blade and slice Makara to pieces now for his effrontery as to introduce her to an emperor as one of his companions.

Kugosu bowed as deeply as Samnang had. Makara held his breath.

"My Lord Emperor, it pleases my Father the Shogun to welcome you and your Household to *Ellariel*-jo," she said now. "We hope that your stay will be pleasant, as we have not been so blessed in many years."

Makara had looked. Centuries was a better term to use here, but he was just a lowly Harbinger of Doom. What did he know?

At least the Emperor recovered quickly from whatever indigestion had filled his eyes for a long moment.

"Indeed, Lady Kugosu," the man said now, allowing a ghost of a smile to appear. "I look forward to it."

Makara froze in place and stepped back emotionally as far as he could. It was a lesson fourth sons learned early and well.

Lady Kugosu extended both arms and indicated the rest of the chamber.

"As we were uncertain, the Shogun thought to make available this entire staff to assist you while you are with us," she said. "You have but to ask, and if they are unable to fulfill your needs, we will find ways to accommodate you."

Makara noted that the Prince was frozen with indecision, but the Emperor seemed ready to take things more in stride. Had he only gamed out arriving at the platform, and then was lost as to what his next moves may be?

No plan of battle survives contact with the enemy. Had they beed reduced to such stakes now?

Was this supposed to be a battle? A free-for-all on all sides?

"That would be excellent," Emperor Osamu said now, turning right and left to take in the various flunkies who might have all drawn the short straws today. "I will need some time to freshen up and prepare for the investiture later. Please, guide me to my chambers."

Makara wanted to step back. To just remain here in the chamber, alone perhaps with Samnang, but something in Lady Kugosu's posture forbade that, in ways that Makara could not spell out clearly, until it hit him.

She's making it all up as she goes. Just as the rest of us are.

Fourteen(?!?) and thrust into this impossible situation. At least Makara had known *Morninghawk* for many years. Heavy Escort, occasionally prepared to make the ultimate sacrifice in order to protect more important players. Such as the Emperor of *Dalou*, the Crown Prince, and two Personal Representatives of the Shogunate, including a favored daughter.

Even *Wulfa* hadn't been that dangerous. And she just intended to kill him.

Still, it framed things for him. Perhaps elevated him to a new place. *Makara Omarov, Harbinger of Doom*, turned enough in place to look back without turning his back on anyone. He found an older clerk in the surrounding group that looked like maybe he knew what the hell he was talking about and pointed at the man directly.

"As the Emperor instructed," Makara called over the utter silence. "Lead us."

Around them, the others began to shift inward. To turn away from whatever weird confrontation this had begun as, and wherever it had ended. They started to move to the far door to the chamber.

Makara had no idea where the hell they were going, but the rest didn't seem to even know what they were doing right now, so he supposed that he had exactly that much advantage on the rest.

And Lady Kugosu had ordered him to continue being Morninghawk.

Makara Omarov would not disappoint.

He just needed to know whose doom he would herald next.

TWENTY-FIVE

Phil had a hard time not acting. Not even reacting. Just sitting there perfectly still and hoping nothing crazy/stupid/bad/terminal happened while he was watching. A *Dalou Incident* and he probably needed to go at least as far as *Meerut.* If not all the way to *Ladaux.*

He sighed heavily when the Emperor's shuttle landed safely. That eliminated an entire subsection of contingency plans. *Junkyard* would have been in heaven. Phil already had tasted hell.

Heather was projected around his table as a holographic ghost, as was Iveta. With Harinder, they all watched him. Now would be a good time for Markus to deliver a little coffee with a hard slug of rum in it, but the current wardroom staff weren't nearly that ambitious with the boss. Nor had any of them served with him long enough to have their own piratical nicknames.

"Now what?" Heather asked. "Should we head over immediately?"

"Absolutely not," Phil growled at her. Then he stopped and breathed again. "Sorry. No, they need time to process this shit internally. Harinder, what's my current schedule look like?"

"Shower in about thirty minutes," she said immediately.

"Departure in two hours. Short trip over with your team. Reception when you arrive. Then progressively bigger receptions for the next six hours after that."

He nodded and considered.

"Heather, you move immediately to dress uniform and everything, so you're there if something happens while I'm busy," he said. "Iveta, you take the flag, and bring the squadron down exactly one notch. No more. No less. I have left you an order packet to be opened if something prevents me from returning from the station, and we've covered your other orders. I'm not going to pretend I'll get any work done in the next thirty minutes, but I'll be in my office. Do not bother knocking. Clear?"

He got nods, but this team knew him. Knew his tendencies and foibles. He could rely on them to keep the waters calm. Thus, he retreated to his office. The things he wanted to say could not be committed to even in his personal log, so instead he pulled down that leather-bound notebook that Casey *zu* Weigand had sent as a birthday present last year. Complete with an ink pen. Hand-written notes.

She had asked for observations from him. Poetical things that she might turn into symphonies, as that was the art she was best known for. All of the paintings that a young princess had done had perished with Werder, save for a few that had been given as gifts and happened to be off-planet or a continent away when *St. Legier* nearly died.

Her music had survived. Had even held the Empire together in many ways. Especially the memories of a young woman who turned to music to remember her father.

So he wrote. None of it made much sense, as in his mind it was more a letter to a retired comrade than anything. Impressions of *Ellariel,* after coming directly from *Ishiokoh.* The chaos of an emperor doing things that did not fit with established patterns, which he suspected she would find amusing in ways almost nobody else in the universe might understand.

Eventually, the door opened and Harinder stood there.

"Time to move," she said simply before withdrawing.

Phil closed the notebook and rose. Time to turn himself into First Centurion Kosnett.

And wonder if he had miscalculated.

TWENTY-SIX

ELLARIEL-JO ORBITAL PALACE

Makara was somehow the shepherd getting this flock where it needed to go, however insane that concept sounded, even in his own head. The man he had randomly selected had had the brains to grab a deputy and send them off ahead, even as the mob walked sedately in a ring around their Emperor and Lady Kugosu. Samnang paced him ahead of the others, just to one side as though being escorted into battle. Behind him, low murmurs and snatches of conversation as the three key players worked out a new battlefield from the last one.

He dared not speak, uncertain how even his voice would sound, let alone what he might say. The clerks and assistants moved like the damned, raised from their eternal slumber as modern zombies.

They traversed through several corridors and frames to a spot close to the center of the station. Not all that far from where Makara had been staying, so he presumed the guest wing. Hopefully, they had rooms sufficient as to not terminally insult the man walking behind him.

We shall burn that bridge next.

Around a corner, a welcoming committee awaited and

Makara found the weight sliding some from his shoulders. More aides. More clerks. More something. The older man leading them walked to an ancient crone of a woman and bowed deeply to her. She did not return it with more than a nod, so Makara promoted her to *Hausfrau* in his mind and hoped she was smart enough not to argue with him right now.

Making it all up as everyone goes. Because that's what you did, right?

He moved to stand before her slowly, giving both of them time to judge things. She bowed first, promoting him to a position of power high enough to give her orders.

He did NOT release his held breath loud enough for even Samnang to hear it, but it was there in his mind.

"I herald the Emperor of *Dalou* and his Crown Prince," he said simply. Makara had no idea what he was supposed to say here anyway. "Are their chambers ready?"

"They are, Lord Morninghawk," she replied carefully, nearly knocking him on his ass with such a title. Not even Omarov or Sugawara. *Morninghawk.*

What the hell?

"Then I place them in your care," he said, speaking as if all this had been scripted out weeks ago and memorized. "The Shogun will send more heralds soon, so prepare your charges well."

He blinked once to somehow just get himself past this moment, then pivoted on his heel to face the four killers that had trailed him. Their looks of deep concern DID NOT help his calmness.

Nothing, however, would ruffle the *Morninghawk's* feathers, though. *Wulfa* had been a distant second to this.

"My Lord Emperor," he bowed again. "Crown Prince. Lady Kugosu. All is in readiness for you."

Then he stepped backwards until his ass touched the cold steel wall of the corridor.

If the old lady calling him Lord Morninghawk had been over the top, the Emperor of *Dalou* nodding and smiling now nearly caused Makara to have a heart attack.

"It is well, Lord Morninghawk," the man said, sweeping by like he suddenly remembered how all of this was supposed to work.

The Crown Prince followed at bit more jerkily, then the entire suite of minions who had been dragged along for this performance. Quickly, the hatch closed and Makara found himself alone with the Shogun's two women. He did not smile. They did not smile.

The awkward pause stretched to stupid lengths.

He would not speak unbidden.

Samnang was watching the daughter. Lady Kugosu was watching him. Makara was counting his heartbeats, but the damned thing refused to slow down.

He was going to need a shower soon. And any food he ate right now might not stay down long.

Wulfa had been a walk in the park.

Lady Kugosu addressed herself to him by pivoting her entire body this way.

"Thank you," she said simply. Quietly. They were alone in this corridor right now, so perhaps she was allowed to be human.

He didn't know. These were games of empire.

"Inspector Sobol, you will accompany me," the young woman continued. "We need to report to the Shogun what has happened."

"No," a voice of perfect doom suddenly filled the corridor.

Male. Not angry. Still, only about as soft as the alloy used to cast starship hulls.

Implacable.

"Father?" Lady Kugosu asked.

Father? The SHOGUN was listening to all this??? Had been, perhaps from the beginning?

Fortunately, Makara had the wall to hold him upright. Nothing else might have sufficed at this moment, and he'd look silly fainting in front of these two woman.

Except that he already suspected they were both tougher than him. Maybe not meaner. But *something*-er.

"All of you will return to my office," the man's voice proclaimed.

The tone of the air changed in such a way that Makara understood he had cut the line from his end.

Orders given. Now, follow them.

He drew a breath and forced his legs to hold him upright. In spite of their wobbliness. He still towered over the two women physically. Just as he did most people.

Makara turned to study both women. They were as white as he felt. That was good. He had been afraid for a moment that he'd fallen in with a troupe of demigods in some terrible, twisted fable.

Which was likely what would happen tomorrow, when all these rumors and stories began to mutate horribly.

Samnang looked like she'd been run over by a ground vehicle. Lady Kugosu had more poise, but that was a low bar at this moment.

"Shall I lead?" he asked her.

"Do you know where you are going?" she asked pointedly.

"No," Makara replied. "That's never stopped me before."

She wanted to argue with him. Say something flip and perhaps biting. He could see it in her eyes. Fourteen years old and charged by their Supreme Lord with handling this insanity. Old age and treachery, against youth and skill, as it were.

He was no traitor, but he'd seen and done things this *child* had never imagined, though he would never say that out loud. She seemed to sense that now, as she nodded.

"Follow me," she said instead, waiting for him to nod, then setting off.

Samnang fell in on his flank. It was weird, *being* escorted instead of escorting.

He wondered how bad this next meeting was going to get.

TWENTY-SEVEN

Heather watched the other Command Centurions mill awkwardly in the lounge as everything got organized. All of them were here as guests of Phil, rather than their own stellar nations, so they didn't have any of their staffs with them. Phil had specifically wanted this as small and discrete as circumstances would allow.

She was in her dress uniform with the epaulets and some of her better awards, including the *Intrepid* she'd gotten for *CS-405*'s long voyage, and another one the Emperor of *Fribourg* had personally pinned to her chest for the same thing. Additionally, nobody got to see the *Seventeenth Imperial Police Protectorate* tattoo on her back, matching the smaller medal on her chest.

Those folks had petitioned the Crown directly to be allowed to award Phil and his team something for the legends that had arisen around *Persephone* and their rescue of the imperial prisoners. *The Lost.* The *Aquitaine* Senate had been required to pass a second bill authorizing her and the others to accept it.

Phil was leaned in with Harinder, covering last minutes details, so Heather turned to Cruiser-Captain Adham Khan, off *Juvayni.* Short for a man, shorter than her by a handspan even, though he did not come across as *small.* As dark as anybody she'd met from the Cluster, but not as dark as the African Diaspora. Van Dyke, trimmed precisely on the sides but growing almost long enough to become a goatee.

She didn't know the man that well, for all he'd been with them a while. Long on glory in battle, dressed in a uniform that combined black leather, bronze-colored chain mail and a few plates, and tall, leather boots. Starkly primitive, at first glance, but it had the feel of something rather more anachronistic. Probably intended to contrast with the simple cloth uniforms everyone else wore.

He glanced at her now, moving this way as if her look was an invitation to speak. Him and Omarov had been the two Death-or-Glory types, but Makara was quiet about it, while Khan tended towards the braggart end. Also a cultural thing.

"I would like to register my complaint…" was as far he got before she growled at him. At least the man shut up as his eyes got a little wide.

"*Nobody* goes to this with even a pocket knife," Heather quietly reminded him with a snarl no one else would hear. "If that's too much, you are free to return to your ship and await our reports."

Heather wondered if slapping the man upside the head right now would have gotten him to stare at her so openly, jaw hanging a little slack. Though with his kind, that might be mistaken as foreplay.

"Security Centurion Dar isn't even allowed a weapon, as we are guests of the Shogun," Heather continued in a quiet, angry voice. "She can protect you, as Phil trusts her with his own life. Now, did you have anything else to say, Cruiser-Captain?"

Give the man credit. He blinked hard. It was like watching his brain reboot. Nobody at all home for about five seconds.

"No, Command Centurion," he said quietly with a nod that barely stopped short of being a bow.

She nodded and stepped past the man, just to get out of range, in case she did feel like punching him for something he said. Striker Gotzon Solo, Command Centurion of the *Ewin Principalities* Light Missile Bombard *Shadowbolt*, nodded to her from a safe distance, like he'd heard the exchange. Or at least enough of it. And didn't want to try his luck.

Ewin and *Gloran* saw themselves as warrior societies, but Heather had to not laugh in their faces right now. They were all show. Pretty uniforms and loud manners. The *Republic of Aquitaine* Navy would have gone through their entire fleets like shit through a goose, even before the Expeditionary-classes. Now, her colleagues wouldn't even break a sweat.

She came to rest next to *Stunt Dude* and Sam, with Captain Xue close enough to form a small bridge quartet if they'd had a table and cards.

"Problems?" *Stunt Dude* asked.

He'd been a Dragoon. Close combat was in his blood. And he didn't have that high of an opinion of *Gloran* martial glories, either.

"Khan wanting to score points," she said, blowing out a breath. "I offered to ship him back to *Juvayni* instead of having him come with us."

"Rude," Sam grinned. "As I understand it, he's about to become the first line-serving officer of the *Gloran* fleet to ever set foot on this station."

"That is correct," Captain Xue nodded. "Just as I will be the first among my kind."

"Really?" Heather asked. "I mean, I know you've said things like that, but you never do port calls? Ever?"

"That is correct, Heather," Xue Dao Zhiou nodded. "How does *Aquitaine* operate?"

"Even when we were at war with *Fribourg*, there were certain vessels granted neutrality to carry diplomats and freed prisoners between worlds," Heather explained. "Since the war ended, I've been into port with all the neighbors. *Fribourg, Lincolnshire, Salonnia,* and *Corynthe.* Plus others outside that, places that are largely isolated enough as to be pocket nations.

Meeting people is how you learn to talk to them. You don't do that?"

"Heather, we don't talk to anybody," Captain Xue laughed quietly. "We're *Yaumgan*, that terrible, dangerous, isolationist nation in the back corner of the Balhee Cluster that frightens everyone off."

Heather had to grin. There was something to that.

"Well, hopefully, all this sets a precedent," she said. "Phil wants to make friends throughout the Cluster. The only way that happens is if the rest of you start talking as well."

"Do we know where he's going next?" Captain Xue asked.

"No," Heather shrugged. "We have open invites everywhere, but both *Meerut* and *Ellariel* kind of took precedence. From here, there will be time organizing everything. I wonder if he might not make it to *Yaumgan* until last, especially if *Ewin* needs to be placated and warned off. And *Gloran* will likely get into a snit over something as well. The Philosophers will be more phlegmatic, one hopes."

"One hopes," Captain Xue nodded.

"Okay, people," Phil's voice suddenly filled the lounge. "We're ready to load and depart."

Heather nodded and moved to the rear of the group, letting him lead them out into the flight bay and onto the shuttle that would carry this group across. Not much better protected than the Emperor had been.

Hopefully, that didn't matter.

TWENTY-EIGHT

Phil led them aboard the shuttle and let Heather bring up the rear. Nobody else had felt like trying their luck after Khan; so they were, for the most part, behaving now. Iveta had the flag and a full, working set of instructions, as well as all the many contingencies as he'd felt like covering.

Getting *Urumchi* back to *Meerut* and digging in like a tick if something happened tonight, while sending messages home, really covered it.

Unless someone pissed *The Junkyard Bitch* off. Then heaven help them, because hell wouldn't want to get involved.

"Any updates?" he asked Harinder as the shuttle lifted out of the bay.

"None, so far," she said. "The Emperor landed safely, then the station pretty much went radio silent, except for answering our calls about maintaining the previous schedule. Second thoughts?"

He laughed so heartily that heads turned this way, but everyone had been studiously ignoring him up to this point.

"Seventh thoughts," he managed when he got the mirth under control. "Not that it will slow me down. We have a job to do here. And just dragging along all these Command Centurions helps. Still sure you didn't want the job as Governor-General at *Meerut*?"

It was her turn to laugh.

"Too many marriage proposals would have come with it, Phil," she grinned. "Those fools might think they are socially advanced, but most of them think women are a second class. If you ever look at the pirate ranks, it runs four to one male across the crews. *Meerut* was smart enough to import a lot of females along the way, and a bunch of them traditionally were widows several times over, because the lifestyle of the men was so deadly. They can't even really do more now than outlaw duels and mostly look the other way, at least until those hard-headed fools get some of that out of their system."

"Marry them off, settle them down?" he asked.

"Maybe," she shrugged. "Milose Dexter, the former captain of *Aggregator*, is probably the right man for the job today, as he has plenty of experience with the hospitality side of things."

Phil thought about that for a second.

"What?" she said.

But then, Harinder Abbatelli knew him almost as well as his wife Xue Yi these days. Technically, he supposed he had a whole string of women like that, when you added all his senior officers up and noted how heavily skewed female it ran.

"Hospitality," Phil said. "I might have an idea. The entire population of *Meerut* is about thirty million currently, right?"

"A little low, but close enough," she nodded. "They are crowded along the one coast and two rivers, for the most part, with a few feisty ones inland from that."

"Much of the planet, however, is open?" Phil asked. "Just wilderness left over from the original terraforming packages, thousands of years ago?"

"That's correct," she nodded.

"Tomorrow, let's talk about investing," he said. "Civilian investing, in the sense that maybe we form a governmental body and task it with raising funds back home. And use that to establish resorts in nice places elsewhere on the surface. Those will require support services and other things. That will require people."

"Okay," she said. "To what end?"

"Those people have to come from somewhere," Phil said. "*Aquitaine* might send some. I'd send a note to Karl VIII and ask her if she could send some. But I don't want true colonies. What I want are kids looking for an adventure or a way to make their fortune, far from home. *Aditi* kids. *Ewin*. *Gloran*. Heaven help me, even *Dalou*, if they'll come. Let's talk to Milose about making all of *Meerut* just a much bigger version of *Aggregator*. Neutral ground where everyone can come if they behave."

"*Dalou* might not appreciate it," Harinder noted dryly.

"I'm more worried about *Ewin*," Phil replied. "The Shogun can issue orders and expect them to be followed. The *Ewin Principalities*, I'm reasonably confident, can't even spell organized."

He said that quietly enough that nobody but her could hear, as he had Striker Solo aboard. Nice fellow. Spoke with his hands a lot. Emotional in speech, but extremely competent when it came to salvoing missiles down on hostile targets according to Phil's battle plans.

Touchy about his honor in ways that certain elements of the Fifty Families back home, or some of the more fussy *Fribourg* Dukes, might be.

"Should we sail there next?" she asked. "That's the question everyone is laying bets on now."

"Anybody not betting to see me at *Meerut* next is a fool," Phil growled.

"Oh, that's a given, Phil," she chuckled. "The next step has them on pins and needles."

"Gotcha," he said. "Let's see what the Shogun has to say. He might wish to complain about how I've handled things."

"Does he get a vote?" she asked sarcastically.

"No," Phil nodded. "I'm not sure anybody has told him that, though."

TWENTY-NINE

ELLARIEL-JO ORBITAL PALACE

Jirou had moved to the conference room where he met with his Ministerial Staff. More formal than his office. Less so than the grand auditorium where he could receive visitors and make them feel small and insignificant.

More importantly, more official. In the last two hours, he had come to realize just how old some of the men around him were. Jirou personally didn't consider forty anything more than a mid-point, as his own father had retired after a generation in power had largely sapped him of the enthusiasm to continue.

Hopefully, he himself would be wise enough to not attempt to die of old age in office. That sort of foolishness had been what allowed Kugosu to ascend in the first place.

A knock of warning, then the hatch opened to a bodyguard leading the three others in.

"No," Jirou pointed to the guard as the man moved to take up a position. "Outside. All of you. I shall meet in privacy with my advisors."

He watched the bodyguard's face fall into shock for exactly a half beat before stolidity returned and the man withdrew.

Thus, we have grown stale and predictable. I must shake up my entire holding, in order to keep us fresh, while somehow not falling off in the process.

Jirou contained his sigh of frustration and watched the others approach.

Kohahu sat in the same place when she had first joined him. Sobol sat on her right. Morninghawk dithered for a long moment and then sat on Kohahu's left.

An escort position, where a warrior with a smaller sword held one-handed might add a shield.

For his daughter.

It left Jirou alone on this side of the table, so the three were arranged almost as supplicants, rather than advisors. He wondered what they would have done had he taken his customary spot at the head of the table.

For a moment, he watched them. Traditionally, now would be the moment aides and servants would deliver tea or beverages, but he had ordered them all outside. Ordering any one of his advisors to do it would demote them in front of the other two.

Easy, then.

Jirou rose and watched them spring to their feet.

"Sit," he ordered, waving them down. "I shall prepare tea."

Gods, the shock on their faces. It almost warmed him that he could catch them so off-guard.

We need this, going forward. Dalou *has become predictable. Staid.*

Dull.

Comfortable.

Never.

Jirou moved to the tea service and flipped the switch on the heating element. The water was pure. The leaves fresh. He mixed things and returned with it all on a tray, giving his people time to recover.

The service got prepared and he sat to watch it steep.

"I am pleased with the Emperor's reception," he began, watching them all relax in their eyes, as they had been expecting the worst.

For what is the Shogun, but a terrible dragon that must be appeased, lest he eat you?

Hida Taro could testify to that.

He let the silence stretch now. The three remained calm. Proper courtiers, as he had not asked them anything.

"How soon until Kosnett comes?" he asked, studying the way the tea was slowly darkening.

"According to the schedule, he will depart from his flagship in roughly twenty minutes," Kohahu replied.

Jirou nodded.

"Send a reminder to the captains around us that they should continue to have everything locked down," he said. "Kosnett and his party are favored guests and I look forward to making their acquaintance."

That last, spoken as he stared at Morninghawk's face. Lord Morninghawk, to hear an old woman and later an emperor proclaim it. But what was this event, if not a way to allow the foreigners to honor one of his own captains for bravery in battle?

The man was on his way to forming a legend, though all the reports, from Sobol and others, discussed how little he wished for such publicity.

"What instructions do you have for Kosnett's arrival?" Kohahu asked carefully now.

Jirou poured four mugs of tea and took the last one for himself.

"I lack a Minister of Protocol to advise," he announced, as if suddenly discovering that he had fired that incompetent fool this afternoon.

"Shogun?" Kohahu asked.

He could see where the other two would hang back, allowing his daughter to speak as the most prominent advisor he had present. Foolish notion, but he had brought it upon himself, so Jirou turned to Sobol.

He had…concerns about the woman. Her reports had been incisive and precise, but looking back at the early ones, compared to recently, he had his doubts that she had maintained her…*objectivity*.

Still, nothing Morninghawk had done suggested that causing Sobol to adjust her thinking was a bad thing. Had she fallen in love with the man, or just his commitment to the *Hegemony*?

Although, was there a difference to be found there? Morninghawk was exactly as he seemed. Dedicated to the *Hegemony*, even at such personal costs as others might have quailed at and rejected.

Not many of Jirou's captains could have issued that order at *Meerut*. Fewer still would have shrugged it off later as *duty*. Perhaps none of them.

Save one.

"You have spoken with Kosnett the most," Jirou said to his Inspector. "Will he prefer a grand performance, as we might have given the Emperor with enough warning?"

"He would prefer a cocktail party that lasted several hours," she spoke carefully. "Informality, stretched over several chambers, both large and small, where the guests he brings with him have a chance to talk in a relaxed setting with your people, Shogun."

"Why is that?" Jirou asked.

"Kosnett has said repeatedly that he feels that diplomacy is the art of making friends," she noted. "Of knowing one another well enough to horse trade later without risking offense over tiny misunderstandings. He has made arrangements for a small party to join him. Himself, his Command Centurion, his Flag Command Centurion, captains off the other three cruisers, and a variety of ambassadorial and support staff, plus that one, tiny bodyguard who so intimidates the men she encounters."

"Xochitl Dar," Jirou nodded with a hint of a grin. "Security Centurion. Make sure I am introduced to her formally at some point. As you said, she intimidates men twice her size. That is an impressive feat."

Sobol nodded and grabbed tea, last of the four.

Jirou sipped and considered how the day should progress. Once upon a terribly long time ago, perhaps three days past, there had been formal plans delicately hammered out by Sobol, Kosnett, and Jirou's staff. Precise locations for each of the clans and foreigners, in a carefully orchestrated dance that was meant to show the aliens that Jirou was not impressed by their power and their fleet.

He understood far better today than he had six months ago, how much of his government had been funding and illegally trading with the now-broken *Zen-Mekyo Syndicates*. The Pirates of Balhee.

Certainly, his finance numbers next year looked much better, though he had his doubts that taxation income would be anywhere close to what it had been. Most of his people were smart enough to pay excise taxes on their stolen goods, pretending to be dealing with honest-yet-misunderstood merchants.

He would deal with that with Tsuma Toshei, Minister of the Treasury, another time. Or perhaps retire that old, sexist pig and replace him with a younger accountant. Worse, maybe find a woman who had trained and never been allowed to practice her magic.

Kosnett's staff were almost all female. The shuttle arriving, even with captains from *Ewin* and *Gloran*, would be dominated by females.

He would ask what they knew that he didn't, but Jirou already understood that the last month, and especially the last two days, had been a rude, cultural awakening for a man who had never considered the other sex as competent to advise, let alone triumph. He did not think there were any women on any of his warships. And only a few serving in his government.

Samnang Sobol must be an utterly amazing woman, to have risen to *Inspector* before coming to his attention. How had he never realized that until now?

"Has the Emperor or the Crown Prince registered any complaints?" he asked his daughter now.

"None that I am aware of, Shogun," Kohahu replied carefully. "However, I returned here immediately from his presence, so he may have said something that is slowly working its way up the hierarchy."

Morninghawk stirred, but did not speak. Hardly moved, such that only Jirou's tightly-wound nerves had noticed it.

"Morninghawk?" he asked. Then he smiled warmly at the man. "*Lord Morninghawk*, I should say."

The man's instantly-passing grimace told Jirou volumes about the man inside that shell, all of it good.

"I had the impression, Shogun, that he would be less of a social threat going forward," Morninghawk explained in a quiet, deferential voice.

"How so?" Jirou demanded.

"His actions were not carefully calculated instigation, sir," Morninghawk replied. "They struck me as a…"

"Yes?" Jirou prompted when the man fell silent. "Speak freely. We need that today. Especially today."

Morninghawk nodded. Sought within himself for the words.

"They were almost a reflexive cry of outrage, Shogun," he said. "At least that was my impression. He rebels not against you, but against himself. Kosnett's arrival disrupted the carefully-calibrated lifestyle that is the Imperial Household, and the man seemed to sense an opportunity for newness. Upon his arrival at the station, however, he was lost as to what his next step should be. He had not expected to succeed in his gambit and had not gamed it past that. Thus, I took the risk of offending him to step in and help provide…*direction*, if nothing else. The look in his eyes was a man spotting an emergency suit in a hull breach."

The audacity of the words almost caused Jirou to snarl at the man. How dare he?

And then he realized that this was exactly what had been missing from this room. Honesty. Everything was always couched in elegant, defensible tones and misdirections, such that nobody ever took responsibility for things.

That fool Emperor might have stood there all day, waiting for someone—anyone—to step up and *do something*.

Morninghawk had.

Jirou made a snap decision, rather than spending months on the topic and consulting hoary sages and ancient tomes.

"Kohahu, you and Sobol will greet Kosnett when he arrives," Jirou said. "Just as you did the Emperor. You will convey him to the auditorium where we will quickly move to the investiture, then a reception. Warn the kitchens to adjust everything to a… cocktail party with finger foods. Have them remove half of the tables then adjust what remains into a more random pattern."

"More disorderly, Shogun?" Kohahu smiled at him.

He flashed back to the earlier conversation.

"Yes," Jirou nodded.

"With your permission?" Kohahu asked.

"Go," Jirou said. "I shall make sure the guest of honor arrives in time."

The two women rose and withdrew quickly, leaving him with this man whom he had originally tasked to travel to *Aditi* and *merely* uphold the reputation of the *Hegemony*.

Morninghawk had gone far beyond that. Kosnett was about to explain to the entirety of the Balhee Cluster what he thought of the man. Again, Jirou caught the grimace of a man who would rather be anywhere than here, in spite of being so honored.

Makara Omarov would rather be walking the decks of his ship. Jirou had never served, but he could imagine having to spend an extended period below at the Sunflower Palace. And how little he would like it, or say anything about it, even when pressed.

"Omarov, what do you really want out of life?" Jirou asked, just to watch the man's mouth fall open.

THIRTY

ELLARIEL-JO ORBITAL PALACE

Makara drank some of the tea rather than answer. The honest answer was so obnoxious as to be irrelevant. To serve. Except that service came with a price. Commanding *Morninghawk* meant that the fourth son was always lesser than his brothers. As it should be, with *Dalou* culture. At the same time, freer, because he was only a Heavy Escort, and nobody important.

He'd certainly fucked that up by sailing into *Vilahana*.

He could say any of a number of things right now, all of which would be true.

None of them would be honest.

And yet, the man across the table had demanded that he speak freely. Damned if you do. Damned if you don't.

And when was the next time the Shogun was going to be so foolish as this?

"My ship and my crew are both hard-won successes," Makara replied finally. "The fourth son of Omarov was always viewed as unlucky. Thus my brothers command *Wraithruin*, *Kestrel*, and *Wraithhawk*. I was raised on duty, sir. And strive to fulfill it to the best of my ability. At *Meerut*, that came with costs, but Heather saved me from having to pay them."

"Heather?"

"Command Centurion Lau," Makara said automatically. He thought of them as Phil and Heather, in spite of their official titles. "Captain of the *Aquitaine* flagship *Urumchi*. Between her, the squadron, and the *Yaumgan* Immortal *Zhang Guolao*, I was not called upon to fulfill my oaths."

"But you would have," the Shogun pronounced quieter than he had at any point so far.

Makara shrugged. He would have. Had given the order, and expected it to be his death.

In that one thing, at least, he had failed.

Makara could live with that failure, though he supposed that more enemy captains might have nightmares about *Morninghawk* these days, to quote Beridze's line just before that battle.

The Shogun watched him. It was not unlike the Emperor doing the same. He wondered if this man was also operating without a net or a plan.

They all seemed to be, caught up in circumstances greater than any of them and at risk of being carried down the side of a mountain while trying to stay ahead of a wall of snow.

For Makara, that was almost a way of life, whereas the others still seemed to be trying to find a new equilibrium.

There was none. Phil Kosnett has assured that.

"I would ask what you need of me," Makara said. "For now, that seems to be, as your daughter said, to embody all that *Morninghawk* implies. I can do that. Afterwards, I will go back to what I have always been."

"And that is?" the man asked.

"The fourth son of a minor lord of a lesser Komyo, Shogun," he said. "Nobody that matters, save that I have a duty and I will fulfill it."

"And a promotion of any kind threatens to take you away from the place you most desire," the Shogun of *Dalou* spoke.

"In serving Kosnett's will, I serve yours," Makara fell back on platitudes. The man had cut him almost to the quick. "In bringing glory to my house, it is reflected upon yours. *Dalou* is seen as a place of importance. As the leader of *Dalou*, that brings you power and glory."

"And the revolution that you have brought to my doorstep?" the Shogun asked.

If the man hadn't been smiling, Makara might have tried to will himself to just die right there and be done with it.

"Sir?" Makara managed to sputter.

He didn't even drop his tea.

"No enemy squadron has ever visited *Ellariel, Morninghawk*," the Shogun replied. "No enemy captain has ever walked these corridors."

"Kosnett is not your enemy," Makara managed.

"No, but the others might be," the man said with a half-smile. "And an emperor has stepped outside the rigid bounds of protocol and duty as well, so the revolution appears to be catching. How virulent do you suppose it is?"

Makara opened his mouth to speak, then closed it again. The answer was a contagion of galaxy-shattering consequences, but he didn't dare say that. Did he?

"Speak, *Morninghawk*," the Shogun ordered in a harder voice. "I do not fear what you will say."

Oh, but you should.

He didn't say that, either. Thought it maybe too loud.

Makara swallowed. Facing down the Emperor of *Dalou* did not raise to the level of *Wulfa*. Speaking his mind with his sovereign lord, right here, right now, might.

"What could be so bad, *Morninghawk*?"

"Revolution, Shogun," Makara said. "It is probably worse than you imagine, because the *Zen-Mekyo Syndicates* and the Emperor are merely symptoms. Kosnett is the vector, though he did not realize it at the time. At least not all the implications of it."

"What threatens my throne?" the Shogun asked in a hard,

cold voice. "What fool thinks that the *Hegemon* of *Dalou* can be toppled?"

Makara nodded.

"At *Meerut*, we encountered pirate warships, sir," Makara said. "Their guardships were equipped with condors and cranes. Lesser ships had falcons as well, even a few shrikes."

"Powerful weapons," the Shogun said. "As well they should."

"Those powerful weapons were utterly nullified by *Aquitaine*, Shogun," Makara said, finding his voice matching the man's hardness as he chopped a hand down like a butcher splitting meat. "Irrelevant. *Urumchi* and her corvettes simply blasted them into ghosts with their rapid-firing beams. At *Vilahana*, one of those corvettes took a crane to the bow and barely noticed."

"What are you saying?"

"Kosnett's current force might not be sufficient to overwhelm our fleet, Shogun of *Dalou*, but ship for ship we are no match at all for *Aquitaine*'s technology," Makara said. "We need to send diplomats to the east. To *Aquitaine* and probably *Fribourg*, so that we can gain access to their technology. Otherwise, we might become as *irrelevant* on the greater stage of Balhee as *Ewin* already threatens to be. Our military superiority is a thing only when measured against *Aditi* and the lesser nations. And then only today, because the *Consensus* has allied themselves with Kosnett. *Yaumgan* is already beyond us. Now *Aquitaine* is as well. The revolution need not be political. At least not much. It must also be social, only in that we as a culture never move with any great alacrity. Such reticence would be a terminal mistake today. We must find a way to build new ships with new technology. New fleets, before pirates or conquerors from outside the Cluster discover that we are too primitive to stop them. We must start over. And we must do it now, because tomorrow will be too late."

Makara fell silent, certain, yet again, that he was about to be struck down for his effrontery. And yet, he wouldn't have said anything different. These were words that needed to be heard. This was the one man who needed to hear them.

All the others might scoff and ignore him, even as *Morninghawk* was being honored.

The Shogun would hear him. Or they were all doomed.

More than once, losers in some terrible social fracas had fled into the wilderness of those uncolonized stars, waiting for a time until they were either hunted down or managed to arrange marriages that created new alliances, allowing them to return.

You might run into all manner of such folks in certain places he'd seen. Exiled *Gloran* warriors. *Ewin* Barons in disgrace. Even, it was rumored, the older brother of the man seated across from him now, though Makara had never heard of a place offering Ichiro Kugosu succor.

He also hadn't looked.

The silence stretched. Makara dared a lightning bolt and sipped at his tea.

The *Hegemon* of *Dalou* watched him intently.

Makara had a moment of pure evil levity pass through his mind, and worked hard not to let it into his eyes. It had been his mother's favorite saying when he'd been young.

Ask a stupid question, get a stupid answer.

The Shogun had asked. After instructing him to speak freely.

Fool.

The honored guest could always run like hell later when nobody was looking.

The Shogun opened his mouth. Closed it. A second time. A third.

And now it was Makara's turn to panic.

Makara waited. He'd thrown enough kerosene on the fire for one night.

"Tell me, *Morninghawk*," the man finally said. "How would you do it?"

Oh.

Shit.

MORNINGHAWK

THIRTY-ONE

Phil figured he had probably spent more time arguing about shuttles than he had the reception, in the lead up to this night. Who would be allowed to land on whose ship, when such a thing represented a tremendous risk, had anyone the notion of a Trojan Horse.

He'd given concessions elsewhere, because it would be his pilot or he wouldn't come. Simple as that.

The landing was just as smooth as he'd expected. These crews were all prepared to handle ambassadors and important visitors, so he'd made it a point not to allow Heather to have anyone like Keller's old favorite *Gaucho* flying around. Not that there were many like him, but the *RAN* was a big place, and that man had been insane. Probably still was, retired, assuming he hadn't broken his neck somewhere.

They landed and gravity took hold. Phil unbuckled and rose faster than anybody except Xochitl, not that he was surprised. He had picked her out personally, since it would be his ass she ended up protecting. Executive prerogative, and all that.

The others rose almost as quickly.

"Phil, you'll want to see this," Heather said, so he made his way next to her and the screen showing the flight lounge beyond the airlocks.

"Huh," he grunted.

Sobol he recognized. Enough arguments with her over these negotiations. The other woman with her was taller. Bigger. Felt young. Like, even younger than his daughter Yi Wen. Shogun's colors, so he assumed someone with important connections.

Nobody else, save the obvious bodyguards that went everywhere with big players. Phil was not armed. Nobody was. Xochitl had a lifetime of beating up people bigger than her, and that described just about everybody. Again, *exactly* why he'd hired the woman.

Harinder was there on his other side.

"Casual, it seems," he observed in a light tone. "Somebody might have actually listened, for once, though I'm both shocked and concerned."

"Waiting for the other shoe to drop?" Harinder grimaced.

"Something like that," he agreed. "You suppose the Emperor broke them, somehow?"

He asked that last, glancing back to Kaur, but she just shrugged. They were all operating in the dark. Fortunately, he'd spent years planning for these sorts of things.

Mostly, the open-mindedness to just roll with punches. Like now. Absolute worst case scenario, Iveta could escape and call for help. Pet could bring down a big enough sledgehammer to rescue him.

Or avenge him.

He forced the snarl deep and let the smile relax. Friendly event with loosely allied neighbors. Stiff and a bit stuffy. Rather like how most of *Fribourg* had been, right up until the moment the Commandant of the Seventeenth Imperial Police Protectorate himself had pinned a medal on Veitengruber's chest for valor.

He studied the screen as the bay pressurized, but nobody was making to roll out a red carpet and bring in a brass band.

"We'll do this like a mob," he decided aloud, turning to include everyone. "Captains and Command Centurions up front."

He nodded at Fleet Ambassador Aliza Babatunde to step close and felt her smile. She would end up paying off on her bet later, because she'd been certain that the whole thing would be a performance lasting into the wee hours of the morning with nobody ever actually saying anything of any value.

Like most diplomatic events. The point wasn't to negotiate treaties over canapés. It was to become close enough to the other person that you could call them at seven in the morning when new instructions had arrived from home and meet them for breakfast somewhere quiet, where all those little details could be hammered out quickly and politely, for the big shots to include in a major news release later.

Chatting.

He let Xochitl open the hatch. Heather followed her out, and both women watched for him and the rest to emerge. Harinder. Kaur Singh off *Aranyani*. Fleet Ambassador Aliza Babatunde. Cruiser-Captain Adham Khan of *Juvayni*. Striker Gotzon Solo from *Shadowbolt*. Captain Xue Dao Zhiou off *Li Jing*, with both *Stunt Dude* and Sam, the three of them forming a little knot of whispers and occasional giggles that probably would have concerned another First Centurion. Another dozen or so after that, the Centurions and Yeomen that made the Navy work.

Markus would have been here, but he had more important things to do right now. As long as the man still had ten fingers when Phil got back, he didn't care. No greater threat.

"Dar, you lead us in," Phil said, following Xochitl as she moved.

He felt like he sat at the center of a fighting squadron, escorts up front and on the wings. Support ships back a bit for safety.

The only thing that was missing was *Morninghawk*, down in

his forward shadow challenging every other ship and threat on the board. Phil smiled.

Hopefully, the best part was yet to come, as Omarov had traveled here aboard *Morninghawk*, while his father and eldest brother had come on *Wraithruin*, a vessel that apparently had almost as much prestige in *Dalou* as the name *Auberon* did, back home.

The twin airlock doors did their thing with all the deliberate speed you built into equipment designed to protect your life in an emergency. Phil watched everyone settle and put on their game faces, as it were. The inner hatch opened.

Phil was standing between Heather and Harinder, and the three of them stepped forward together.

Samnang Sobol was to the right of the young woman, as a herald or escort, so Phil addressed himself to her, stopping the polite, requisite distance *Dalou* preferred, rather than getting close enough to touch hands in greeting, like *Aquitaine* did.

"Inspector," he nodded as the mob of people came to rest.

"First Centurion," she replied, a hint of a smile in her eyes that didn't show on her face. "Allow me to introduce you to Lady Kohahu Kugosu, daughter of the Shogun."

Yeah, that made sense. The Shogunate was an aristocratic thing, dating back to a civil war that had elevated the winning lord and generals to a position of control over the imperial house that had been on the losing side.

Phil supposed that just keeping the Emperor in place helped with long-term stability, as opposed to those places that would have replaced the entire house. York and Lancaster would have made for a more interesting history, but might have also brought the *Hegemony* down, since there was no Channel in place to keep invading armies at bay.

You might have ended up with the chaos of Renaissance Germany instead.

Phil bowed deeply to the young woman. She was obviously the representative of his host, important enough and trusted enough to handle this. Phil had already caused enough revolutions, just being here with the mob around him. He could be exquisitely polite now.

He came back to his full height and smiled at the young woman. Teenager. Tough and well-trained, but fourteen or maybe fifteen at most. It was there in the eyes. Tall. Almost as tall as Heather. Black hair. Dark eyes. Broad shoulders tapering down to hips that hadn't yet begun to develop curves.

"Lady Kugosu," he said. "Thank you for hosting me and allowing me to have this event on your station. Your loyal retainer greatly impressed both myself as well as my squadron with his performance."

She returned a lesser bow, but that was to be expected. He was here not quite hat in hand, but close enough to try to charm these folks.

He needed *Dalou.* Needed them intact. Needed them in a position to push back on *Aditi* on some future date, should it become necessary, much like *Fribourg* was going to be needed in a few generations to keep *Aquitaine* honest.

"First Centurion Kosnett," Lady Kugosu replied. "We are honored to host you. The Shogun has proclaimed that we should move quickly to the investiture for *Lord Morninghawk,* so that we can have more time to converse as individuals, rather than listening to prepared speeches. Come, I will convey us to the place."

She and Sobol turned and began to walk.

Lord Morninghawk? What the hell had happened in the last six hours? Something big.

He supposed that he would find out shortly, when he went to pin a medal on the man's chest. Perhaps the Shogun or the Emperor had sought to blunt the effectiveness of the Republic Cross by elevating the man at the same time? A cunning move.

Phil fell in behind the two women as they walked to the exit, with Dar handy and everybody else trailing behind that. The rumbles of quiet conversation behind him let Phil know that the others had seen the radical changes from what had been on the schedule.

Had the Emperor made his opinion known? Was that man being catered to or scoffed at? Phil had wanted as relaxed as he could manage without insulting his host. Looked like the Shogun had suddenly decided to do it, instead of formality.

With any luck, the wheels weren't coming off of *Dalou* right now, while Phil had a front row seat to the festivities.

And if they did, how the hell would he put it all back together again later?

THIRTY-TWO

THE SHOGUN'S PALACE

Osamu had gotten all of the servants out of the room. He and Shingo were alone, with whatever monitoring devices were pointed at him. Hopefully, the Shogun hired competent spies. He could deal with that. It was the gossip of retainers he distrusted.

They were dressed in imperial finery dating back centuries, to a happier time. At least he supposed so. Were emperors ever happy? Or were they merely pretty songbirds?

It would not be wise to ask him today, which one he felt like.

"We have a few minutes," he said to Shingo. "All I ask is that you learn well from all the mistakes I have made, and will continue to make tonight."

"Father?"

"We appear to be engaged in a dance to the death, my son," he expanded. "Kugosu and I. Each of us is stepping farther and farther from anything anybody else would recognize as proper protocol. The man even fired his Minister of Protocol and handed us off to his daughter. I cannot tell if that was a mark of desperation on his part, or a masterstroke, as I cannot say anything to her without offending him, even as he makes me wait on a girl child."

Shingo, smartly, kept his mouth shut. Osamu approved.

"So there are no precedents for today," Osamu continued. "None, whatsoever."

"Could this not form the basis of a new pattern, Father?" Shingo asked now.

"How do you mean?"

"No emperor has been here in many decades," the Crown Prince said, gesturing to the room about them. "Just as you have never done many things because it has been several generations since such activities might have been acceptable. I was allowed to train for fleet service, though both of us understand that I will never be allowed to serve properly. Never put at risk. Instead, I will be a different kind of symbol, at least until such time as you, like your father, choose to retire to a period of quiet contemplation."

"So, already a revolution?" Osamu asked.

"Kosnett threatens one, Sire," Shingo replied. "He broke the pirates. And *Meerut.* Such was his vast authority that the Shogun had no choice but to allow the man to bring outsiders to *Ellariel* in order to reward *Morninghawk.* Do you supposed the Minister of Protocol resigned, when the Shogun overrode the man's objections?"

"You never knew Hida Taro socially," Osamu laughed.

"Father?"

"My own father would have described the man as roughly as dumb as a bag of hammers, Shingo," Osamu continued. "Political and loyal, but not able to make great leaps of intuition. If anything, the Shogun probably got tired of the fool and did something to set him up. Maneuver the man off the board in disgrace without offending the rest of the Taro clan. Our opponent is a dangerous, cunning man, Shingo. Do not ever forget that."

"I see," his son nodded. "And the mistakes you expect to make tonight?"

"It was entirely possible that the Shogun would have ordered someone to open fire on my shuttle during our flight," Osamu replied. "Had you not been aboard, the odds go up. Except that he would have had to handle a much greater problem had he killed both of us."

For a tough, stubborn young man, it was still good to watch his son pale a little at the implications. This was an entirely different arena. Points scored here were sometimes measured in lives, rather than embarrassment.

"Now, we are here without my Premier, nor with the Minister of Protocol, both of whom should be supervising things," Osamu continued. "That means that we will be operating without a net of any kind, if we place a foot wrong. All of us."

"Are we doomed?" Shingo asked.

"If we did not have *Morninghawk*, I suspect that we might be," Osamu replied. "Even I wasn't sure what sort of reception awaited us. It would not be a stretch to say that he alone saved us from my irrational belligerence in coming here as we did."

"The old woman called him Lord Morninghawk," Shingo noted. "And you agreed. What will that mean? What will that do to all our calculations?"

Osamu shrugged. Then he considered it.

The man was not married. Had never been, nor had any of the other houses expressed any great interest in the fourth son of Omarov. At least until he became a major player overnight.

Who would be lining up to find a daughter or a friendly widow for the man?

Dare Osamu dangle one of his own daughters in front of the man? Sota was seventeen. Moriko fifteen. As political alliances went, the age gap was great but not impossible. That would draw Omarov and likely Sugawara closer to the throne. Both had been loyal for centuries. They had even suffered with the Imperial house when the Shogunate came into being.

Should Osamu demand that Sugawara be elevated to Great House status? Or that Omarov become a house on its own?

Or would that bring down the entire *Hegemony*? Were those the actions guaranteed to unravel the Shogunate, at a moment when alien barbarians threatened the entire Cluster?

Osamu needed to measure this First Centurion. And the Shogun.

What games were being played out around him?

THIRTY-THREE

ABOARD ELLARIEL-JO, ELLARIEL SYSTEM

Lingyi Omarov considered the image that his eldest son presented as they stood in his chambers wearing their best robes. Like Makara, Darra bore a strong resemblance to his father. Makara was the tallest of the four. Lingyi had the excuse of seventy-eight years bowing his shoulders to have lost height from his glory days fifty years ago. Darra did the family and the clan glory, commanding *Wraithruin*, just as Pich did with *Kestrel* and Soth aboard *Wraithhawk*.

Darra was watching him now. They both wore Sugawara black laced with forest green. It would stand out, as there were only a few houses that still wore colors so close to the Emperor, and only he and Darra had been allowed to travel here, along with Lord Sugawara himself and a few retainers.

This was the Shogun's Court. Lingyi had never met the man, but his father had been a powerful and decisive leader in his time. As has the grandfather.

They had a few minutes alone before someone would come to round them up.

"Have you considered all the marriage contract proposals one might expect when this is all done?" Darra asked with a grin.

The eldest son of a hero had been married off well, and had his own family now.

"Makara has made it clear time and again that he would rather command *Morninghawk* than engage in politics," Lingyi replied.

Darra held out his hands to indicate their surroundings.

"Does this look like he will have a choice?" the man asked.

Lingyi smiled.

"He will always have a choice," Lingyi said with solemnity. "*Meerut* guaranteed that. *Ellariel* is just to reinforce it to the rest of the Cluster."

"What haven't you told me, Father?" Darra asked. "If you keeled over tomorrow, what should I be prepared for, as the new head of the family?"

Lingyi grinned fiercely now. Darra only talked that way when he wanted to be a pain in the ass.

"Makara is the fourth son, Darra," he replied. "No other clan wanted to deal with the unluck. Doubly so when he wasn't going to be a famous warship commander, like his brother."

"That's changed," Darra scoffed.

"Indeed it has," Lingyi agreed. "However, if I were to press my other son for an answer, I am certain what he would eventually admit to."

"Oh?"

"The Imperial Inspector who accompanied him on his mission," Lingyi said.

"Sobol?" Darra was aghast.

Lingyi was not surprised at his eldest. Darra was a strong personality. Growing up as the eldest, he was never going to be matched on love. Only on alliance. That he had managed a good marriage afterwards was luck and hard work.

"The same," Lingyi said. "I took Makara aside and asked him that question at *Ishiokoh*. He did not deny it."

"Would that mean a direct tie to the Shogunate?" Darra asked.

Lingyi could see the calculations begin. As he expected. If he keeled over tomorrow, Darra would have opinions.

Makara might even listen to them patiently. As long as Darra didn't push too hard. Then he might discover that his three brothers could be just as stubborn.

"That is a conversation for later, Darra," Lingyi said, sobering. "The Emperor is disrupting things. The Shogun has reacted with greater disruptions. All is going to be in turmoil today."

"What do you know, Father?" Darra asked.

"I have my spies, just as Sugawara and others do," he grinned again. "We will remain calm in the face of all challenges, just as *Morninghawk* is now famous for, and I expect we will emerge on the morrow without trouble. Let the Great Houses experience great pains, as the saying goes. Sugawara is a minor house, and Omarov a minor family, for all that we command three of Sugawara's cruisers. Let *Morninghawk* set your example."

"Calmness in the face of death?" Darra asked sardonically

"If the fear of death cannot touch you, Darra Omarov, then nobody else can, either," Lingyi said. "Let that be my lesson to you today."

Darra nodded and fell silent. Makara had expected his death. Had gone into it at *Meerut* head up and stubborn.

His own father could do no less.

Even if the Emperor and the Shogun were apparently intent on starting a war with each other that might spill over and involve Kosnett and the outsiders before it was over.

THIRTY-FOUR

SHOGUNATE ORBITAL STATION

Kaur followed Phil and Heather, surrounded by the others. The *Yaumgan* cruiser had brought Trinidad Mildon and his wife, but they were special cases in Phil's diplomacy. Kaur was alone, as were the other two captains, Khan and Solo.

Still, she had made it a point to walk close by Babatunde, Phil's lead Ambassador, so Kaur had a nice view. Lady Kugosu herself, the daughter of the Shogun, was escorting them through elegant corridors to the central portion of the station. The hallways had been cleared ahead of time, so she only saw occasional people in the distance, hanging back as if she might bite.

She supposed that from their perspective, Phil might be seen as a terrible danger. He had defeated the pirates twice, at *Vilahana* and *Meerut*. Had brought an enemy squadron to the beating heart of the *Dalou Hegemony*. And now the Emperor of *Dalou* had emerged from the slumbers of his palace below to become involved.

She had explained to Phil and Heather what that meant, but neither Cruiser-Captain Khan nor Striker Solo seemed to grasp how revolutionary such a thing was.

Nor how dangerous. She did not like relying on the patient benevolence of others to survive.

Thus, she was both surprised and relieved when they followed the young aristocratic woman through a short side hallway and emerged into a ballroom. Enormous. Perfectly flat floors with checkerboard in the crimson and gold of the Kugosu. Enormously vaulted ceilings overhead that seemed to vanish into the murk and lighting fixtures.

There was a mob awaiting them, rather than mathematically precise lines and clusters. Had you asked Kaur what to expect from the Shogun, this would have not been it. Nor anywhere even remotely close.

Every color of the rainbow was evident around her. Outfits seemed to take one of two styles. Men frequently wore baggy pants tucked into leather boots, with a tunic or half-length kimono wrap held with a belt. Otherwise, they would be in full kimono-style robes that didn't quite reach the floor. Women were in such robes, with exceptions such as Lady Kugosu or Inspector Sobol.

To Kaur, it suddenly reminded her of her original impressions of *Dalou*, where the men held all control, and women had to mirror them in order to be accepted. Almost the exact opposite of the *Consensus*.

Lady Kugosu led them to a large cluster to the left as they entered. Kaur didn't recognize anybody in the group. And then she did, but only because the outfit the older of the two men was wearing bore the Imperial Sunflower design, worked elegantly into the fabric. Green and white.

She had never even seen pictures of the Emperor. He was generally a nobody, outside *Dalou*, as the Shogun controlled everything.

Or had, until yesterday.

Kugosu came to stand close to the two men, father and son from the similarities of their features, then turned sideways.

"Your Divine Majesty, it is my pleasure to present to you

First Centurion Philip S. Kosnett, Ambassador and Governor from the *Republic of Aquitaine*, on a voyage of exploration that has brought him to our shores," she said, bowing deeply.

Phil started that direction as well, so Kaur matched him and his officers. Solo and Khan took a moment to catch up, but neither of them were prepared for this situation. Plus, they had to try to look tough.

Xochitl Dar made them look like pikers anyway.

Nobody could see Kaur's grin while she was looking at the floor, though. Her face was neutral by the time she rose again.

"First Centurion," the Emperor spoke. He had a thin voice. Maybe on the verge of reedy, in that odd range at the bottom of tenor or the top of baritone. "I have heard much about your mission and your squadron. It pleases me that we are finally able to meet in person. My son, Crown Prince Shingo."

"Thank you, Your Majesty," Phil was saying now. "I look forward to establishing bonds of friendship with the entirety of the *Hegemony*, that we can all learn valuable and useful lessons from one another. My Command Flag Centurion, Harinder Abbatelli. Heather Lau, Command Centurion in charge of my flagship *Urumchi*. Fleet Ambassador Aliza Babatunde, my personal advisor on all things diplomatic. And my guests that were able to join us as we recognized the incredible bravery in battle of your Captain Omarov: Captain Kaur Singh of the *Aditi Consensus*; Cruiser-Captain Adham Khan of the *Gloran Empire*; Striker Gotzon Solo of the *Ewin Principalities*; Captain Xue Dao Zhiou of the *Yaumgan* Domain; my Chief Medical Officer Au Aqal Corven Sam, formerly of the *Holding of Man*; and her husband, Trinidad Mildon, who once served as my own Dragoon."

Kaur bowed again, though not as low. *Aditi* had some level of friendly relations with *Dalou*, but again, no other serving *Consensus* captain had ever walked these halls. Only diplomats. Would *Dalou* allow her to return for a port call when she commanded a Ship of the Line? She hoped so.

Dalou did not shake hands, nor touch, so the two groups remained at a discreet distance from one another, smiling politely.

"If Your Majesty will forgive me, I would be grateful if I could introduce the Shogun's guests of honor to others," Lady Kugosu continued, when the silence had stretched just far enough.

"Indeed," the Emperor nodded regally. "We shall speak more on other topics."

Again, a quick bow.

How often was an emperor just an honored guest in the middle of his own Empire? But this was *Dalou,* and that discussion had been settled centuries ago. They withdrew. The next group of people included Lord Sugawara, and the members of Omarov's family that had been allowed to attend. Not much had changed since *Ishiokoh,* so things went quickly and smoothly.

Everyone seemed to be on their best behavior, which was good. *Dalou* leaders had a reputation for brittleness that caused issues at time, more wound up in their honor than in the ethics of a situation when the two diverged.

At the same time, Kaur noted that the Ministers she was introduced to all seemed to be a little off-center. As though uncertain if the Shogun was going to fire them next. She had not yet gotten any hint of a rumor as to why the Minister of Protocol wasn't here, but it must be good.

Especially when the Shogun had apparently replaced the man with his own fourteen-year-old daughter. Who was doing an excellent job. It helped that Phil and the others were working hard to support her.

Did they think that she might ascend to become Shogun, someday? Kaur had never heard anything remotely like it.

But then, no *Consensus* captain had ever been invited to *Ellariel*-jo, either. And no Emperor of *Dalou* had ever met with barbarians from across the vast darkness.

Kaur had a jolt pass through her as they moved off to one corner now, to become their own island that allowed others to circulate. The *Aditi Consensus* was the single most egalitarian place she'd ever known. Only *Aquitaine* and *Yaumgan*, both relative newcomers to this modern stage, had the same mix of genders in senior positions. Almost everyone in here was male, excepting only the two women that had met them at the shuttle bay and a few others who had the look of senior bureaucrats rather than wives or mistresses. There were none of those, interestingly, even though rumors always swirled.

In that, *Dalou* wasn't that much different than *Aditi*.

Servers began to move through the crowd now, bearing trays with either small plates or drinks. Phil turned to one of his security people and got the requisite orange juice that he drank when off-ship. The others did the same, having been warned ahead of time.

Kaur had a flask she could get into, but felt like being bold and adventurous today. And not spending all her time merely hiding in Phil's shadow like Solo and Khan. She flagged down a waiter and received a glass of red wine that she intended to stretch for a considerable time.

Around her, the groups began to dissolve slowly, like sugar cubes dropped into cold water. Perhaps she had triggered something?

She found herself standing close to Inspector Sobol. Kaur noted that the woman seemed to have the entire range of human emotion visible in her eyes when she glanced this way. Fear, triumph, exhaustion, calculation. Everything.

"We appear to be successful so far," Kaur murmured as she came to rest next to the woman, companionably looking out over the crowd as Phil's other guests began to migrate.

Sobol glanced at her sidelong for an extended moment.

"What does *Aditi* think of all this?" Sobol asked.

"The *Consensus* is thrilled that Phil was able to arrange such a thing," Kaur replied. "But for *Morninghawk*, *Wulfa* might have destroyed *Urumchi*. What would that have done to the Cluster?"

Silence. Not unexpected. Sobol was a diplomat, rather than a naval officer, so she would see things through that lens.

"Perhaps delayed the revolution for an entire generation," Sobol replied quietly.

Kaur felt an irresistible force drag her around to stare at the woman in surprise.

"Revolution, Inspector?" she asked, keeping her voice down to a whisper that would not carry.

Sobol gestured with the hand also holding a full wine glass.

"Outsiders," she said carefully. "Neighbors. Enemies. Even the Emperor himself. Lady Kugosu might end up being the Minister of Protocol formally tomorrow."

"And how does the *Hegemony* feel about that?" Kaur volleyed the question back. "Is this revolution good or bad? Or should it wait a generation?"

"That djinni has already awoken, Captain," Sobol said. "*Morninghawk* believes that the Hegemony must move today, if it is to keep up with the *Consensus*, even as *Gloran* and *Ewin* fall further and further behind."

"And *Yaumgan*?" Kaur asked. Whatever she had been expecting, this wasn't it. And she had a responsibility to gather information. Possibly intelligence. Her superiors on *Aditi* would spend weeks debriefing her when she finally got home.

Sobol shrugged, which was even more impressive.

"Who knows what they might desire?" she asked. "We share no common border with them, so they hardly impinge upon the *Hegemony*'s thinking."

"Unlike the other three," Kaur nodded.

"Unlike the other three," Sobol agreed.

"So you see a generation of struggle between *Dalou* and *Aditi*?" Kaur dared ask.

The woman was an Inspector. Not that far below the

ministers around the room in rank. And female, which meant that she had to be exceptional at her job.

"Only if we maintain our strength, Captain," Sobol replied. "Otherwise, the *Consensus* might decide to push everyone out of their way and take charge of the entire Cluster. You would already be doing that, but for the pirates that Kosnett has smashed. Who will stop you tomorrow?"

Kaur started to reply, then held her tongue.

Who, indeed? Phil had hinted to her that he would force *Aditi* to hold existing lines, if they started to trespass on *Dalou* territory. Warned her to warn her bosses explicitly not to tamper in *Hegemony* politics. No wars, as it were, but spies would be acceptable.

Was he setting up a duality to hold the Cluster in the future? *Ewin* and *Gloran*, as Sobol had noted, were weak and fading with every day that passed. *Aquitaine* technology could disarm an *Ewin* fleet without even working up a sweat. *Yaumgan* gave all impressions that they would return to their pocket and hold their current lines.

Should *Aditi* draw hard lines and force everyone to remain contained within them? Was that Phil's goal? As a conqueror, it made no sense whatsoever. That would be the last thing he would want, when he might cause every nation to fall on their neighbors and destroy themselves.

Ergo, Phil wasn't here to conquer. And it had to be an official position, because his superiors would have to know what he was up to, and could overrule him. Could send that warfleet that he occasionally threatened, in order to get people to behave.

Kaur decided to take a risk. Possibly a tiny one. Maybe career-ending, if the wrong people chose the worst interpretation.

"Phil Kosnett warned me," Kaur said, watching the woman's own curiosity drag her around, until they were almost face-to-face. "He said that if something had happened to the Emperor, and *Dalou* descended into any sort of civil war, he would order all *Consensus* ships to depart. And for me to convey to my superiors specifically that *Aditi* meddling would not be tolerated. That he would enforce such a thing."

"Why in heavens would he say that?" Sobol asked.

"I have been wondering the same, Inspector," Kaur replied. "He is not a man given to make light of threats, so this was serious. In fact, if something happened to him, my orders were to immediately fly to *Aditi* itself and tell them. Even as *Urumchi* headed off to *Meerut*."

She fell silent. Sobol watched her. Neither of them had anything to add to that, and it became irrelevant as two guards bracketing a hatchway on the far side of the room suddenly lifted spears they had been holding and slammed them to the deck in unison, causing all conversations to cease.

Heads turned. Bodies turned as well. Silence.

The hatch opened and two figures emerged. Kaur had wondered where Omarov was. He was with the Shogun, obviously.

More interestingly, the two men walked side-by-side. Kaur was aghast. Omarov was being treated by the Shogun as something of an equal, if she understood *Dalou* Court culture adequately.

More revolution.

Where would it end?

THIRTY-FIVE

Phil felt a charge in the air. Like lightning gathering, in the way all the hair on his arms suddenly rose. All the maneuvering to get here, then all the craziness that had occurred over the last forty-eight hours, it all came down to this moment.

Kaur Singh was having a conversation with Samnang Sobol that seemed involved. Sam and *Stunt Dude* were having a chat with some locals, with Captain Xue close by, possibly being protected, or possibly protecting the other two. Sam was the key here, once you got below the level of command politics.

She'd been *Buran*, once upon a time. The enemy across the battlefield that became a friend. There was fantastic power in that. Just look what Jessica Keller had been able to do to *Fribourg*.

And Casey.

Solo and Khan were talking to Darra Omarov and some of the folks from *Ishiokoh*. Safe, as they all knew each other a little before today. A dozen other clans were hovering nearby.

Aliza and Harinder had stepped forth, forming little knots on his right and left as they worked their magic on *Dalou*. A few brave folks had even come over to greet him before withdrawing.

Nobody of earth-shaking importance, but people who might wish to establish trade later.

And that was what this was all about. *Fribourg* had accepted a bad treaty and forced *Aquitaine* to trade with them. That had given way to negotiations for better ones, to the point that the thing that had been an armed frontier when Phil was a lowly Centurion was now mostly just a line on a map indicating that you were subject to a different tax regime.

Hopefully, it would stay that way for the rest of his life, too. Denis's letters did not fill him with imminent dread, but they both had low opinions of what the future would bring. *Fribourg* had to catch up to the *Republic*. *Lincolnshire* might never, nor would *Salonnia*. But if the Balhee Cluster remained intact, it became a place to go. Far enough away to not entice an invasion. Big enough to be worth sailing with goods.

Phil studied the approaching Shogun. Maybe one hundred and eighty-five centimeters, compared to *Morninghawk* walking beside him. Built solid, so the two men might weigh the same. Phil would be between them in height.

Everyone was dressed in their good stuff. He had on his best uniform, the one that he only wore for things like this, with the array of weird medals and ribbons he had accumulated from *Fribourg* as well as the *RAN*. Diplomacy in bronze and gold, as it were.

The Shogun wore crimson and gold, as was to be expected. The clan colors. *Morninghawk* wore black with green. In that, he was a dark spot in the middle of a room that was otherwise colorful.

Except that *Aquitaine* wore black and green. Phil's dress uniform was different than his day gear. The same gray/black pants and shoes paired with a white undershirt that had a standing collar. Instead of a tunic, the dress uniform was more of a blazer, buttoned up the front in bronze and with no collar. Gold epaulets with fringe, going back to the days when they were called Fleet Lords. He would have been a First Fleet Lord then. He even had gold cuffs on each wrist, with two small, bronze decorative buttons on each.

This jacket was cut to fit him, and he had a tailor on staff to keep it perfect. *Aquitaine* Green—which just happened to split the difference between Omarov and the Emperor—with the same gray/black covering his upper arms and a broad stripe across his chest.

It would make his people look like *Morninghawk* to the casual glance. Or make *Morninghawk* look like he belonged to the *RAN*. Not the worst thing. Let folks draw their own conclusions.

Phil watched the whole room pivot inwards to watch the Shogun and *Morninghawk* walk directly his way. Centurion Dar shifted sideways like she did. Not in the way. Not out of the way, either.

Phil found it instructive that the Shogun's bodyguards took up stations around the room, rather than surrounding him as he walked. Here was a man fully in control of the situation. And he knew it.

That would help with what was to come. Especially as the original plan had called for speeches and formality utterly at odds with what Lady Kugosu had delivered them to.

Phil drew himself up and smiled as the two men stepped close.

"First Centurion, it is my pleasure to introduce you to the Shogun of *Dalou*," *Morninghawk* said now. "Jirou Kugosu. Shogun, this is the *Aquitaine* First Centurion, Philip Kosnett."

They all three matched bows now. Interesting. Just as *Morninghawk* was allowed to walk beside the Shogun, the man was acknowledging *Aquitaine* as the equal of *Dalou*, and him the Ambassador.

Phil could work with this.

"First Centurion, welcome to *Ellariel*-jo," the man said now.

He had a rich voice. Used to issuing orders and having them obeyed the first time. Sharp. Raised from birth as the son of a

Shogun, though *Aditi Consensus* folk always tittered with nervousness when talking about how this man had outmaneuvered his own brother to ascend, driving the other into hiding from which he had never emerged.

Phil nodded.

"Thank you for allowing me to so honor your man, Shogun," Phil replied. "Captain Omarov has set an exceptionally high bar for others to strive against in the future."

He paused, glancing around at the audience which he and the other two men were playing for.

"I am at your disposal, sir," Phil continued. "How shall we proceed with the events that we had planned?"

Past tense. They were already off the script that Samnang Sobol and Aliza Babatunde had spent weeks negotiating. Not that he could blame anyone.

At no point had an emperor intruded on their thinking. And yet the man stood about fifteen meters away right now, watching with shining eyes.

Kugosu's eyes glittered as well.

"I have spoken with my representatives, First Centurion," he replied. "Let us move quickly to lionize Lord Morninghawk, that he may have the longer to accept the congratulations of his friends and peers."

Lord Morninghawk? *Again, that title.*

Phil was certain he had heard the man correctly. At the same time, it appeared that the Shogun was about to wander further afield than they already had.

Maybe it was time to just chuck all his plans for the *Dalou Hegemony*. Go with the flow of things and let *Dalou* handle it. Eventually, they would settle into a new stability. The only question at that point was how weird, dangerous, or violent the interim would be.

The Shogun turned and located his daughter, nodding her close. Inspector Sobol, standing next to Kaur Singh, got the same, though Phil caught a hint of concern that those two women were talking.

Nobody but the *Aditi Consensus* represented any sort of military threat to the Hegemony, after all.

Lady Kugosu and Sobol moved quickly, gesturing folks into a pattern. Interestingly, the Emperor and the Crown Prince remained in place, and everyone moved around them, like moons orbiting a gas giant.

Phil found himself at one point of a triangle, with the Emperor close across the base and the Shogun somewhat removed at the top. All his people were along this flank, along with Lord Sugawara and Omarov's father and brother. Between him and the Emperor, a clan whose colors were purple and jade stood formally, as if instructed to separate the two parties.

Phil knew where that order originated, but he wondered how far out of date those instructions were already. He kept his face somber and let the smile only show in his eyes.

At the head of the triangle, Makara Omarov stood next to the Shogun, with Samnang Sobol on his outer side and Lady Kugosu standing next to her father. To Phil, it looked like the start of a new gravity well forming. What he didn't know was how that would impact on *Dalou* politics.

At some unheard signal, Kohahu Kugosu stepped forward into the open triangle of space, pausing to bow to the Emperor first and then in his direction. Both were of equal depth. Interesting.

To Phil, he had to wonder if that young lady recognized that the old ways, with the Shogun dominant and everyone else submissive, were in the process of giving way. Her behavior spoke the loudest, as she was advising a Shogun, but could not become one herself.

Not without a civil war, he amended himself.

And that was the thing Phil most wanted to avoid. *Aditi* as Empire would be no better than *Aquitaine* as Empire.

"Servants of the *Hegemony* and welcome guests," the woman

called now, drawing the room to silence so stark Phil could hear blowers in the corners circulating air. "We are gathered to recognize one of our captains for exceptional service to the Shogunate. All the more so, because those offering honor are strangers only recently come to our lands. We have heard stories of distant *Aquitaine,* but it has been generations since the two spoke directly. Now they have arrived, and chosen to honor Captain Makara Omarov, of the Sugawara. First Centurion Kosnett, would you join me please?"

He stepped into the arena now. Xochitl Dar had apparently won an arm-wrestling tournament to be the one to accompany him. She held a small, purple pillow, upon which rested the Republic Cross. Only the Legion of Valor was higher in the *Republic of Aquitaine* Navy. Technically, it wasn't even his authority to award it, as such things had to come from the First Lord herself. However, Petia Naoumov had specifically authorized him to speak in her stead on something like this.

And it was appropriate. Especially here.

Morninghawk stepped out now, moving with brittle stiffness, as if he was afraid that he might shatter if he moved too quickly. Phil understood the man well enough to appreciate that he was only doing this out of a sense of duty to his nation and his various clans. Nothing for himself.

That would just make it all the better, because Omarov wasn't any sort of gloryhound. Others would take note, hopefully, and work towards that quiet excellence that was Makara Omarov.

Never to be intimidated, regardless of the odds.

The man came to rest and they were both turned sideways, with the Shogun and his staff to Phil's left, and the Emperor on his right forward flank. Heather had his back, as always.

The Professor figured he'd never have another moment like this, so Phil paused and looked once around the room. *Morninghawk* had fallen into more of a relaxed stance.

"The First Lord of the *Aquitaine* Navy charged me with

exploring the unknown west, as we see if from our home at *Ladaux*," Phil lectured nicely. "Our wars were over, so peace and trade could break out everywhere that upright, honest people might gather. We came to Balhee, because it was midway to the next galactic arm, where it might be a place to rest on a greater journey. But it also became a place where we could make friends. And fight common battles against the enemies of civilization. Those wolves at the edge of the firelight that seek to bleed the nations of the cluster and tear them down."

Phil smiled at folks. A few tentatively smiled back, but nobody relaxed as much as Omarov or Sobol. They'd been there. They understood. It was necessary for the rest to do the same. To join them on a new plateau.

"At *Meerut*, we faced a place that some might have called a pirate kingdom," Phil nodded to the man standing across from him. "It exists inside the walls of the cluster, and thus outside the lands claimed by others. The pirates had assembled a mighty fleet to protect themselves from the forces of law and order. When attacked, they fought like cornered rats."

Again, a pause, letting people settle on those words. He'd spent years teaching young officers how to be better at their jobs. Better thinkers. Better sailors. Better people. It worked here as well. Everyone was leaning forward, hung on his words. Even Makara Omarov wasn't immune, and he'd seen it with his own eyes.

At the same time, Phil supposed that the man might be there right now. His eyes had a faraway look to them.

"At the climax of the battle for *Meerut*, the pirate Salvager *Wulfa* locked in a course to ram my flagship," Phil let his voice drop now, causing more lean from all directions. "Rather than attempt anything fancy or elegant, Captain Omarov ordered his crew to intercept *Wulfa*. To ram the enemy vessel with the expectation that both *Wulfa* and *Morninghawk* would be destroyed, so that *Urumchi* would be safe. Ladies and gentlemen of the Court, I am not aware of many officers who would not hesitate one bit before issuing such orders. The Republic Cross is awarded to recognize bravery in battle that is frequently but not always posthumous. *Morninghawk* did not pause as he fought his own battle with the pirates. For that, it is my exceptional privilege, speaking in the name of the First Lord of the Fleet, as well as the Senate of *Aquitaine*, to award Makara Omarov, Captain of the *Dalou* Heavy Escort *Morninghawk*, the Republic Cross."

Xochitl was there, calmly poised. Phil took the ribbon and medal from the pad and turned back to *Morninghawk*. They were both there again at *Meerut*. Omarov had gone a little white, and his teeth were clenched, but you had to be this close to know it. And Dar would never gossip.

Phil pinched cloth and attached the back of the ribbon. It had an adhesive that would hold for several days, after which Omarov could mount whatever backing he needed to make it a permanent part of his uniform, much like some of the ones on Phil's chest right now, put there by Karl VIII herself. Others would see that and remember *Meerut*. And that *Dalou* had stood with *Aquitaine* on that day.

Thus were friendships forged in the crucible of battle.

Phil stepped back now and turned to face the Emperor and clans on that side of the triangle. Xochitl slid behind him and out of sight. She was good at that.

Before Phil could speak, the Shogun sudden strode forward, coming to rest as the third point of a much smaller triangle. Himself, Omarov, Kugosu.

Phil and Makara were poised and ready for action. Off script, if they had ever been on one.

"Let it also be known from this day forward that the Shogunate can do no less to honor one of our own," the man said in a calm, loud voice.

Surprisingly, the Shogun turned to Phil's side of the group.

"Lord Sugawara, with your permission, I will remove one of your captains from Sugawara service," the Shogun said.

Phil heard the gasp all the way around the room. Almost silent, but multiplied by nearly a hundred mouths, all drawing that little bit of air simultaneously.

"It is good," Lord Sugawara replied serenely.

Phil wasn't watching the man, but his voice suggested that Sugawara, at least, had seen some of what was coming. There was no surprise there. Nor resentment. Calm acceptance, tinged with happiness.

"Servants of the Shogun's Court, I present to you *Lord Morninghawk*," the Shogun continued now. "As our Emperor himself suggested was most appropriate for the man."

If Phil understood things correctly, and he had people he could ask, Makara Omarov had just been promoted to roughly the same political and social rank as Lord Sugawara. *Komyo.* Lesser clan lord, or rather, Lord of a lesser clan, when there were several Daimyo around them for this event.

Makara bowed. Once to Phil. Once to the Shogun. The third time to the Emperor himself, standing so close. Phil could see the tears in the man's eyes, but wasn't certain what they heralded.

Harbinger of Doom. That much he knew from spies and rumors.

Harbinger of Revolution as well?

VIKING

Markus knew that if he wasn't careful, Phil would end up turning him into a Centurion. On the one hand, better pay in retirement. On the other, he'd have to start acting like management. Didn't help that the last two weeks he had been doing exactly that.

Not quite a foretaste of hell, but Markus could smell the brimstone from here. It just looked like the Command Centurion's day office on *RAN Viking*. And CC Silver didn't look like the devil. At least most of the time. Just let Markus handle things because First Centurion—1C—had ordered it.

Worse, Markus had organized a third team. Rednecks to weld stuff. Engineers to design better sensor arrays. Scientists coming up with a theory of astrophysics as related to the walls of the Balhee Cluster.

That last group had even tentatively started producing mathematics, but the shit was so far beyond him that Markus was already lost, just looking at the executive summary. CC Silver, however, seemed to think that it worked, so Markus was happy to let the man handle it. As Command Centurion, he was technically senior officer in the system right now.

Even the new governor was keeping quiet, but that man had

to build a third government in six months, after the pirates had come in and executed most of the first one, before dying or being arrested the second time by Phil.

"You sure you don't want to transfer back to Engineering proper, Markus?" CC Silver asked now, looking up from the document that might tell his people how to predict gaps in the stellar wall and all the crap around them. "You've done an amazing job with this stuff."

"Rather not, sir," Markus replied. "Phil gets better coffee supplies."

CC Silver laughed. Didn't argue the point. Might have something to do with Markus being in charge of some of those supplies, and making sure the quartermaster didn't skimp. Gotta keep the boss happy, you know.

"How soon will your teams be ready to start installing new equipment?" Silver asked now.

"We can move reasonably quickly, sir," Markus said. "My personal preference on waiting only comes from having to take apart a good chunk of your bow to do things. We can ask the locals to do it in their yard, but they'll figure out what we're up to pretty quickly. Ain't none of them dumb. Just lazy and parochial. If we do it ourselves, you're offline for at least a week. Do we trust the locals to behave?"

"Good point," the man replied. "Phil would, but he's like that. We've got a few corvettes to handle search and rescue kinds of tasks, plus the two former enforcers, both of which are repaired now. The crews, however, are all still former pirates at this point."

"Yeah, but they got nowhere to run to from here, so I expect them to largely behave," Markus said. "It's everybody else."

"Oh?"

"Natural paranoia, CC," Markus said. "Right about now, the First Centurion is pinning a medal on our boy. That means *Urumchi*, *Morninghawk*, and escorts aren't here. If I was gonna cause somebody grief at *Meerut*, now would be the time. That's why I've been lagging a little with my teams, before letting you know we might have invented the future when nobody was looking."

"Truly?" Silver asked.

"Well, *CM-507* has the sensor power," Markus shrugged. "The others have to lose some space forward and aft to rearrange things. Maybe a cabin at each end, but you know how lean they already run, so we sacrifice crew comfort or sailing supplies."

"What about the locals?" Silver pressed.

"Nobody else in the sound of my voice could do this," Markus said. "Look at page 143."

He waited while the man did, then waited for the whistle.

"That is a lot of power," Silver noted.

"For them, yeah," Markus agreed. "We've got it, because that Corynthian pirate built us this way. Doubt anyone could retrofit anything to do it, but they already know they need to build new hulls once they buy or steal tech from us. This is merely a tweak during the design process. For us, just a new way to build a scout corvette. More likely the locals take a freighter, overload it with enough generators, and slow-sail until they pick out the gaps they've been too lazy to locate before now."

"Assuming they are still secret," CC Silver replied.

"Yeah, that," Markus nodded. "*Vilahana*'s value goes way down fast, if *Meerut* can access the outside directly. Hell, I could see the boss building a new Citadel just outside, and having purpose-built wall-runners hall cargo inside. Great way to make a lev around here."

"Gonna retire and become a shop keeper?" Silver grinned.

"Bar owner, maybe," Markus grinned back.

CC was about to say something when his comm chirped.

"Silver here," the man said.

"I'm bringing the ship and the squadron to alert, Barnaby," First Officer Alma said quietly. "Need you on the bridge now."

Silver was moving, but Markus was used to sudden alerts, so he was already out the hatch and running. Didn't have anyplace else to be right now, and Silver was in charge, so it would be just like getting Phil coffee.

Forty steps and they were on the bridge. Expeditionary-class. Everyone more or less facing in so they could communicate with faces as well as tones.

Markus found a station out of the way as Aurelius "Auke" Alma moved his giant self out of the command chair. Silver slipped in.

"What have we got?" the CC asked.

"Since we snuck up on the ships at the mouth and bottled them in, standing orders have always been for them to keep a runner ready on zero notice to bring alerts inside," the man said. "One just did. Haven't even read the report yet, but it is a good training exercise if nothing else."

"Alright," CC said. "You take over Tactical now. I'll handle the flag. Anybody coming for trouble thinks they have a chance."

He turned this way and smiled at Markus. Markus was already grinning.

"Good thing our bow is still in one piece, Markus."

It was, as Markus read the message.

THIRTY-SEVEN

Barnaby looked around. Folks were piling in and senior officers were displacing juniors to side stations. First-team, with backups.

Auke was settling in here instead of moving aft to the Emergency Bridge like he normally did. The First Centurion had made it clear that he expected officers to rotate through all command spaces routinely, just to keep training sharp and make sure everyone knew everyone else at an unconscious level.

Barnaby still wanted his killers up here.

Expeditionary Survey Cruisers were big beasts, designed to travel alone into hostile territory. No escorts. Nobody lagging out at the edge of the system you could jump to in an emergency.

At the same time, they were built on an Expeditionary-class hull. Lots of power. LOTS. Two Type-4s and a lot of Pulse-Twos. No bubble gun, but that space was filled with cargo capacity, more generators, and the best sensor equipment in the galaxy.

What he missed was the rest of the escorts. *CG-505* and *CM-507* were better than anything in the system, but they were just two. Pretty much just escorts for a flagship here, because the locals hadn't had anything like fleet or even adequate squadron training.

And he had a fox sniffing at the hen house.

"Gunner, unlock everything and prepare for battle," Barnaby called, just in case Centurion Terje Rasmussen hadn't already. "Pilot, make sure the corvettes are close and know to stay in formation as you move. Let's not rely on the pirates to cover our asses. They'll be too busy with their own."

Centurion Riny Van Akkeren looked up and nodded. She was used to delicate maneuvering, having come up in scouts originally.

Battles were a whole other beast.

"Okay people, look sharp," Barnaby called. He clicked a few buttons and the scan log from the lagoon appeared on his screen. "This is the scan that got shipped in. What do we know?"

Sunan had been at her station already, she reacted quickly.

"*Ewin Principality* transponders," she called. "Three big hulls. Four small ones. Cruisers and frigates, looking at my notes."

"Armaments?" Barnaby asked.

"Could be anything," she replied. "*Ewin* have two versions of every hull. One based on strike fighters like we used to do. The other is a missile platform like *Shadowbolt*."

"Seriously?" Riny asked. "Strike fighters?"

"The future has not caught up with the Balhee Cluster," Barnaby called over the room.

"Hadn't until today," Terje laughed rudely. "How friendly are we feeling?"

"That's up to them," Barnaby said. He looked over at Markus with a smile. "While you're there, feel like grabbing us some coffee? Mine's not as good, but this might be a while."

Markus laughed and rose. Barnaby turned to Sunan.

"Get me everything, as soon as they emerge," he said. "We have some time, as folks outside reacted fast enough, and it looks like the raiders are deadsailing around the mouth like we did last time."

"Would you want to try taking that mess on?" she laughed.

A comm chirped. Auke.

"Got Governor Dexter on the line asking for you, Barnaby," his first officer said now.

Barnaby switched his screen.

Milose Dexter. Formerly the captain of the resort ship *Aggregator*. Closest thing to a common leader the pirates had been willing to accept, when Phil gave them the option of a military governor instead. Generally good. Businessman, though, so not really a warrior type.

Lots of the warriors had retired to the ground in the last few months. Those that had survived him and Phil arriving the first time.

"Governor," Barnaby nodded.

"We're not really a nation yet, Captain," Dexter replied. "Pickets and Raiders aren't warships. What do you expect to happen today?"

"Will know that as soon as our friends arrive," Barnaby smiled grimly. "Was just having a chat with one of my advisors and owe him because his bet was an attack today from outside the lagoon. If this is it, I will send flag signals to everyone, but I don't expect them to react as crisply as a trained military. Not yet, anyway. Still expect them to go for the throat if this is an attack. That good enough for now?"

"It is," Dexter said. "Just getting settled into the governor's mansion, but the last two guys that held the job both died in office. I'd rather be on a beach somewhere when it happens to me."

"The force arriving does not appear sufficient to take the place, Governor," Barnaby replied. "And I have firepower. Tell all your people to follow orders and we should get through this."

"Understood."

Barnaby cut the line. Phil did diplomacy. And combat.

Barnaby was an old hand who'd come up from the scouting side of things.

Who happened to fly in the most dangerous scout ever built.

Time to make use of it.

"*Meerut* Squadron, this is Command Centurion Silver," he announced over the general line. "I have the flag. Everybody come up to combat readiness and stand by to receive incoming missiles from what appears to be an *Ewin Principality* invasion force. My suggestion is that those of you close to the station move into defensive positions around it. Everyone else cluster into tighter groups where you can overlap your fire defensively. *Viking* will bring the offense for now. Once we know what they're about, *Tango* and *Blade of Kunke* will lead teams as well. Everyone signal your understanding and readiness."

He nodded to Sunan. She'd handle that part.

The two Enforcers had new captains, since Utkin had killed Harper Zemke to start their revolution and the few surviving senior staff of *Tango* had retired to the ground under amnesty after Utkin died in his last duel. The new folks aboard were still getting used to a light cruiser, having come over from a Raider that *CB-502* had dismembered so badly it wasn't worth repairing.

One more Raider wouldn't have meant much today, but having two Enforcers might.

"Riny, we have the range," Barnaby said. "Move us to a spot where the Fours can hit someone coming in to a standard landing pattern. Terje, don't fire until I tell you, even if provoked."

"Back to *First Vilahana*?" his Gunner asked.

"That's right."

First Vilahana. *Tango* and a pair of missile platforms throwing spears at *Aranyani*. Would have worked, but Phil had ordered everyone to intervene. Missiles weren't worth a shit against First Centurion Whughy's Pulse-Two. Strike fighters weren't much better, save that *Viking* didn't have any Type-3s or Type-1s. He did have a pair of corvettes.

"Sir, do we want to move to the edge of the gravity well ourselves?" Riny asked now. "If we chase them off, they still have to land and deadsail. We might capture them at that point. Or pound them into submission."

"Yes, Pilot," Barnaby ordered. "*CG-505*, *CM-507*, stand by to exit the gravity well for combat."

Just about the opposite of the old days, when a squadron would drop out, organize, and then sail down to fight in high orbit somewhere. When you got high enough, it was possible to go straight to JumpSpace without maneuvering. Assuming you charged your drives.

"Engineering, be ready for a Jump," Barnaby ordered. "Auke, you have Tactical."

Auke looked over, then nodded.

Half the reason Barnaby was so successful was his First Officer. Auke was a bear of a man, with the energy of a hummingbird and the brains of any three other officers combined. He'd been the key scientist handling math for Markus Dunklin, once they identified the need.

He was also pretty damned good as a Tactical Officer.

"All hands, enemy force should begin arriving in ninety seconds," Auke announced.

Barnaby assumed that he'd done the math of flight, jump, and organizing themselves into whatever trouble they thought they might cause while the cat was away. Markus returned with fresh coffee and Barnaby settled in to see what happened next.

THIRTY-EIGHT

Auke scowled at his screens, as if he could make everyone conform to his needs by sheer force of will. He had Tactical, but that was just inside the hull. Barnaby had the flag. Still, Barnaby listened.

"Flag, have *Blade of Kunke* shift up eight points and draw those seven ships with them," Auke said now. "That forces the enemy to shift across or risk being caught in a crossfire before they understand what happened."

Barnaby listened and relayed the order, without even asking. That was good. Auke wasn't sure he could express what he saw in words. Everything was numbers when he thought about it like this. Vectors that he could program a screen to display if he had an hour or so to work out the math. Probably a third derivative estimate, but that would shift down the curve as soon as he knew what the enemy commander had brought with him.

Chaos offended Auke. Battles always began as contained chaos, at least until you knew what someone's opening moves were. Then it became chess.

Iveta Beridze was a warrior. Thinker, but killer first. Auke was a mathematician who liked to play with guns occasionally.

Today, he had to stand in for *Junkyard* and handle these assholes like she would have.

"Also," he continued. "Have *Tango* drift their flank outwards a bit and bring those two Pickets into forward escort positions like we have our corvettes. A missile force shouldn't be able to overwhelm them while still dealing with us, but the Enforcer lacks the Point Guns to defend themselves. Does anybody around here use strike fighters besides *Ewin*?"

"*Yaumgan* is rumored to have something," the Science Officer spoke up now. "Supposedly looks like the bigger ships, but one- or two-crew biped ships. Likely at least as advanced as what we used to build before *Buran*."

Auke nodded. That would be something to see. *Li Jing* and *Zhang Guolao* had impressed the hell out of him, because all those moving parts made it a far more complicated set of equations than just welding steel and attaching guns. It needed art. But it needed math more.

"All hands, stand by for enemy emergence," he called.

Others had a sixth sense for the flow of battle. Beridze was like that. Auke had math on his side. And an expectation of human nature. He didn't always understand Humans, but that was because they were only predictable up to a point.

Lack of professionalism on their part just made it harder for him. Pissed him off. Trained forces could be predicted.

He waited. Tried not to fidget. Any other maneuver orders had to wait until he was sure. The two Enforcers just anchored portions of his flanks against end-sweeps, because he had Type-4 beams with which to chastise annoying people.

And anyone deadsailing around the guardships was trying to annoy him.

Assuming that they hadn't seen the messenger fleet and decided to withdraw.

Of course, if they were honest folk, they wouldn't have brought a war squadron, and would have knocked politely.

"Emergence detected," Sunan called. "Seven signatures as

before. Strike that. I am detecting what we used to call a crash launch from the main vessel. Transponder code *Pioneer*."

"Sunan," Barnaby called. "Hunter-class cruiser?"

"That's my guess," she replied. "First time we've actually scanned one."

"Hit him with all sensors then," Barnaby said cruelly. "I want to know what the captain had for breakfast."

"Stand by."

Auke heard the hard ping that played when the Science Officer went to work. *CM-507* had adequate sensors as well, and a good parallax. They should be able to count frames on the ships, even at this range.

Pioneer. Two other cruisers calling themselves *Dragonfly* and *Merchant Venture*. Four things he would rate as frigates, based on what other nations in the Balhee Cluster built. Smaller than the corvettes in front of him, but those ships were almost the size of the destroyer/scouts he'd served on when he was a pup.

"Okay, I have twelve fightercraft deployed from the flagship," Sunan called. "Also, *Merchant Venture* looks to be a Light Missile Bombard. They scan just like *Shadowbolt*. *Dragonfly* might be a Heavy Bombard, based on numbers and mass."

"Attention enemy squadron," Barnaby's voice filled the bridge. "You are trespassing. I repeat, trespassing. You will remove yourself from this system immediately or we will be forced into hostilities. Reply on this channel."

Auke had a bet going with himself. Human chaos and arrogance, against estimated tonnage comparisons. The *Ewin* ships were outnumbered and outmassed, but maneuvering in at least a semblance of a military formation. Not as good as *Viking*, to say nothing of the entire squadron, but better than the former pirates.

It took a lot of training and practice to sail as a unit.

"I have missile launch from all warships," Sunan announced. "Shit. Those are missile frigates."

Auke nodded. He'd assumed something like that. Nothing else made sense if this was a raid.

"Order all warships to fire defensively," Barnaby called.

It was good. Most of the missiles were coming this way, which just meant that *Pioneer* had identified *Viking* as trouble.

He doubted they understood what trouble *really* meant.

"Gunner, I have identified Frigate Four on your boards," Auke purred now, watching the various vectors intersect in his mind. "Hit them with both Fours, recharge, and then again. Gun teams can handle all the hornets."

"Frigate Four, aye," Terje replied.

Auke listened to the big beams beep on his board. Sunan was scanning, but not generating much electronic mush. She'd be blinded if he fired the big guns while she was trying. And it would take a bit for those missiles to arrive.

"Second salvo in the air," she called a moment later. "Repeat, they had hot-launched a second wave. These are coming faster. Assume time on target impact."

Auke growled quietly. Someone thought he was being cute over there. Slow missiles first, with faster missiles overtaking them. Double the hassle. Absolute shitshow, except that he'd clustered Pickets around Enforcers. And most of the missiles were inbound.

Still, Frigate Four turned out to be a tin can. Even at this range, Type-4 beams were rude. First one hammered his forward shielding. Second one collapsed it and dinged the hell out of his bow. Normally an effective deterrent, but missile ships had all their ammunition in the middle.

So when the third bolt hit, someone got his nose bloodied. The fourth one was almost a curb stomp.

"Are missiles losing tracking?" Auke asked.

"Negative," his Gunner replied. But he'd trained Terje, so the man knew how he fought battles. "Self-guiding in terminal mode now."

Too bad. He'd been hoping that they weren't bright enough

over there to do that. Losing a frigate—and that one was *lost*—might have caused their missiles to go ballistic.

"Gunner, target *Dragonfly* next and begin hammering him with the Fours," Auke decided.

A Hunter was a flagship that carried fightercraft. Utterly useless at these ranges, but intimidating as hell if someone decided to rush them. A Heavy Bombard had a lot of spare power, so Auke assumed it would be routed to the forward shields right now. Hopefully, he had their attention.

"Barnaby, I could use the cannons off the Enforcers now," Auke looked up and made eye contact. "Even at this range. Maybe have them start forward at a sedate saunter, too."

Vectors. Movement in three dimensions. Bright colors that just happened to have names and lives, but that didn't matter right now.

Assholes had shown up and opened fire without any provocation.

Time to teach them some manners.

THIRTY-NINE

Barnaby watched Auke work. It was like standing there as a jeweler cut diamonds some days. One frigate over there was just rolling like a dead fish at this point. Power curves were good, which suggested that the bridge had been destroyed and nobody on the Emergency Bridge was taking over.

Out of the battle for now.

"*Tango* and *Blade of Kunke*, begin engaging at long range and remain on the flanks," Barnaby called to his two wings.

Neither would be good up close, but they were a distraction right now, and that seemed to be what Auke was about.

"Tactical, should we close?" he asked.

That would disrupt the delicate timing of the double missile salvo. A third had been launched, but it was moving at the speed of the first. Barnaby assumed that the second wave were all specially loaded for just such a stunt. Only useful once. Then it became a duel of weight and luck

"A slow walk heading to starboard would be excellent," Auke replied. "Pilot, pick a path that brings the rear port batteries to bear and have everyone transition across. Gun Teams, continue engaging as you bear. Gunner, keep the Fours on *Dragonfly*."

Barnaby watched Riny plot the maneuver and saw what Auke was doing. Herding them a little, maybe.

Tango had firebirds. Ineffective at this range, but surrounded by other vessels with firebirds and missiles. *Blade of Kunke* had titan bolts. If the *Ewin* force didn't turn away soon, *Viking* could get close, where the Fours would get devastating. Turning towards *Tango* meant that they had to deal with incoming plasma torpedoes, while the starboard wing was heavier on beams and direct fire weapons.

All that, and Barnaby knew that Auke wouldn't be able to explain to mere Humans how he had arrived at that conclusion. The best never did. It became an instinct that let them act decisively on little preparation.

Still, it was just one of the many reasons he had hired the man.

"*Meerut* squadron, continue engaging at current range," Barnaby called. "Prepare to maneuver as we force his hand."

He noted a signal from one of the vessels on *Tango*'s flank. *Hollywood*. A Raider whose captain had the same nickname.

Hollywood Ward, because she'd been in vids as a teen and young adult. Older now. Not quite a senior statesman, but one of Milose's advisors.

And a fighting captain.

"Go ahead, *Hollywood*," Barnaby said when her face came up on his screen.

"Are you driving him our way?" she asked now.

Didn't sound fearful. More curious.

"Driving him backwards, if he has any sense," Barnaby replied. "If the fool turns to close on you, this whole wing pounces on him from behind. I don't care if they have titan bolts. Ships like that don't mount enough to be a threat to you."

"You expect him to flee?" *Hollywood* pressed.

"Those that can," Barnaby countered.

"Then what?"

"Then we have a general chase, *Hollywood*." Barnaby smiled

cruelly. "You and I both know where they're likely to come out of Jump, in order to escape the lagoon. If you are feeling bold, feel free to grab a couple of Pickets and camp where you'll be behind them when they emerge. I want prisoners, but that's just because I want answers."

"That's Baron Russand on *Pioneer*," she offered.

"Know the man?"

"Only by reputation," she said. "Something of a renegade House. *Dalou* does the same thing. Competition, in the old days, just because they qualified as other kinds of pirates."

"Any love lost today?" Barnaby asked.

He hadn't expected any of the pirates to turn on their old friends. At the same time, most of them were only safe as long as *Meerut* was independent. Otherwise, maybe the gallows.

"None here," she replied.

"Then take command of a team and move to intercept them at the outer barrier, *Hollywood*," Barnaby offered, just to see if she would take formal orders. "Right now, you are not doing much besides walling them in. Out there, you might have complete surprise. Ships you capture might be bought by the *RAN* and impressed into service, but that's up to Phil."

He liked the way her eyes lit up at that. They were still pirates if you scratched them at all. Still, he could put that to use.

"See you in hell, *Viking*," she said cheerily and cut the line.

Yup, pirates. He wondered if she had just promoted him to assistant pirate warlord after Phil.

He'd had weirder days.

A few seconds later, the Raider of the same name pivoted and began to accelerate with a pair of Pickets. Up and out. Might look like they were running. If so, that silly-ass Baron Russand just might forget about them until she put a couple of titan bolts into his ass at short range. Plus, she had extra beams on the wings, in case he did launch missiles. And that team of Pickets that pretty good escorts against that sort of thing.

Assuming they weren't facing a force capable of overloading them.

"*Aquitaine* squadron," he said now, switching channels. "Be prepared to move to high speed, then to Jump. If this works, they'll break, but they can't escape us immediately. Instead, they have to deadsail. That means we can stern chase with the Type-4s while they launch backwards at us Parthian-style. *Hollywood* and escorts will be moving to cork things, but don't have the throw-weight to do much, so we might be rescuing them shortly."

"We trust the locals to assist?" Command Centurion Isabèl Pan asked from the bridge of *CM-507*.

"Not in the heat of battle," Barnaby replied. "Tomorrow, we need to start organizing squadron training, since we won't always be around to curb stomp people."

"Minefields are always an option," she said.

"Add it to the list," he said. "Governor Dexter can pay for it if he wants to. And can hire us to handle it."

"Barnaby," Auke's voice intruded. "They're about to break."

"*Meerut* squadron, stand by for General Chase."

FORTY

DATE OF THE REPUBLIC NOVEMBER 16, 411
RAN VIKING, MEERUT ORBIT

Auke could almost smell the fear wafting across space from *Pioneer*. This Baron Russand had made one critical mistake at the top of the battle, and Auke wasn't about to let him recover.

Dropping a full squadron of fightercraft meant that he had a tremendous amount of firepower nearby, in case someone tried to overload him with firebirds or missiles. Or to get too close.

Viking didn't have to. The Type-4 had a stupendous range and those fools hadn't internalized what that meant.

They thought that they could just sit over there throwing arrows at him all day until he ran away. Except that the *RAN* could just swat them all aside. Plus the two wings were slowly drifting inward, as they each faced few enough missiles to keep them honest, but not to stop them.

Viking didn't have to close. Auke could hurt them from clear over here. And eventually, they'd run out of ammunition. He could do this all week.

The slow movement inwards from the flanks had also pinched them, but only on a mental scale. All those ships were so far apart that you needed a telescope to spot someone. On a screen, Auke was practically breathing on them.

And he'd left that little gap on his port side. As if taunting them to dive in and maybe attack the planet below. That would just trap them below him in the gravity well, too close to the one station with guns, and nowhere to run.

Plus, *Dragonfly* was having a hard time flying in a straight line. He'd been holding his forward shields to keep the Fours from kicking them in. So *Kunke* and a Raider close to *Tango* had weaker shields to snipe at.

Some of those titan bolts had gotten through.

Right now, he could smell a change in the breeze, so to speak.

"Gunner, hold the Fours at recharge," Auke ordered. "Shift your targeting point to *Pioneer*."

On his screen, he watched the bow of the Baron's flagship.

The man could drift now, letting his fighters race home and try to land. Or he could keep fighting, but that just meant that Auke would move on to cripple *Merchant Venture* in the meantime.

He saw movement.

"Science Officer, confirm that *Pioneer* is coming around," he barked.

"Affirmative, Tactical," she replied immediately, watching the same thing no doubt. "I have redshift on the bow."

"Gunner, put both Fours into his ass, as soon as you have a clean shot," Auke ordered. "Not until. I want them softened for *Hollywood*. Pilot, maximum acceleration. All gun teams go to rapid fire and damn the cooling circuits."

Endgame. Fool had made a bad situation worse by not just leaping to JumpSpace and THEN turning around. Thirty seconds when Terje could get him from here.

"*Meerut* forces, charge," Auke said, swapping over to the general channel. "They are about to run. Capture all the fighters for me for later, though. They have nowhere to go."

Auke leaned back and felt a preen coming on. *Blade of Kunke* was already in motion, so maybe they'd seen it, too.

Terje hammered a pair of destructive green spikes into *Pioneer*'s ass. Metal erupted, because the ship was a carrier that expected to sit at the edge of battle while missiles and fighters handled things. Front shielding was exceptional. Rear was hardly nav levels, and the fool had kept his shield projector on his bow, just like the others had.

The bow that was suddenly pointed at deep space.

"*Dragonfly*, if you surrender now, your crew will be repatriated," Barnaby said over an open line. "Otherwise, you are pirates. And you know how we feel about piracy."

Then he was talking to empty space. Not surprising. *Pioneer* and *Merchant Venture* were only slightly injured, for all that they had been hammered. Two of the frigates remained, but only one struck his colors.

The other one would need to weld a new flag pole to have hung them from first, in order to strike.

Auke was willing to give them the benefit of the doubt.

They were probably down to a junior engineering centurion trying to take command now, from the way that bow had been crushed by Terje's Fours.

"Pilot, General Chase," Auke ordered. "You know where I expect him to land, and we have better drives than he does, so we might get there first, even over this short a distance."

And then that silly asshole would be trying to run across deadspace.

That sort of situation was what Type-4 beams were invented for.

FORTY-ONE

RAIDER HOLLYWOOD, MEERUT LAGOON

Everyone called her *Hollywood*. Occasionally, someone would forget and call her Captain Ward. Her real name was Kim. She couldn't remember if anybody she'd met in the last twenty years knew that.

Everyone called her *Hollywood*.

Once upon a yesterday, she'd done bit parts in a few *Aditi* video productions, but knew even then that she'd never make it in the big leagues. Not after she saw how tiny most actors were. Skin and bones, because the camera added bulk and mass, so those skeletons looked like normal people on the screen.

She'd never been willing to diet to that level of insane.

Instead, she'd taken her pay and some residuals and invested well. A lot of the old pirates had gotten into the business after trouble with the law meant that nobody else would hire them. Basant Utkin had been born to it, on the planet behind her. Some of the old *Ingham* crews as well.

She'd parlayed a lot of smarts, some money, and the right connections to get an officer slot on a merchant raider. Then been smarter than the folks above her, to the point that the crew had eventually picked her to lead.

Luck, charm, and cheesecake posters of her as a kid hadn't

hurt. She might be in her mid-fifties now, and not a video babe, but the years had been good.

Plus, she'd built the crew she wanted. In front of her she had McKenzie Bonham in the Pilot seat, with Holman next to her. Nobody but *Hollywood* knew Holman's first name, as the redheaded woman refused to tell them. *Hollywood* only knew because she had to make sure payroll processed correctly, but had been sworn to secrecy.

They all had secrets. You didn't become a pirate when you could have lived an upstanding, legal life. Unless you were that boring in bed.

"Status?" *Hollywood* asked, looking around and making sure everyone was sharp.

"Hiding in the dark, waiting on a fat freighter to waddle by," Holman replied.

"Gunner?"

"Got my shots. Ready for a weekend in port," McKenzie said with a flip of her blond bob.

McKenzie liked to play the part of a ditzy blond with a big chest. Got people to underestimate her. Here, having a female command crew meant no men of size thinking they could use it on a smaller crew member.

Hollywood had only had to kill a few of them over the years before the word got around.

"Stand by and stay sharp," she said. "*Viking* was playing possum, too, but we don't know how badly bashed they'll be when we get them. Plus, a lot of missile launchers that probably aren't empty."

"Got a weasel in the port launcher," Holman said, turning her evil smile this way.

Homely, but that smile promised all sorts of fun and trouble for the brave.

"Load one to starboard as well," *Hollywood* decided. "They might be smart enough to give us a half-launch, burn the first weasel, then fire the other half."

Weasels. Old term for a missile or shuttle designed to mimic the electronic signature of the ship. She had a pair of short-range missile launchers aft, mostly to kill incoming missiles. Nothing that could save her if that group let loose at short range. Instead, you shut everything down, launched, then pretended to be a hole in space as the weasel screamed at everyone and raced off.

Usually, it worked.

This time, she'd landed a little bit short here, all of them back a reasonable distance from the edge of the lagoon where she was expecting all of the trouble to appear in front of her shortly.

A Raider was no match for even one of those missile frigates, at this range. Twin titan bolts on the bow would be a bit of a surprise, but just initially.

"Got a target!" McKenzie called. "Shit, it's *Viking*."

"That means the rest are right behind them," *Hollywood* said. "And we've got cover, so prepare to shitstorm someone."

Then all hell broke loose.

FORTY-TWO

Auke watched them drop into the real universe with a moment of pleasure.

He'd gotten here first.

"All gun teams, cover your quadrants against incoming fire and extend the Threes to protect *Hollywood*," he ordered "Fours, prioritize *Dragonfly* first, then *Pioneer*. We might force a surrender, if *Dragonfly* is as hurt as I think."

He listened for assents and leaned back. Barely.

The first missile frigate came in high on his starboard bow, already going away at full speed. A battery of Pulse-Twos would be tracking, but those folks seemed more interested in running. Let them go. He had bigger fish.

Dragonfly and *Pioneer* dropped out almost in synch. *Pioneer* had run harder, so they were a little farther away. Almost to the edge of the gravity well where the inflection might mess up their controls and force them to rebuild their matrix.

He could be so lucky that they'd make that kind of mistake later.

Merchant Venture and the other frigate appeared a moment later.

"*Dragonfly*," he said aloud, reminding Terje.

"One," the Gunner replied as he pressed buttons. "And two. Type-3s next."

Yes, that would do nicely. The Heavy Bombard staggered. Weak rear shielding, unreinforced. Still hadn't thought to spin his Shield Projector aft. Too late now. *Hollywood* slammed a pair of titan bolts into his ass as well.

The invaders launched a weak wave of missiles in reply. Ragged and scattered. More likely panicked Gunners pushing buttons and hoping they had locks, as they seemed to spread things perfectly even on *Viking*, *CG-505*, *CM-507*, and *Hollywood*, ignoring her two little Pickets. One of those put a titan bolt into *Pioneer*'s flank now, hitting metal. The other launched a falcon-scale firebird after the enemy flagship. Pretty good for a little ship. Pretty ballsy, too, but Auke had never found a victim or a coward among the pirates.

Bunch of stubborn, opinionated gits at times, but didn't that describe most of them?

"Missile threat?" Auke asked.

"Not today," Terje replied sarcastically.

Auke smiled. Terje had held back three of the Type-3 beams. They started stuttering through the missiles almost as far as the enemy ships could launch them. The few that got far enough came under the withering fire of the Pulse-Two teams. Ants thinking they had an invitation to a picnic, when a hungry anteater was waiting for them.

Everybody always thought of *Viking* as a simple Survey Cruiser, and forgot that this version was built on a standard Expeditionary-class hull. All he lost was the Bubble Gun forward. All the Threes and Twos remained, just as deadly as anything *Buran* had ever faced.

These folks were no *Buran*.

Auke smelled more panic.

"*Meerut* ships, hold in place here," he yelled, looking over at Barnaby in case the boss wanted to override. Barnaby nodded.

"All vessels, remain in place on this side of the gravity well. Sniping and defensive fire only."

Titan bolts could be fitted with a proximity warhead. Less damage, because it exploded as soon as it got close, but more likely to hit at long range. That meant *Hollywood* and her one Picket. The Type-3s could keep firing for a while, eventually fading out as the range got too great.

The Type-4s would hold on like a rabid badger.

"*Dragonfly* is striking their colors," Sunan yelled across the bridge.

Auke nodded. It was that or die right this moment.

He turned his attention to Barnaby.

"I assume they split and run right now," Auke said. "Do we chase? Which one should we punish?"

"We've got two frigates and *Dragonfly* surrendering," Barnaby said. "I assume Phil sells hulls to *Meerut* if he doesn't want them. And if that's a nobleman over there, we might be in a Death-or-Glory mode, so let's see if we can get *Merchant Venture* instead. If somebody strips out most of the missile racks, they have a nicely armed cargo carrier for cheap."

"Turn *Dragonfly* into a flagship?" Auke asked.

"Heavier than *Tango* or *Blade of Kunke*," Barnaby nodded.

"*CG-505* and *CM-507*, stand by to chase down *Merchant Venture*," Auke ordered.

On his screens, the two remaining cruisers began diverging, with the two frigates forming the other points of a compass rose. That was the best part here. If you flew straight, you got to the place where you could jump the soonest, but you had to go right down the throat of the five remaining guardships to do it.

Auke could see where those folks might not be as understanding about passage right now.

"*Hollywood*, take charge of *Dragonfly* and get them back to *Meerut* orbit soonest," Barnaby called over the squadron line. "Honorable surrender and all that. We'll lock them up and figure out who we can send home after we talk to Kosnett."

Auke tuned that part of the battle out. *Merchant Venture* was fleeing. And trying to run faster scared than *Viking* and his two escorts could run mad.

And Auke was pissed.

The Light Missile Bombard unleashed a solid wave of arrows now. Auke smiled. He'd spent enough time around *Shadowbolt*, which might be a sister ship to *Merchant Venture*. Both hulls had a single titan bolt and two Main Guns, but they were all pointed forward. Four Point Guns paired on the flanks that could fire aft, if Auke had any missiles to throw at them right now.

Waste of time and space in a battle like this.

505 and *507* were riding escort forward, so Auke let them handle the twelve missiles trying to reach back.

"Pilot, let's close to Type-3 range and finish him," Auke called. "Accelerate two points and come to this rough heading."

He transmitted a vector that would force *Merchant Venture* to get too close to the guardships if they tried to evade him now. The other three ships were all running like hell, so they would get away from him today.

Today.

"Gunner, start pounding on his Shield Generator with the Fours," Auke said. "As soon as it goes down, give him all of the Threes in a single salvo."

You could reinforce that rear shielding, but even reinforced it still wasn't as good as *Viking* had normally. They relied too heavily on the Shield Projector.

If he was feeling really mean, Auke could slide *505* and *507* out some and force *Merchant Venture* to try to cover his entire rear hemisphere.

Actually, that might make him surrender faster.

"*CG-505*, I am transmitting you a new vector," Auke said. "*CM-507*, same. Come to these new headings and stay sharp, in case he catches on and tried to overload you with missiles."

Auke watched Terje work.

"Next shot," the Gunner said abruptly.

"Agreed," Auke nodded. "Stand by the Threes."

Boom. Shield Projector collapsed. Normally, those took thirty to forty-five minutes to rebuild. *Merchant Venture* didn't have that long to live.

A battery of Type-3-Pulse cut loose. Six across the forward arc, plus one down the left hemisphere. Angry flock of rabid woodpeckers.

Something broke on *Merchant Venture*. Plasma started bursting out of seams along the aft starboard flank. Must have lost a reactor and they were trying to vent it before an internal explosion gutted the ship.

"All guns, stand down!" Auke yelled. "Assume they'll surrender as soon as they get their shit together. Where's *Pioneer*?"

"Running lateral and diverging rapidly," Sunan replied.

Auke studied the plot and did the math. He might be able to chase them down, but only maybe, and that gave *Merchant Venture* the time they needed to maybe fix whatever had just broken. Both ships might escape.

"Barnaby, bird in hand?" he asked.

"Affirmative," Command Centurion Silver replied. "We've annihilated the Baron's navy today."

Auke nodded.

"Damage control teams and marines, stand by to transfer to *Merchant Venture* as soon as they surrender to us. We'd like to save the ship if we can."

Auke smiled at Barnaby.

"That's that."

FORTY-THREE

RAIDER HOLLYWOOD, MEERUT LAGOON

Hollywood watched *Dragonfly* drift. *Viking* had done something to disrupt their gyroscopes, so the ship was tumbling on three axes. If they lost gravplates, that would just be an utter mess inside, but it looked like they were intact so far.

"*Dragonfly*, this is *Meerut* Port Authority warship *Hollywood*," she called over the line, promoting herself slightly and running a colossal bluff in the process. Undamaged, *Dragonfly* could savage her little Raider. "You have struck your colors and surrendered honorably. What assistance do you need to return to *Meerut* orbit?"

The line came live now. Smoke and sparks were visible in the background as the man focused on her. Bridge hit. Bad one, too. She wondered how close one of the Fours had come to decapitating the ship.

"I need time to stabilize everything, *Hollywood*," the man said. "We're fighting fires on three decks. Permission to transfer crew to your vessel for now?"

Hollywood considered it. Great Trojan Horse move, but she expected that *Viking* or Kosnett would put his face on a *Preferably Dead* poster in every post office in the Cluster if he tried anything after surrendering. Still, better safe than sorry.

"Acknowledged, *Dragonfly*," *Hollywood* decided. "Stand by."

She studied her two Pickets that she'd carried with her from orbit.

"*Varmint* and *Tralfa*, close with *Dragonfly* and begin evacuating crew with your shuttles," she ordered.

She could do that. *Viking* had put her in charge today. She keyed an internal channel.

"Flight deck."

"Stand by to launch medical crews on shuttles to evac *Dragonfly*," she said. "Include a couple of marines, just in case, but we'll set up passwords to land everyone. I'd prefer officers came here and enlisted went to the Pickets, as you start organizing things."

"Got it, *Hollywood*," the woman said.

Hollywood cut the line and watched her screens.

The invading force had started with three cruisers and four frigates three hours ago. One of the cruisers had been captured, along with two of the frigates. The remaining group was running, but *Merchant Venture* was already being overtaken by *Viking*, so they'd be done shortly.

Bad way to invade someone. Baron Russand apparently hadn't done his homework. Or had expected a mob of poorly trained and undergunned ex-pirate ships, Might have even worked, if they'd gotten the element of surprise and overwhelmed one of the Enforcers fast enough. And *Viking* and her consorts hadn't been around.

Not that many Raiders in-system. Bunch of Pickets.

Hopefully, Kosnett and Silver would let them keep all these hulls as the start of a new *Meerut* Navy.

It had been fun, being a pirate. Looked like she might have to go straight if she wanted to survive this new galaxy.

FORTY-FOUR

Barnaby studied the plot. *Merchant Venture* was done. Damaged bad enough that they'd come close to losing something and having a cascade blow through the entire interior before they managed to control it. Too many missiles on ready racks with detonators inserted.

Add open flame and the ship might have ruptured. Instead, they'd vented huge chunks. Right now, every shuttle he had was busy picking up stragglers that had been blown out in the explosion. Most of them were alive because they'd had the smarts to be wearing suits rated for damage control, rather than simple softskin suits.

Pioneer and the two frigates had made it to Jump, though not without a few passing shots from the guardships. Barnaby could see mounting rear-facing turrets and maybe a few minefields out here one of these days. And a couple of Type-4-armed stations back in the throat itself.

You could still sail around the outer edge, but in that case the voyage would be measured in weeks if you had to avoid Fours.

Tomorrow's problem. Something for Phil when he got back.

He checked the clock. After midnight local. Long day of

fighting, then fire-fighting. And the day wasn't over. He had the bridge so Auke could eat and nap. They'd swap in a few hours.

Barnaby turned to the man seated in the corner.

"Markus, I need to detach you for special duty," he said.

The man had already perked up, but probably expected to go get more coffee. He was like that.

"Sir?"

Barnaby waved him closer and opened a comm.

"*Hollywood*, this is *Viking*," he said.

"*Hollywood*," she replied.

The woman looked almost as ragged as Barnaby felt, but she'd also taken a Light Destroyer and set herself up to ambush a force that outweighed her by about a dozen. Without much help.

"I have a task for one of your Pickets," he said. "Figure out which one is in better shape to sail to *Ellariel* immediately and carry a message packet to Phil. Include outstanding warrants in your thinking, but I'd like them to rendezvous promptly and set out, rather than stopping at the guardships to resupply if we can."

"Stand by," she said, and then cut the line.

Barnaby turned to Dunklin.

"You'll take command of the ship as a supernumerary," Barnaby continued. "I'll have packets for Phil in a few hours. Everything with *Morninghawk* should have happened already, and you're still a couple of days hard sailing to get there."

"We keeping the prizes?" the Yeoman asked now.

"Phil's call," Barnaby nodded. "I could see him keeping that one barely-damaged frigate and thinning down our crews to man it. We're overstaffed already for exactly that reason. The two cruisers got beaten so bad that I expect time in drydock before they can do anything, but both are missile platforms, so they could sit in orbit being repaired and still threaten folks. Again, his call. I need you getting him up to speed, just in case he decides to sail across to wherever this asshole Baron lives and dropping a warfleet on top of him to finish this job off. Or not. Questions?"

"None, sir," Markus replied. "Need fifteen minutes to pack and I'm ready to go."

"Go," Barnaby nodded.

"*Viking*, this is *Hollywood*," she came back. "*Varmint* is in better shape to make your journey. Vectoring them down on your position now."

"Excellent, *Hollywood*," Barnaby replied. "Thank you."

As everything around him started rolling, Barnaby wondered if *Hollywood* might end up being the first Admiral in charge of *Meerut*'s new fleet.

That would be extra special, considering how sexist *Ewin* and *Dalou* tended to be.

He couldn't wait.

CHAPTER
FORTY-FIVE

Markus looked around as he emerged from the airlock and felt the shuttle detach behind him through the ringing of the hull under his feet.

"Dunklin?" the man in front of him asked. Markus nodded. "Captain Jones. Follow me."

The tall man reminded him of a menacing tornado. Broad shoulders and mobile hands just reinforced the image.

Captain Jones had deep-set brown eyes and fine, straight, soot-black hair worn in a braid that reminded Markus of a comet's trail down his back. Big and tall, like Auke Alma would have been had he spent a lot of time lifting weights to get the same, overmuscled build. Jones's skin was deeply-tanned.

The pirates didn't do uniforms, per se, but Jones and the others nearby all wore red, so Markus supposed that was the ship's color.

He fell into step behind Jones and ahead of a couple of folks that looked like typical boarding marines. Him and *Stunt Dude* could have taught them a few lessons in toughness, though.

Pickets were tiny vessels, compared to a beast like *Viking*, to say nothing of *Urumchi*. Smaller than *CS-405* had been. Maybe midway between the old *405* and *RAN Persephone*, back after they'd captured her to go raid *Buran*.

Quickly, they were on the bridge of the ship. Crowded, dark, and a little smelly, but he'd just come off *Viking*. Yan Bedrov had loud opinions on the proper way to build command spaces. He just hadn't gotten around to telling these pirates how to do it.

Yet.

"You sit here," Jones said, pointing.

Markus was in a jumpseat off to one side, just like when Phil might need coffee. Or Barnaby. His travel pack went between his feet until they found him a bunk.

The others got seated quickly. Captain at the apex of a triangle. Pilot and Gunner in front of him facing forward where a big screen could display things, as well as their own consoles. Science/Comm officer opposite Markus. Couple of engineers monitoring things and able to talk to the folks aft.

"*Viking*, this is *Varmint*," Jones said. "Got your boy aboard and we're about to head out. Any last minute details?"

"Negative, *Varmint*," CC Silver replied. "Good luck and remind those folks at *Dalou* that you'll need resupply as soon as you offload Dunklin."

"You think we're going hunting, Silver?" Jones asked.

Markus didn't even have to wonder. But then, he'd known Phil since *CS-405* got her plank crew. Small ships meant you got to know your officers way better than you did on dreadnoughts.

"I think that it gives him options, Captain Jones," CC replied. "Baron Russand screwed up royally by attacking *Meerut*. And he just lost better than half his fleet in the process. Phil might want to go have a chat with the man about it."

"We allowed to fly *Aquitaine* transponder codes when we drop out at *Ellarie*?" Jones asked now.

"That's why I sent Markus," CC Silver laughed. "Consider him your good luck charm."

"Roger that."

They cut lines and Markus found the whole bridge crew

looking over at him in a new light. More than just a messenger boy, after all, hey?

"So I guess we're the *Aquitaine* Navy now?" Jones asked with a laugh.

"Fine by me," Markus replied. "Not the first pirate vessel I've flown on with that distinction."

"No?"

"Fourth," Markus grinned, holding up fingers. "*Queen Anne's Revenge. Packmule.* Then *Persephone. Varmint's* just the best armed of all of them, but I don't expect we'll need to launch an assault against an orbital station, like we did with *Persephone.*"

"How big was this *Persephone*?" the Gunner asked now.

Smaller guy than the captain. Looked more like a terrier than a bulldog. Markus thought his name was Whendez but hadn't been introduced yet.

"Stolen police cutter," Markus grinned. "Single Main Gun on the bow. Point Guns on each rear corner with wide firing arcs."

"And you attacked an orbital fortress in that?" the man asked.

"We also had a scout version of an *RAN* corvette," Markus replied. "Smaller than *CM-507* but similar. Half as many guns. And we liberated a whole prison planet with it."

"A prison planet?" Jones asked.

"We're the *RAN*, pal," Markus replied, echoing his favorite story from Phil. "That's what we do."

The others wanted to scoff, but Markus had told the story enough times now that folks heard the ring of truth, rather than any bullshit fables. And he could have someone pull out the records when they all got to *Ellariel.* If they got feisty, he would.

"We'll talk more later," Jones promised now, before turning to the Pilot. "Hellee, take us out of the Lagoon and get us to *Ellariel* as fast as you can push. I'm looking forward to what the First Centurion has to say about all this."

Markus sat back and watched this crew go to work. He'd

talked to CC Silver about maybe recruiting for the new hulls they expected 1C to keep. Phil would want Markus's opinion of this crew over the next couple of days before he did anything.

URUMCHI

FORTY-SIX

Phil had put an entire week's worth of schmoozing and conversation into the last five hours. The original plan for the event had called for probably an hour or two of speeches in the middle, plus several hours more for something approximating a state dinner.

Neither had happened. Instead, he'd been on his feet, flowing with unseen currents, for nearly the entire time since Lord Morninghawk had been proclaimed. Thus, he'd had a front row seat as the politics of the *Dalou Hegemony* had shifted subtly and not so subtly.

Sugawara had lost a minor captain-turned-hero, and gained an ally of equal stature, though how it would all work out in terms of economics remained to be seen.

A figure emerged from the mob around him, walking in his own bubble of space. The Shogun had that effect on his people, as all worked assiduously to remain several meters away from the man at all times. Samnang Sobol accompanied him.

Looking around, Lord Morninghawk was off to one side, with a few folks from other clans. Lady Kugosu seemed to be in conversation with the Emperor. That would be interesting, to just be a fly on the wall nearby.

But he had a Shogun suddenly attentive.

Phil nodded deep enough to be something of a bow. They'd danced socially all night, but mostly it had been just two starships passing in orbit. This felt like something more serious.

Phil noted that the only person close right now was Centurion Dar. Everyone else had managed to be five or maybe ten meters away.

Serious business, then.

"Security Centurion Dar," the Shogun said, turning and nodding deeply to Xochitl.

Phil watched her turn a little umber, but she remained perfect silent. She was like that.

"First Centurion, I have had a chance to talk to the man known as *Stunt Dude*," the Shogun continued. "As I understand it, he has been serving aboard the *Yaumgan* Skycruiser *Li Jing* as an advisor."

"That is correct," Phil agreed, wondering where the man was going.

"I am also given to understand that he was a Security Chief before he retired, serving you aboard an earlier vessel?" the Shogun asked.

"Indeed," Phil nodded now. "He was the *Dragoon* aboard *CS-405*."

"And now the man still occasionally trains your security teams, as well as, apparently, similar staff aboard the *Yaumgan* ship?" the Shogun asked.

Phil hadn't delved too deep into happenings on *Li Jing*, but wouldn't be surprised. Those folks had entirely different martial traditions, so Trinidad might be introducing them to forms and patterns they had never encountered before. He wondered where all this was heading.

"He does," Phil said simply.

"I have heard many stories about Security Centurion Dar as well," the Shogun said next, indicating the small woman with a nod. "Given prior precedent, would it be possible to have her spend some time training my own staff while you are at *Ellariel-jo?*"

Phil didn't blink, but that was a lifetime of command saving him.

He'd sent *Stunt Dude* because the man had the most experience with learning and understanding strange cultures. Xochitl was a tough woman. The absolute minimum height and weight to graduate the Academy and be commissioned. Small in every *physical* sense.

Enormous as a warrior in close combat. Dangerous. And she'd won an arm-wrestling contest with his other marines to get to stand there holding the Republic Cross so Phil could award it.

Phil could order it. The needs of diplomacy overrode all else in the service. Still, he turned to the woman. Caught her hopeful grin, rather than grimace of distaste. Phil smiled. Xochitl smiled.

Yet another arena for her to compete in. And show off.

"I think that we might trade officers for a bit, sir," Phil said. "I am not aware of anyone training in kendo or steel in a manner similar to your warriors, so I am certain my own staff would have an interest in learning. Everything in Balhee is as new to us as we are to you. At least for now. I look forward to the day when all this might be old hat."

The Shogun nodded and smiled. That was the promise that they would become old friends, rather than bitter enemies. He turned to Sobol and she took a half-step closer. Into the center of the conversation, as it were.

"Trade is a topic of interest now, First Centurion," she began.

He nodded, assuming that they were finally getting down to the interesting bits of the entire evening. Folks had all horse-traded up until now, with all the various clans present able to talk on neutral ground. Marriages might be arranged. Investment deals. Feuds negotiated or initiated, depending.

And everyone had to deal with *Morninghawk* as a new factor, perhaps.

"Trade is my primary interest, Inspector," he replied. "I am aware that *Dalou*, as with all the others, tends toward autarky whenever possible, only trading with their own worlds, rather than other nations. That was a significant part of the reason smuggling has been such a problem for so long. Folks couldn't trade aboveboard, so had to resort to criminal means. My hope is that folks finally stop dealing with pirates and start dealing with their neighbors instead."

"Your arrival has altered certain calculations, First Centurion," she said with a faint nod.

Understatement of the century, but nobody asked him. He nodded politely instead, letting her work her way through whatever speech she had prepared.

"You are aware of that long stretch of stars that tends to wrap about the *Dalou* periphery," she continued. "That Neutral Zone, as it were. Many of those stars currently have habitable worlds, but few of them have more than illegal mining colonies or bases for smugglers that must be cleaned out from time to time."

"I am aware," Phil said, waiting for the other shoe to drop.

If the Shogun wanting to recruit Xochitl to train made the man Good Cop, then it was possible that Sobol was here to play Bad Cop. To let her fall on her sword, as it were, protecting the Shogun.

"Both the Emperor and the Shogun have chosen to elevate Makara Omarov to the rank of Lord Morninghawk," she said. Phil nodded and smiled. He agreed with that much. "That suggests the need for a new fiefdom for the man to ascend to."

Ah, yes. Adding something without disowning someone else meant that those stars were open territory. Marches, to use the ancient term, where a Marcher Lord was one on the border facing hostile enemies, while the inner duchies and baronies were not as immediately at risk.

"The Shogun has several worlds that might be appropriate, but has determined that it might yield more favorable outcomes to consult the *Aquitaine* ambassador before deciding," she said.

"I would be happy to offer suggestions and ideas," Phil countered. "Is this something that needs to be determined tonight, or would we have time to sit down around a table and chew over all the options, that I do not offer bad advice with unforeseen repercussions that end up being net negative for the *Dalou Hegemony* over time?"

Mousetrap. Did you want to bull ahead and announce something now, or let everyone settle into the new galaxy a little first? First mover advantage or best strategic calculations?

Phil had seen from all the faces around him tonight that a lot of what had gone down had been off the cuff, rather than the elaborate scripted theater everyone had originally planned for. The Emperor had really thrown a monkey wrench in everything, hadn't he?

Sobol was caught off guard. The Shogun was, too. Phil caught a ghost of a grin, gone almost as quickly as it arrived, as everyone turned to the man.

"My Lord?" Sobol asked now.

"The First Centurion already provides me excellent advice, Inspector," he announced. "Let us take a few days to consider all the ramifications. As he notes, this would appear to be the dawning of a new era. It is incumbent upon all of us to step out correctly. First Centurion, would you and some of your staff be available the day after tomorrow for a series of exploratory sessions? I suspect that your other vessel, the Surveyor *Viking*, has maps at least as up to date as anything we have. Perhaps better, in certain instances. Hopefully, I can persuade you to make some of them available."

"Detailed maps of the Balhee Cluster was one of those things that I intended to produce and distribute for free, to anyone interested, Shogun," Phil smiled. "What better way to make sure merchants from *Ladaux* or *St. Legier* can make it here safely, laden with cargo to trade?"

"Excellent," the Shogun nodded. "My new Minister of Protocol will contact your staff tomorrow to make arrangements.

And with that, I believe that this evening has been an exceptional success. I will withdraw now, to allow some of my more exhausted retainers the ability to do the same. Some will likely stay up all night drinking my whiskey, but that's what such an event is for. Those will not be ready at dawn tomorrow to take up a new future. I look forward to engaging you on the possibilities, First Centurion."

Phil bowed deeply to the man. This evening alone might have made the entire trip worthwhile, over and above everything he had already accomplished at *Vilahana*, *Aditi*, **or** *Meerut*.

How many people had a chance to shape the future of such a large space with their own hands? Karl VIII and Jessica Keller were really the only two that came to mind immediately. He'd be happy to be a few chapters after that with Balhee.

The Shogun withdrew and walked immediately out of the room without any announcement. Still, heads followed him. Conversation grew louder when he and his bodyguards were gone. Sobol had remained close, but she turned now and walked towards Lord Morninghawk.

Phil nodded to Xochitl Dar. They were alone.

"Try not to embarrass them too badly?" Phil asked.

"No promises, First Centurion," she grinned up at him. "They are a sexist sort of place that thinks any man is automatically better than any woman."

"Agreed, but we want them as friends, not nursing badly bruised egos."

"Then don't step out on the dojo floor," Xochitl said with calm certainty. "They might think they are impressive with those blades, but it is a dojo art. Flat floors. Good grip. Rules for fighting. Nothing like rumbling in a bar or back alley. I only know a few people around here with experience storming an enemy warship under fire. And all *that* implies."

Phil let his face fall into a lopsided grin. *Stunt Dude* and *Ground Control* were in the room with him, while Markus was back at *Meerut*. Phil had just been a pirate warlord in those days.

Still, there was a reason he'd selected Xochitl as his principal bodyguard, from all the folks applying. She could step onto a training floor here on *Ellariel*-jo and teach them some things, even as she learned.

"Just so you understand," he said. He looked around and caught Heather's eye across the room. "Let's get back to the ship."

FORTY-SEVEN

ABOARD ELLARIEL-JO ORBITAL PLATFORM

Makara, now Lord Morninghawk, watched Inspector Samnang Sobol approach. He knew his first uncertainty in days as she did. In spite of everything.

He had lived his life by a certain reticence, constrained by the values of *Dalou* itself, where all things were done in carefully measured increments and shades. Fourth Son. Unlucky.

And yet…

Harbinger.

Of what, he could not say, as so many things had already succumbed to the revolution he had felt take hold the first time he had seen *Urumchi* navigating into port at *Vilahana*. Since then, it had only grown worse, like an avalanche building speed and mass as it carried itself down the side of a mountain, seeking lives to destroy below.

Around him, the unwary had begun to hear the distant rumblings and were only barely starting to look at the mountain above, previously oblivious to the onrushing devastation and thus unprepared.

Not that he considered himself ready for it, but he had risen to the moment. At least he hoped so. The Emperor had thrown all protocol out the window and rushed in to have his say in something that no previous holder of the throne had considered. The Shogun had cast aside a blinkered Minister of Protocol and ordered his daughter into the breach to try to hold things together.

And the servants and minions of the station had elevated him to Lord Morninghawk, even before the powers he was striving so hard to save did the same.

Now Inspector Sobol approached.

Doom, it seemed, had finally caught up with him.

Makara looked around, but nearly half the important lords and visitors had already begun to withdraw in the absence of a Shogun. The Emperor and Crown Prince departed with almost no fanfare at all, which somehow struck Makara as correct, however unseemly. Kosnett was in the process of gathering up his flock and removing them from the game board as well.

She came to rest in front of him, dressed in the seriousness of her station as an Imperial Inspector and the person who had seen him at his worst. And perhaps his best. He couldn't say.

The others were ignoring him now. Servants seemed to have picked up on it as well, letting a bubble develop around them where he could pretend to be alone with her.

Makara decided that the time had indeed come to throw all caution to the wind. Time was short and there was a wall of angry snow coming to destroy all of them, if they could not escape it first.

"Samnang," he said, using her given name in public for the first time, however quietly he did it.

Her eyes still got big as she considered him. For a moment, he saw past that hard, terrible shell she kept around her in the power of her authority.

"Makara?" she answered just as quietly, sliding perhaps a half step closer now. Closer than an Imperial Inspector addressing a Captain, or even a minor Lord, as he had apparently been transformed into by the weight of opinion around him.

Even if they were all wrong.

Except that he knew they were not. *Harbinger.*

Even the Shogun had not struck him down, when Makara had answered the question.

"Tell me, Morninghawk," the Shogun of the Dalou Hegemony *had asked when they were alone. "How would you do it?"*

And he had. That memory still paled before the woman standing in front of him.

"I have a problem, Samnang," he continued, trying still to find the right words and no closer than he had been three hours ago. Or twelve. Or two hundred.

"What is that, Makara who is now Lord Morninghawk?" she asked.

"I am Lord Morninghawk," he agreed. "That means even more things must change than yesterday. And in unpredictable ways. Perhaps unfathomable to the people we were a year ago."

Something changed—perhaps matured—in her eyes at the word *we*, but he wasn't sure and hadn't seen the woman inside enough to predict the meaning.

"What things must change, Makara?" she asked, reverting to the *personal*, even as the *social* threatened to overtake them like that terrible beast of snow and rage coming for their souls.

He paused. Considered. Shrugged.

"I must step out ahead of everything again," he said. "Harbinger of Doom, though at this point both Shogun and Emperor might be disposed to listen. That just means I transform from a man too insignificant to have meaningful enemies into someone that the Great Clans might find a threat, if only because it has been so long since something like this has occurred."

"Agreed," she replied, stepping close enough that they might whisper.

He still wasn't touching the woman, but the instinct to reach out and take her hand was close to overwhelming.

"The Shogun will expect things of me that even I was not prepared for," Makara continued. "When we were alone, he asked me how I would shape the future revolution of *Dalou*, were that power in my hands."

Again, a flair of something in her eyes. He was close enough now to almost see his own reflection in them.

"And?" she murmured.

"And I told him," Makara replied. "All of it. All of the things I might have only mentioned to you in one of our other conversations. Things I barely mentioned to my own father, let alone Lord Sugawara, who was until today my Lord and is now my peer and hopefully ally."

"Many will seek to ally with *Morninghawk*," she nodded. "You have the ear of a shogun as well as an emperor, if you chose to exercise it."

"Those are merely political issues that can be observed and resolved," he waved a hand between them, as though swatting a fly. "You represent a greater thing that I must address."

"Me?" she asked, surprise suddenly overtaking her.

He hoped it was a good surprise.

"I would have liked time to handle such a task with greater delicacy and care," Makara said to her. "Circumstances force my hand, because I have begun a revolution that might yet cause the collapse and destruction of *Dalou* as a power, perhaps as a culture, even as we all strive to save it. The Emperor and the Shogun have made me Komyo, Samnang. That brings with it expectations and maneuvering. I will need to build a house. A fief. Everything. From scratch, in the middle of everything else."

"It will be a challenging task," she agreed, voice cool and only starting to show any traces of emotion because he was so hyped up at this moment that he wondered if he could leap into JumpSpace on his own, straight from this very deck.

"I need help," Makara said. "I would like your help. Your formal help, but I am not sure how I might have gone about it before now and time has run out for me to ask others who might suggest a path. I would like to ask you to join with me and become *Lady Morninghawk* if you still feel as you did the last time I kissed you."

He fell silent. Not out of words, but out of things to say. Too much depended on the next words out of her mouth.

The audacity of what he had just done would have probably caused the woman to punch him in the mouth a year ago. Drawn the blade she had on her hip, and chop him into fish food. *Dalou* women were not to be trifled with.

But by her own words, he had seduced the woman. She wasn't the first to show an interest in him: however, she was the first social or political peer.

He held his breath. Held himself perfectly still as those dark eyes seemed ready to swell up like the mouth of a leviathan and swallow him whole.

At least then he'd be dead and none of those future problems would be his.

"You are serious?!?" she asked/said now.

"I am," Makara answered. "You believed in me when I might have been denounced as a threat to our society and driven into hiding. You believed in me when I was prepared to die gloriously in battle because the situation called for it. I hope you believe in me now, and will continue to going forward."

"*Lady Morninghawk?*" she asked. "But I am only a commoner, from a family of little note but bureaucrats and scholars."

"And I was the fourth son of a minor retainer of a Komyo," he answered her. "Someone recently reminded me that four does not have to be doom. At least not for me. It might be doom for the enemies of the Shogun and of all *Dalou*. Harbinger of Doom, you called it. Harbinger of Revolution now, perhaps, because the Shogun might actually listen to me. Lord Morninghawk, because others seemed to believe that was the wisest path forward."

"*Morninghawk* is a Heavy Escort, Makara," she replied, eyes serious. "Your position in battle is to stand between *Urumchi* or *Wraithruin* and the enemy, blunting their threat with your own."

"As it always has been," he agreed.

"That also makes you a Herald, Lord Morninghawk," Samnang continued, rocking him back on his heels. "You lead, and the rest will follow. *Vanguard of Revolution*, if you will."

Makara blinked, uncertain how they had gotten to this new plateau. At the same time, it felt right.

He even felt the first stirring of hope. The last several months had been a bed of quicksand threatening to swallow the unwary. Such a thing could be defeated, but required patience and mental focus to escape without going under.

"You are serious, Lord Morninghawk?" she asked. "Certain that I would be the best to stand beside you?"

"You have been," he answered her. "Nothing in that bright or bitter future will change that."

"I am not certain that I might bear you children to continue the line," she countered.

He wondered if she was seeking an excuse to elude him, then decided that she was giving him an option to reconsider.

As if he'd done nothing but consider all the options and outcomes for the last several hours.

"If so, I am certain that I have nephews and nieces I might adopt," he decided. "Or you might, though I have never inquired as to your family. Will your father object to such a match?"

She laughed warmly.

"He has loudly objected several times that I have not been interested in any sort of marriage of convenience and alliance that might elevate our family to the fringes of the aristocracy," she smiled. "I cannot imagine him objecting now."

"Then we should send Lingyi Omarov to announce the news?" he asked her leadingly.

"If you are certain, Makara."

"I am, Samnang," he replied. "The revolution we have

discussed previously continues to grow. Some will fall beneath it and there is nothing I can do to save them. But *Dalou* must survive."

He felt bold enough to take her hand, no doubt scandalizing everyone left in the room, but most of them had clustered on the far side of the room, close to one of the several bars over there that would continue to serve until ordered otherwise, or they ran out.

Lord Morninghawk made a note of the colors that remained to drink, long after the principal players had retired. It was rude to mark them as less serious, but nothing would come of drinking this late save mutterings of rebellion and hangovers, neither of which he had any use for.

Lady Kugosu stepped closer to him. He had been tracking her unconsciously. She entered his mind now.

He watched the young woman study them, holding hands. Samnang made to let go and he held her all the fiercer until her grip strengthened.

"Congratulations," Lady Kugosu said, nodding to them. "I will let my father know the joyous news."

"Thank you," Makara said to her, bowing.

"No, Lord Morninghawk," the young woman said firmly. "Thank you."

FORTY-EIGHT

P hil noted the way that the Shogun's marines had changed as he exited the airlock and got fully surrounded. It was just him, Harinder, and Dar today.

The men around them were far more respectful than they had been last time. Polite and almost smiling, rather than growly and tough.

Phil put it down to the revolution Lord Morninghawk had mentioned to him was coming.

Apparently, it was about to arrive.

Quickly, they walked through the station to a conference room done to look more business and less social. Phil measured his life in hours and days spent in such spaces. Best way to pull together a small group and get everything you needed quickly. More than once, he had considered having Markus remove all the chairs from his favorite room back on *Urumchi* and elevate the table so you were standing around it like a bar. Meetings tended to run much faster when nobody was sitting down and could relax.

There were chairs here, but not comfortable ones. Enough to be functional, and keep folks on their toes. He approved.

The Shogun was seated. His daughter was there, along with

Morninghawk and Sobol. The latter two were holding hands, which would be an utter scandal in most of *Dalou*, so that told Phil all he needed to know about that situation.

The other men were folks Phil had studied the other night. Ministers who had served the Shogunate for years and decades, or generations in the case of Tane Eiton, the oldest present.

None rose as he entered.

"First Centurion," the Shogun smiled. "Command Flag Centurion. Centurion Dar. Welcome and join us. Can we get you some tea?"

"That would be excellent," Phil replied as he pulled out a chair next to Lady Kugosu and put Harinder next to Tane Eiton.

Somehow, the arrangement of the room did not strike him as accidental. Xochitl took a spot behind him on the wall and an aide delivered a fresh tea pot. Phil noted that there were already cups.

The Shogun was treating him like a friendly advisor rather than an alien barbarian, as some of the rumors and a close reading of *Dalou* history might have suggested.

Revolution, indeed.

They made small talk for several minutes as Phil got to study the Shogunate Staff at close quarters. Other than Lady Kugosu and Minister Eiton, he was not much impressed. But then, the Shogun had defenestrated his own Minister of Protocol literally on the lip of the events the other day. Had he been looking for an excuse to clean house?

Food for thought.

"First Centurion, we have been reviewing logs and messages since you first joined us in the Cluster," Lady Kugosu said now, sounding much older and more mature than her fourteen years.

Phil was impressed by her. And wondered how he might tip the scales to allow her to ascend to the Shogunate, rather than the old traditions that meant some other male got the power when all of Kugosu was cast aside.

Phil turned his polite and friendly attention to the woman now. He nodded for her to proceed.

"Trade and diplomacy, but always trade," she prompted him now.

"We brought a fleet capable of both sailing tremendous distances, as well as protecting ourselves because nobody was certain what reception we might find," he replied. "And indeed, the *Ingham Syndicate* squadron under *Tango* was immediately hostile. You have seen how that played out."

He watched the shivers of anger and terror sweep around him. It could just as easily be *Ellariel* on some future date, though Pressor Beams were still experimental technology not widely accepted.

"At the same time," he continued, "we have considered asking the Governor at *Vilahana* for permission to build a naval base in their system, so that we could more readily explore the darkness beyond the Cluster in all directions, as those are still blank spots on all our maps. We know where the stars are, but not the people."

"And your plans for *Meerut*, First Centurion?" Eiton asked now.

Elder statesman. If anyone else held the Shogunate, Phil would have said the power behind the throne, but perhaps consigliere was a better description. Someone who could have honest conversations with Kugosu, because he was powerful and respected.

Phil studied the man for a long second. He'd had all this out with Sobol previously, but she was merely a bureaucrat at the end of the day. Or had been. Imperial Inspector put her at the top of the local Civil Service, but these men—and young woman—held the true power. If Sobol was about to become Lady Morninghawk, her role would change as well.

"I have studied the various treaties that the *Dalou Hegemony* and the various *Ewin Principalities* have signed over the last few centuries," he said, nodding to Harinder now. "Her job was to confirm them at a level of depth that none but fussy lawyers might attain, which is why she is my Command Flag Centurion, gentlemen. I trust her to understand those things and advise me well."

"And your findings, Command Flag Centurion?" Eiton asked, turning to Harinder.

Phil caught that the man addressed her by her rank, rather than her position. She was a peer of Heather Lau and Barnaby Silver, having served as a First Officer in her time before realizing that the future would mean fewer command berths. So she'd trained under Enej Zivkovic himself.

"The twin blue giants that generally mark the entrance to the place we call *The Lagoon* are so prominent that all of your treaties have used them as marker stones for establishing boundaries with your neighbors on that side, Minister," she replied coolly. "Rear corners, if you will."

The others blinked with a hint of confusion, but Phil was watching Eiton now. The implications hit him like a fist to the mouth.

"All of them?" he asked, a bit perplexed.

"All of them, sir," Harinder smiled like a crocodile at the men around her, excepting the two friendlies at Phil's end of the table.

"Thus," Phil leaned in and drew all the lightning to him now, "*Meerut* exists in territory outside anything ever claimed by *Ewin* or *Dalou*. Ever. Technically outside the Cluster itself, depending on how you wish to interpret things. Nobody has any legal claim on the system, as even the lagoon is outside your borders. That was the situation when the pirates of the *Ingham Syndicate* claimed it and developed it. It was the situation when Basant Utkin staged a coup and executed the former government so he could take it over. It remains the situation now that I have destroyed Utkin and his force."

"So you intend to hold it against us?" Admiral Toko asked in a belligerent voice.

"I have not yet determined what would be the best course of action," Phil turned a dangerous scowl on the man. The sort of anger that had seen him raid *Buran*'s planets and steal a god's vessels. "*Meerut* currently has an interim Governor in Milose Dexter, accepted by the rebel captains when he killed Utkin in single combat with blades, as was their tradition in the old days. If you chose to challenge Dexter to single combat, they might allow you to accede to power, but they are also in the process of building a new government and legal system at *Meerut*, so perhaps that will not be necessary."

Maybe a bit rude to suggest an aging, unfit First Centurion like Toko might have to don blades and go to *Meerut* himself, but he certainly got the man to lean back in shocked anger.

Eiton leaned forward now. Not much. Such was his power that the gravitational zone in the room shifted anyway. Phil smiled expectantly at him.

"The Shogun had been talking about trade and diplomacy," he reminded the others in a tone that a recently-roused dragon might use.

Phil nodded and took the opening.

"It is my hope, ladies and gentlemen, that *Dalou* and *Ewin* might accept that their current borders are sufficient, and begin to trade with the folks at *Meerut* as well as each other," he said, looking around. "If those former syndicalists have trade options, they are much less likely to revert to piracy or brigandage out of desperation."

He turned to the Shogun now. Eiton might be powerful, but only one man would make the decision. Most of the Ministers in here were just for show anyway. Eiton and Lady Kugosu, plus Omarov and Sobol, seemed to be the ones with the cards.

The future, as it were. Maybe the *Hegemony* itself.

"Diplomacy and trade," the Shogun drawled slowly now, echoing his daughter, his consigliere, and Phil. "You used an interesting term the other night, Kosnett."

"Sir?"

"*Autarky*," Kugosu said. "Economic self-sufficiency, but the kind that borders on social isolation. Hard, frigid borders intended to keep out all others."

Phil nodded. Dead center accurate. All of the Cluster, save the *Aditi Consensus*, seemed wedded—even welded—to that ideal.

"It is my experience that allowing trade better fosters communication," Phil opined. "Social as well as commercial development. Innovation, because no culture has an exclusive on good ideas."

He could see which men around him maintained good relationships with the remaining smugglers, just from who smiled and who scowled at that comment. Getting rid of the pirates would be like dealing with ticks, probably. Slow, painful, and occasionally bloody, but necessary if the host was to thrive.

"And so *Aquitaine* trades now with the *Fribourg Empire*?" The Shogun asked.

"As well as *Lincolnshire*, *Salonnia*, and even *Corynthe*, despite being a considerable distance from our borders," Phil agreed. "Even greater than the direct sailing distance to *Ellariel*, though not by much. Just out to the end of that galactic arm, where the stars grow thin and the darkness between galaxies looms."

These folks did not understand darkness. The Balhee Cluster was a hollow sphere of light and warmth, with hundreds of systems one might colonize. It was only outside where the empty space stretched for light-centuries in every direction.

The Shogun nodded serenely.

"I suspect that *Meerut* will be a vast and complicated issue with which to deal," he said. "And as the First Centurion has noted, it does not need to be solved today, as even they are not certain what they will demand from the Cluster."

"All the more reason to crush them now," Admiral Toko growled at the room, slamming a pudgy hand down on the table for emphasis. "Before they build up the strength to resist us."

"*Aquitaine* frowns on invading independent nations," Phil offered, staring at the man like a mongoose.

"You think you can stop us?" Toko snapped.

"I think that if it became necessary, the *Republic of Aquitaine* Navy might take sides, yes," Phil said. "My superiors might decide to base a western fleet at *Meerut* if it was necessary to make a point."

"Your forces cannot challenge the *Dalou* Fleet!" Toko snarled.

"You think so?" Phil asked quietly.

Toko started to say something and Eiton cracked the whip on him.

"Admiral, you will be silent or I will have you removed," the man said in a voice of quiet, deadly menace.

Effective. The fool shut his mouth so hard he might have bit his tongue.

Phil would have expected the Shogun to speak. The Shogun's smile was fleeting, and telling.

Tane Eiton nodded to Phil now. Phil let it go with a matching nod.

Kongō, at the head of a Heavy Dreadnought fleet, might go through those battleships outside this station like shit through a goose, if Raizō Tanaka had a reason to. And maybe the orders from Pet to make an example of someone.

Hopefully, it wouldn't ever come to that.

"Diplomacy and trade," Phil repeated simply.

"Today, we need to begin considering Lord and Lady Morninghawk," the Shogun announced, making official what Phil had suspected.

Both of the new lovebirds were a little white and shaky now, but still holding hands. That was good.

Phil focused his attention on the man who would make that decision. As did everyone else in the room.

"Having elevated the man, it is incumbent upon the Shogunate to make sure that he succeeds, as a reflection of the

Shogunate, the Emperor, and the Hegemony itself," the man continued. "At the same time, there are no systems currently without leaders that could serve as fiefdoms for the new house. And even that outcome would immediately create enemies. Unnecessarily, I might add."

Phil nodded. The man seemed to be speaking directly to him now, ignoring most of his Ministers.

But Phil supposed that *Aquitaine* was the wild card here. He'd upset centuries of tradition, inertia, and entropy by sailing into *Vilahana.*

"You spoke of borders, First Centurion," the Shogun prompted now. "What future do you see for the Balhee Cluster?"

Phil wondered if the man had spies who had listened to his conversation with Kaur Singh, and his warnings to her that the *Aditi Consensus* would not be allowed to intervene in a *Dalou* civil war.

"You have many treaties in place, Hegemon of *Dalou,*" Phil replied, elevating the man to what he really was.

The power that would control this territory.

"As you noted, many such agreements, many dating back centuries," the Hegemon nodded.

"The Balhee Cluster is a hollow sphere," Phil reminded them. "If we consider *Vilahana* as the mouth of an amphora, then the *Aditi Consensus* sits at almost the center, with *Gloran* to the left, and *Dalou* back and to the right from the entrance. *Yaumgan* sits quietly in a far corner, while the *Ewin Principalities* are the second largest grouping behind *Aditi* in terms of stars claimed, but perhaps the least well-organized and governed of the five."

"And how would you change things, First Centurion?" Lady Kugosu asked now.

Phil wondered if she'd been prepped for that question by her father. A wise choice, as her youth could be an excuse for such bluntness, should Phil decide to draw offense at it.

Obviously, everybody else at this table had underestimated him.

Phil smiled at her benignly, like an uncle.

"I wouldn't," he replied.

"No?"

"No," Phil nodded. "My preference would be that every single border treaty in place today assumes the absolute force of law. The *Aditi Consensus* is known to be economically and occasionally militarily expansive, having intruded on all of their neighbors but *Yaumgan* from time to time, necessitating short wars, police actions, and kinetic solutions to return to a status quo. However, they have been successful enough to date that they currently occupy and have colonized *Ewin*, *Gloran*, and especially *Dalou* worlds. Rather than try to push everything back a century, I think everyone should focus on nailing things in place now and trading with one another instead of fighting or funding piracy."

Denis Jež had liked to talk, in the old days, of going out on his grandparent's farm as a child, when both his parents had served in the *RAN*. There had been this one pond that would be calm and still in the first light of a cold morning, with mist rising off of it. Until a youngster named Denis would find the single biggest rock he could lift and drop it off a slight rise, just to see how big a splash he could make.

Everyone around this table except Harinder was covered in water and mud.

Metaphorically.

Phil leaned back and smiled as the voices started talking over each other, growing louder as each strove to be heard. The tea was growing cold, so Phil drank some and caught Harinder's wicked smile.

The Ministers were in turmoil. Eventually, Lady Kugosu slammed an open palm down on the table loud enough to cut through the din.

Worked. The old farts shut up finally.

"Diplomacy and trade, First Centurion?" she asked.

"You'll catch more flies with honey than vinegar, Lady Kugosu," he replied, citing one of his wife's favorite quotes.

Notably, she turned to her father now and nodded. Phil could see a whole new future for *Dalou* in that gesture.

"Would *Aquitaine* be just as aggressive in defending other boundaries as they would *Meerut*?" the Shogun asked.

"If we had the right kinds of treaties," Phil agreed. "At present, we have not signed any, save for an agreement to protect the moorage and lagoon at *Meerut*. Even with *Aditi*, we have only begun discussing such things in great detail, and I will remind everyone that my squadron only first arrived at *Vilahana* nine months ago."

A few of the ministers around him gasped, but they'd been so focused that they might have forgotten how recently the revolution had come to their shores. Then the noise started up again. It tapered quickly, though.

"You have no treaties with the *Aditi Consensus* at present?" Lady Kugosu confirmed.

"That's right," Phil agreed. "I have ambassadors present negotiating things. And unofficial, verbal agreements, such as sent both *Aranyani* and *Khandoba* with me to *Meerut* the first time. But I also was able to take Lord Morninghawk with me then, as well."

"There is a world," the Shogun leaned in now, causing the room to tilt again. "It sits at roughly the corner where *Dalou*, *Ewin*, and *Aditi* come together at something of a corner on a map."

"*Urwel?*" Phil asked, causing all manner of consternation around him.

"You know this place?" Eiton asked, utterly shocked.

"I was frankly surprised that you didn't already have at least a full colony, if not a major forward naval base, there," Phil replied honestly. "According to *Viking's* notes, it was tailor-made for a trade depot, and you've chased out *Ingham* pirates, *Ewin* renegades, and *Aditi* merchant forces any number of times without fully occupying it yourself."

"It is too far from other colonies," the Shogun noted dryly.

"Only if you restrict trade to *Dalou* worlds," Phil replied just as compactly. "Neither the *Aditi* colony *Belamel* nor the *Ewin* sector capital at *Toulouse* are that far away physically, however remote emotionally. If you have trade and not war, it becomes valuable real estate."

"War is the question, First Centurion," the Shogun said. "As you note, our neighbors have attempted on more than one occasion to claim the world for themselves. We maintain that neutral belt of stars to keep our foes at a distance."

"And it served such a purpose for a long time," Phil agreed. "Now, it provides you space to expand into, without having to carve it off someone else's frontier in the process. If you were to fill in all those empty stars, *Dalou* would be larger than *Ewin* and perhaps rival *Aditi* for overall size, though it would take generations for your population to match theirs."

"Would *Aquitaine* sign a treaty to guarantee all these borders, in both directions?" Tane Eiton asked now.

It all felt like a complicated and rotating game of good cop/bad cop, but Phil supposed that Eiton knew the current Hegemon better than the rest. And the Shogun's own daughter had proven her worth at this table, according to all reports Phil had been able to consume.

"We would look forward to five strong, developed neighbors on this frontier," Phil said, turning to include everyone. "My primary fear lately has been that the arrival of *Aquitaine* would cause one or more of the nations of the Cluster to fall in on itself in a civil war that would cause a spasm of violence like an earthquake, bringing down distant buildings unsuspected of being weak."

"So Lord Morninghawk might be able to build at *Urwel*, and count *Aquitaine* as a friend and defender when others complain?" Eiton asked.

"In broad terms, yes," Phil said. "I have ambassadors to credential, both for *Ellariel* and other places, just as I do at *Aditi* itself. The devil is always in the details, but trading with *Dalou* and *Aditi* means that they intend to embrace a future that doesn't have a place in it for piracy or the old ways. Personally, I look forward to the first time a *Corynthe* Mothership manages the impossibly-long sail from *Petron* to *Ellariel*, bringing goods and stories. Those folks are pirates, but their retired Queen is Jessica Keller herself."

More chaos, but a contained kind. Everyone had heard of Keller. And most rightly feared her.

Phil respected the woman, because he'd seen her hold the entire fate of the galaxy in her hands one afternoon, before deciding not to destroy everyone and everything in her rage.

As had Vo Arlo.

"Perhaps, then, First Centurion, we should talk about the kinds of treaties that *Aquitaine* and *Dalou* would both be well served by," the Shogun noted.

Phil leaned back now and nodded to Harinder. He'd brought his legal shark for a reason, after all. If they thought that she was just a woman they could bull over, he looked forward to their impending surprise.

And maybe, just maybe, the *Hegemony* could be saved from itself, after all?

FORTY-NINE

Heather was sitting a watch on the bridge, mostly just because she'd managed to get completely caught up on her paperwork somehow and didn't feel like napping or reading a book this afternoon.

"Hey, boss, got a live one for you," Leyla said from her Science Officer station.

Heather turned to study the woman.

"Boat just appeared out at the edge of the gravity well and beyond a bit, like they didn't want anyone shooting," the woman said. "Identifies itself as *RAN Varmint*."

"Do they now?" Heather drawled. "This the same *Varmint* we left behind at *Meerut*?"

"Is."

"What's harbor control doing?" Heather asked.

"Combination of belligerence and confusion," Leyla looked up and grinned. "*Varmint* asked for us. Claimed that they had messages for the First Centurion. Diplomatic Courier, even."

"Oh, that sounds good," Heather grinned. "Ask harbor control if they'll allow the ship in or if we should go out and rendezvous with them."

"On it," Leyla said.

Heather dialed up a small field to dull noise and opened a line to the flag bridge. Aliza Babatunde was holding the fort back there right now, with Phil and Harinder over on the station for the third day.

"What's up, Heather?" the woman asked as she came on line.

"Picket from *Meerut* just appeared at the edge of the gravity well asking for Phil," Heather replied. "Using *RAN* transponders to make it official."

"I see," Aliza replied. "Should we roust Phil from his meetings?"

"Not yet," Heather replied. With Phil gone, she was in charge of the squadron. "But probably worth sending him a ping letting him know. I'm routing you everything from Leyla now. Can you filter it, compress it, and send it along in a way that doesn't bring the platform to battle stations?"

Aliza laughed. In the background, Heather could hear others do the same. Same on her bridge.

"Will let you know," Aliza said, cutting the line.

"Leyla?" Heather turned to the woman now.

"Since it is a nothing more than a Picket, the locals aren't being as rude as they might be, had a Raider or something wandered in. I'm hearing orders to come down to our location."

"Excellent," Heather said. She keyed a different line and woke Iveta up. "I'm about to bring the ship up a notch. Not any sort of alert, but we might be changing that shortly. Want you on the bridge in fifteen minutes."

"On my way," Iveta yawned.

That gave the woman time for a shower and mug of coffee, since it was late in her day and they'd all been stretching shifts as they scanned and cataloged everything there was to see around here. Including just about every class of warship the *Hegemony* had built in the last generation.

Phil had mentioned how pissy the Minister of War had gotten on that first day. *Urumchi* couldn't take on three battleships. Not without a Heavy Dreadnought squadron backing them.

The folks back home, however, would like to know exactly how many frames and bulkheads made up such vessels, if they needed to saw somebody apart with Type-4s at close range. They would be able to do that.

Heather flipped another switch.

"Flight Deck," came the reply.

"Warm up a second shuttle and crew," she ordered the man. "We're expecting a courier shortly and need to go retrieve them from their transport. At the same time, we might need to pull Phil from his meetings, depending on how things go."

"Second shuttle, aye, sir," he said.

She cut the line and looked around.

"Leyla, tell me about *RAN Varmint*," she called.

"Picket hull," the Science Officer replied. "Originally *Hamath Syndicate*, same as *Hollywood*. Friendly with that woman and her crew. Captain is Esser Jones. Single titan bolt on the bow and a pair of Main Guns. Four Point Guns with good all-around defensive firepower. Nothing interesting in my notes beyond that."

"Good enough," Heather said. "Everybody stand by."

Varmint came down quickly to rest a little ahead of *Urumchi* and above them in orbit. Close enough for the naked eye to pick them out as everybody drifted along in the wake of the big station. The shuttle docked, held for two minutes, then withdrew.

"Boss, Markus is on the shuttle," Leyla said as they watched it return.

Heather grinned over at Iveta. They weren't dating, but they did seem to spend a lot of time together. Occasionally, overnight as well. Iveta had a smile on her face.

"Aliza, I'm coming back to flag bridge," Heather said over the line. "Iveta, you have the bridge, but I'll keep the flag for now."

She rose and went aft. It wasn't far, but still felt like an enormous distance, all of it mental. She got herself settled and Markus Dunklin arrived promptly, along with Captain Jones. Heather vaguely remembered the man from receptions. Then he stepped into the room like a whirlwind and Heather remembered him entirely.

"Sit," she ordered, nodding to the woman who had Markus's job today delivering coffee. "Executive summary first."

"*Ewin Principality* squadron of three cruisers and four frigates attacked the moorage on the Sixteenth," Markus began. "*Viking* and consorts assisted local defensive forces in repelling the assault with minimal damage on our side of things. The cruiser in command and two of the frigates escaped us at the lagoon. CC Silver sent me with a complete message pack for Phil."

Well, shit.

Heather turned to Aliza.

"Phil needs to know this right now," she told the woman. "I'll let you phrase it better, but there's no reason to continue having the meeting without him. Captain Jones, can we offer you hospitality overnight or did you need to return to *Varmint?*"

"My First Officer can handle anything, Command Centurion," the man replied. "Just like that, though? You don't need more?"

"Markus was with me when we were pirates in stolen warships behind enemy lines in *Buran*, Captain," she told him, in case somehow he didn't know. "Were the invaders friends of *Shadowbolt?*"

"Negative, sir," Markus said. "One Baron Russand, who my records show is one of those renegade lords on the outs with the king right now. Probably was looking for a safe place he could capture and hold as a base to rebuild his forces, though that's pure speculation on my part. He got his tail singed hard and took off running. Barnaby and Auke took both of his cruisers down at the lagoon and forced them to strike."

Heather nodded and rose, turning to the Yeoman with the coffee.

"Captain Jones will need a cabin, laundry, and an aide while he's with us," she said. "Put him in an ambassadorial suite for now and have him eat with us. Captain Jones, she'll get you taken care of."

Rather than stay, Heather went forward again to let Iveta know.

Phil wasn't likely to be pleased.

FIFTY

Phil had gone ahead and left his comm on the table top after the first message, resting between him and Harinder. The Ministers around them had taken a break at the Shogun's order, on the assumption that an unscheduled courier from *Meerut* wasn't likely to be good news. Lord and Lady Morninghawk had left as well.

Right now, it was him and Harinder, plus the Shogun, Lady Kugosu, and Tane Eiton.

The old man was even more dangerous than Phil had first understood. At the same time, he was smarter than just about anybody in the room, and most able to adapt quickly to changing circumstances.

Phil wondered how long it was until most of the other Ministers were simply retired and replaced with younger, sharper people. The current staff had a lot of dead weight accumulated over the years.

His comm chirped with a note from Aliza. Phil flipped it over and read it.

A word escaped his lips before he could get his mouth shut. Probably one that Lady Kugosu didn't use frequently, from the way she turned a little red hearing it. Both of the older men perked up.

Phil considered operational security, then just slid his comm across to the younger man across from him.

The Hegemon would need to know.

Markus Dunklin reports: Renegade Ewin Principality squadron of three cruisers and four frigates attacked the Meerut moorage on Nov 16. Viking and consorts assisted local defensive forces in repelling the assault with minimal damage. The cruiser in command and two of the frigates subsequently escaped. CC Silver sent complete message pack for First Centurion. Not friends of Shadowbolt.

Well, there you have it. He'd worried that *Dalou* would launch some sort of surprise while he'd been at *Ellariel*. Turned out that *Ewin* had done it instead. Or at least *Ewin* boats. Renegade suggested another group of aristocrats bickering with their king over something or other. *Ewin* was famous for their governmental and social dysfunctionality.

"Am I to understand that they captured two cruisers and two frigates?" the Shogun asked after a moment, passing it on to Eiton.

"That's my read, sir," Phil said. "Senior Chief Dunklin is one of my inner circle of folks. Nominally my personal aide, but I'd left him with *Viking* to take command of a research project while I was gone. Command Centurion Silver sending him suggests that the rest of the message is rather important."

"I would presume then that we should adjourn our meetings for a couple of days?" the Shogun asked. "To give you time to process and plan?"

"That would be most helpful, sir," Phil said. "At the same time, I think we have made enough progress here that I could send over Command Diplomatic CenturionEvgeni Danchev and have him fully credentialed to continue negotiations with your staff. We've hammered out the important points to the extent that both staffs should be filling in details."

"I agree, Shogun," Eiton said, handing Phil back his comm. "We've covered sufficient ground, especially if the First Centurion needs to depart *Ellariel* shortly. Let the bureaucrats handle things for now."

Phil studied the older man. Dangerously smart. Immediately understood that Phil should return to *Meerut* to reassure everyone. Phil wondered if he needed to go chastise someone as well. Though, losing more than half your force in an afternoon had to sting.

"I had originally intended to sail to *Urwel* with Lord and Lady *Morninghawk*," Phil told Eiton. "To help them establish their own moorage, as it were, as they began construction."

"Perhaps one of your corvettes might be able to accompany them in the meantime?" Eiton asked. "As a show of unity, as it were?"

Phil started to speak but Lady Kugosu interrupted.

"Already, we take away the Heavy Escort *Morninghawk* from his well-deserved space guarding *Urumchi*'s van, Minister," she pointed out brightly. "Now, we ask him to remove a second escort? That sends the wrong signal, unless we intended to replace both vessels with other ships to make up the shortfall. And anything we send will obviously not fill that emptiness, as *Morninghawk* is now a ship that other commanders will have nightmares about."

Phil turned and couldn't help but blink, trying to remember that this young woman was barely a teenager. And yet, she'd heard the recording of Iveta's voice, obviously, talking about *Morninghawk* before the battle at *Meerut*.

Lady Kugosu beamed proudly up at him, all legs and short torso seated next to him.

"Would the First Centurion be amenable to a trade, if we offered a pair of vessels to assist you?" the Shogun asked.

Phil considered it for a long moment. Before Aquitaine, such a discussion would have taken these folks at least a year, from his understanding of how *Dalou* used to be. Now, it might take a few hours.

"Nominally," he temporized. "I will need to speak with the messenger and review the information, but if—and I expect this is the case—I need to return to *Meerut*, then a trade could be something we worked out. With your permission, I will withdraw now and come to a better understanding of the situation that I may communicate my own needs to you on the morrow?"

"That would be excellent, First Centurion," the Shogun replied, nodding and even smiling.

Phil got himself detached, grabbed Harinder, and had Xochitl lead them out.

Things were moving rapidly, which was so unlike *Dalou* that occasionally he wondered if he'd stepped through some sort of magical mirror into another place.

Hopefully, in a good way.

FIFTY-ONE

ELLARIEL-JO ORBITAL PALACE

Jirou watched Kosnett depart, leaving him alone with Tane Eiton and his daughter. The old man rose.

"With your permission, Shogun, I will also withdraw?" Eiton asked.

Jirou studied the man, then Kohahu. He nodded, and quickly found himself alone with her, only a handful of bodyguards around the edge.

"You obviously have a plan," he said quietly.

She bowed her head, biting her lip with a grimace.

"I have an idea, Father," she replied. "I am not sure it works, but it potentially puts you in the strongest position, at least as far as I have been able to calculate the odds. None of this tracks with what I originally learned, but we can place that at *Morninghawk*'s feet."

"In a good way, Daughter," he reminded her. "Lord *Morninghawk* will lead us into this new future he saw first. Keep that in mind."

"I do," she nodded.

"Tell me," he commanded her.

"Kosnett will lose one of his Guardian Corvettes, plus *Morninghawk* itself, if we proceed and he publicly sends a ship with Lord Morninghawk sailing to *Urwel*," she began. "As he cannot be in two places at once, and needs to go to *Meerut*, we must send replacement vessels."

"Which two did you have in mind?" Jirou asked her scrutinously, to see what she had envisioned.

"The Escort *Forktail* is currently available," Kohahu replied. "Having come from *Ishiokoh* with *Wraithruin*. It is commanded by a Sugawara, which honors that Lord for letting us remove his most famous retainer."

"Not as big or dangerous as *Morninghawk*, but still a wise choice," he nodded. "And the other?"

It was interesting, watching her hesitate, though he didn't know what caused it.

"The Command Cruiser *Storm Petrel* would be a good candidate," Kohahu continued. "It is commanded by a Yukimura."

"And the Crown Prince is a training officer aboard, only just returned to duty having attended the events here," Jirou concluded the thought.

She nodded her head and remained silent.

On the surface, a good combination. *Dalou* ships were at great risk facing a mass of *Ewin* missiles. The firebirds were a more effective weapon, but slow to charge when the other ship could keep firing arrows at you until he ran out. *Storm Petrel* had fewer such weapons than others of that scale, and instead supplemented that with extra Main and Point Guns as a ship intended to engage on that frontier.

Also a safe place for a future emperor to learn military discipline, which was something few of his forebears had ever encountered.

Something in her demeanor wasn't right.

"Kohahu?" he asked.

Indecision. That was what he saw in her eyes. Until something crystallized.

She turned to the bodyguards now.

"Clear the room," she ordered in a suddenly hard, almost angry voice.

The men around them hesitated. Jirou nodded and found himself alone with his newest advisor.

"How bad is it?" he asked her.

"You will need a personal representative to join Kosnett," Kohahu replied. "Sobol satisfied that need the first time, but she is otherwise unavailable. Admiral Toko is a poor choice for a variety of reasons. Minister Eiton too old perhaps to make such journey."

"So I should send you?" Jirou asked, calculating all the angles he could see from here, but not finding the thing that made her hesitant. "Put Lady Kugosu aboard *Storm Petrel* to watch my captains and make sure that they answer to Kosnett."

"That is one interpretation, Father," she said. "I can see a second one that might not be obvious to your rivals and enemies at the moment. That would be better."

"Which is?"

"Even now, others prepare for the day that Kugosu has to stand aside from the Shogunate," Kohahu replied, her voice finally finding a solid footing. "As you have no sons, any marriage elevates the son of another house as the primary candidate to replace you. Three daughters suggests any of three Houses might dream of ascending to power if they maneuvered adroitly enough."

Jirou nodded. Such had been his calculations. And why he had not yet begun to even entertain suitors for Kokoro, the oldest at sixteen. He was in no hurry to make any of them grow up any faster than they desired, especially as Kokoro was the scholar of the three, and would demand that she be allowed to complete her formal education first.

"What if Kugosu allied with Yosan?" she asked simply.

Jirou felt the bottom of the station's gravity fall out from beneath him. Since the Imperial House and their allies had lost the civil war, marriages into the Yosan had been strictly controlled. Lesser Houses or old allies could be considered, but the various Great Houses that had been on the winning side, who were those that might become shoguns, had avoided such a taint.

Until now.

Until Jirou Kugosu had only daughters, none of whom could aspire to the Shogunate. Or could they?

Morninghawk had brought home the revolution. Had delivered it to this very doorstep, but done so in a way that Jirou could still retain control, rather than the day it simply overwhelmed all of *Dalou* and swept the Shogunate and the *Hegemony* away before it onto the trash heap of history.

What could they build in a future that was no longer controlled by the past?

"I have three daughters," Jirou said quietly. "A scholar, a warrior, and an artist. What vision did the warrior seek to build?"

"The Shogunate and the Imperial House are separate," Kohahu replied carefully. Almost surgically. "Have remained carefully so for centuries. Tradition. However, we are in an age of breaking with tradition, Father. In a previous era, I could not become Shogun, just as the Crown Prince could not have even asked to become a naval officer outside the Sunflower Palace. Already, new precedents occur, even before *Morninghawk* and Kosnett. What if the Shogunate and the Empire became one again? What if they joined into a new kind of Hegemon?"

He stopped and considered the political ramifications of her plans. Grand. Almost impossibly so.

Then Jirou stopped and studied his middle daughter. She was asking to make a sacrifice that might yet let her transcend whatever he might have planned for her, when several allied Houses had quietly approached him about the future. About her future, as she was the strongest-willed of the three.

"Your opinions of the Crown Prince?" he asked carefully, both as a father and a Shogun.

"Intelligent," Kohahu replied. "Disciplined and committed to doing something more with his life than merely inheriting a cold seat on the surface of a dull planet."

"Sounds familiar," he grinned, watching her blanch, then grin back.

"Past that, how many marriages at that level of power are love matches?" she asked.

"Occasionally, one gets lucky," Jirou replied. "Your mother and I, for one. Emperor Osamu and Empress Aimi as well. But I agree that in both cases, relative strangers ended up being well-matched and able to build something for themselves."

"Thus many things are possible, Father," Kohahu replied. "Even overthrowing centuries of tradition in the guise of forging a new *Dalou Hegemony*. Again, *Morninghawk* shows us the way, with his commitment to excellence and overwhelming loyalty to the Shogunate. Sending *Storm Petrel* and me with Kosnett signals to outsiders as well as the Great Houses that you are serious about a new approach to things. That they should adjust their thinking, and do so immediately. And it allows me a chance to see if such an alliance serves my future needs as well as Kugosu's."

She didn't sound fourteen right now. His own age, perhaps, leavened with a great deal of thought and cynicism about the future.

However, if all options were possible, who was he to prevent her from trying? Ichirou had always been assumed to be the next Shogun. No one had produced concrete evidence of his brother's existence in years.

As long as it stayed that way, Jirou would let him be free. Perhaps Kohahu would as well, but that wasn't a conversation to have today, as Ichirou had sons who might aspire to return from the wilderness and claim that which Jirou had taken from them.

If they could.

He nodded.

"Let us see what Kosnett's news is, first," Jirou told her.

"Then we can figure out a proper response. In the meantime, I will assume you have prepared the research to back up your proposal?"

She nodded carefully.

"Deliver it to me and I will review it after dinner," he continued, rising. "I think we are all done for today."

Tomorrow would be here too soon, anyway.

FIFTY-TWO

Phil had pulled Heather, Harinder, and Markus into his favorite conference room, after confirming the boy still had ten fingers. The two of them had gone over the whole thing last night, then again this morning over breakfast.

A marine stuck his head in the hatch.

"Striker Solo for you, sir," the man said.

Phil nodded. Now the fun began.

Striker Gotzon Danel Solo. Striker was a weird title for a Command Centurion, but went back to when *Ewin* boats were smaller and armed only with missiles. The Striker had been the man who actually launched those missiles. Always men in *Ewin*, just as *Gloran* and *Dalou* for the most part. As technology had made the warships bigger, the title had stuck.

Solo was generally a pleasant person to speak with. Gestured almost continuously when he opened his mouth, but Phil had never had a reason to worry about *Shadowbolt* on his flank, covering things.

At the same time, Solo was something of a *Ewin* aristocrat, and they were as touchy about their personal honor as any of the Fifty Families back home in *Aquitaine*, to say nothing of *Fribourg*.

The man came to attention.

The news wasn't general yet. Would be after this meeting, so he supposed that a sudden messenger from *Meerut*, followed by being ordered to the flagship, might have the man keyed up more than normal.

Twitchy.

"Sit," Phil ordered him. "Relax. We need to pick your brain, Solo."

Confusion, but that was better than other emotions right now.

"A gentleman by the name of Baron Russand attacked *Meerut* last week while we were busy here," Phil began, watching the play of emotions on Solo's face.

"Son of a bitch," Solo said quickly, then panicked a little. "Was it bad, First Centurion?"

"He escaped with his life," Phil said. "Lost better than half his force in the process, though."

The look of utter shock on the Striker's face was both telling and rewarding. He repeated the words silently as Phil watched.

"The Hunter *Pioneer* got away," Phil continued. "The Bombards *Dragonfly* and *Merchant Venture* were captured, as were two of four missiles frigates."

"Casualties on our side, sir?" Solo asked in a tiny voice.

"They launched missile swarms at modern *Aquitaine* warships, Solo," Phil smiled grimly. "Nobody had told them was a waste of time and money that was."

"Oh."

"I had hoped that *Ewin* would behave while I was talking to *Dalou*, Striker," Phil continued. "That the King and his various princes, dukes, and barons weren't stupid enough to try my patience."

"Baron Russand, last I checked, had gone rogue, sir," Solo said now. Carefully. Oh, so carefully. "Not quite in open rebellion to Doysan IV, but close enough. Also, mostly in rebellion to his Duke as well as the Prince of the Eastern Squadron that borders on *Dalou.*"

"Well, *Viking* and friends kicked his ass quite thoroughly, Solo," Phil smiled. "So he might be more willing to return to barracks now. One way or the other."

"Sir?" Solo asked nervously as Phil's voice changed tone.

Phil could see the man's predicament. Solo had been forwarded to this force from *Ewin*'s Central Squadron, what the *RAN* would have called First Fleet. Western, Southern, and Eastern were all smaller Squadrons, broken into fleets and Task Forces that largely had to do with duchies in a manner similar to *Dalou* and *Gloran*. Only the *Aditi Consensus* did it differently, but they were surrounded on all sides and had to maintain their vigilance everywhere.

"I can sail back to *Meerut* and inspect things, Striker Solo," Phil informed the man. "Except that I have an excellent staff, and Barnaby Silver already sent me everything I needed to know in order to plan my next steps. So I think I need to surprise someone."

"What are your orders, First Centurion?" Solo asked, tensing.

He'd hesitated there at the end. Almost called Phil a Prince, which was their term for a First Centurion In Command. The man probably thought he was on shaky ground right now.

Guilt by association, and all that.

"Keep your mouth shut when you get back to *Shadowbolt*," Phil began with a warm smile. "Because my next stop is probably to suddenly drop a major warfleet on top of *Jacoby* and see if Baron Russand is home. And wants to talk instead of just opening fire. I wonder if I should send you directly to *Ewinhome* to talk to the King. To let him know what is coming, so he doesn't think I'm here to overthrow him or something."

"No, sir," Solo said abruptly. "I'm going with you."

"Excuse me, Striker?" Phil demanded, feeling a little hint of rage underneath.

"My orders were to be part of your fleet for the anti-piracy patrols, First Centurion," Solo replied hotly. "Baron Russand is a pirate, by most definitions, so *Shadowbolt* should be there with you. Plus, without *Morninghawk*, you'll need us in the vanguard."

"My corvettes can annihilate any missile swarm that the Baron and his fleet want to throw at us," Phil growled.

"Understood, sir, but this is a political statement," Solo replied. "*Ewin* needs to know that this is a sanctioned invasion. *Shadowbolt* tells them that the King approves."

"And if he doesn't?" Heather suddenly asked, having been so still up until now that it looked like Solo had forgotten her from the way he jumped sideways.

"Then he forgot to tell me something," Solo said, twisting himself around to look at her. "Since Russand attacked *Meerut*, he's declared himself a pirate, and deserves what's coming, sirs."

Phil considered the man. *Shadowbolt* had been solid on the missile flank with *Juvayni*, when he needed *Li Jing* and *Aranyani* on the other side. *Dalou* might be sending more vessels to replace what Phil would lose when *Morninghawk* withdrew to start shaping a new future, but he doubted that *Ewin* was a threat.

They were utterly enamored of ships throwing huge numbers of missiles or launching snubfighters, like the famous *Ishfahan* that had invaded *Thuringwell* with Keller in another life. Or the original Strike Carrier *Auberon*, which was something similar to the Hunter *Pioneer*.

Urumchi was designed to fight *Buran*. *Ewin* didn't stand a chance if they got snotty with him. And he was feeling a little aggrieved right now.

"So I can rely on you to shoot at other *Ewin* ships if it comes to that, Striker?" Phil asked.

That caused the man to pale.

"Rebels and pirates, Solo," Phil amended. "Not Eastern Squadron Task Forces."

"Thank you, sir," Solo sighed. "Absolutely."

Phil considered it. Dropping a load of bricks on an *Ewin* world, even a renegade one, was likely to cause problems. At the same time, *Ewin* was the least well-governed of the six. Five with the Syndicates all coming apart as they retired, sold ships, or ran trying to stay ahead of a law that wasn't as forgiving as the old days.

"Okay, Striker Solo," Phil decided. "When I send a note to the Shogun asking for a full resupply, I'll assume *Shadowbolt* will be sailing with us."

"Thank you, sir."

The man relaxed. Being sent home probably meant that he got cashiered in disgrace, from his reaction. They were a touchy people, but Phil figured that he would need to bloody a few noses to get his point across.

Hopefully, not too many mouths in the process.

"So, Striker, we need to know everything you can tell us about the political, social, and military complications that we're about to face when we sail into *Jacoby* orbit to crack heads together. Can I get you some coffee before we begin?"

The man nodded, and talked. Phil, Harinder, Heather, and Markus listened, occasionally asking questions, but all of it was being recorded and would be added to the encyclopedia that Phil was compiling of life in the Balhee Cluster, both before his arrival as well as after.

There were still a lot of things he needed to get sorted out before he told the First Lord that merchants were safe to call here. At least *Dalou* was moving in the right direction.

Now he just had to deal with *Ewin* next.

Figure out what was going to be the next move in this grand chess game everybody thought he was playing.

Figure out how to win. And how to save the entire Balhee Cluster from itself.

EPILOGUES

FIFTY-THREE
HEAVY ESCORT MORNINGHAWK

Makara, *Lord Morninghawk*, sat on the edge of his bed and studied the woman getting dressed. She was still close enough that he could reach out and touch her. Samnang, *Lady Morninghawk*, though it wasn't fully official yet.

The Emperor had demanded the right to fully invest the two of them, immediately after the Shogun himself officiated at their wedding. As that would take time to organize, everyone was treating it like a done deal already, a whirlwind of motion and activity that sounded more like an *Aditi* vessel or a *Zen-Mekyo* Board of Directors meeting than the *Dalou Hegemony*.

The only downside to date had been their sleeping arrangements. He had a small cabin, because that had been all he ever needed. Samnang had been previously bunked aft, in nicer cabins reserved for the occasional important visitor.

He'd tried sleeping there two nights, but Makara's unconscious mind wouldn't relax, so far from his bridge, even when they were at a safe moorage at *Ellariel*-jo. At the same time, his bed wasn't big enough for two, nor was his cabin, really.

They'd worked out an arrangement. One of them would tuck the other in, occasionally after getting dressed again, and they would sleep separately. Only to wake up early and snuggle again. And maybe fool around some more.

At least he had a private shower. It was too small for the two of them to share, but he could see redesigning whatever flagship he ended up building later, so that they had comfortable space.

"You are daydreaming again," Samnang said abruptly.

She'd finished and he'd moved on from ogling her to staring at the wall, working out electronic blueprints.

"I will miss *Morninghawk*," he said, gesturing to the walls around them. "Lord and Lady Morninghawk will be largely creatures of the ground, rather than terrible privateers and rogues, flying through the spaceways. Even when I have the resources to buy or build new ships, others will command them."

"You should turn this into your private yacht, then," Samnang said. "Do we tear out a few walls, or keep separate bedrooms?"

She was grinning at him. He grinned back. On the one hand, he really didn't know that much about the woman herself. On the other hand, he knew all the important parts.

And she would be there to help, when they began building that most impossible dream.

The Future.

"If I end up with fewer guns and firebirds, I need a smaller crew," Makara replied. "That means more internal volume. On the other hand, we are *Morninghawk*, so the three of us should be prepared at all times to sail into trouble firing. Thus, we should retain everything."

"Will Kosnett sell you Pulse weapons?" Samnang asked. "Or the technology for building our own?"

Makara shrugged. Then realized that she was his other half in all the ways that mattered, and he needed to keep no secrets from the woman.

"I had a conversation with the Shogun, when we were alone," he began, standing now and taking her into his arms.

They were a perfect fit. "Knowing that a thing can be done, he has already ordered scientists to replicate it. *Aquitaine* started with their equivalent of a Point Gun, the thing they called a Type-1 beam. From there, they slowly built up power generators and batteries to handle the Two and the Three."

"Can we do the same with our own Main Guns and Point Guns?" Samnang asked.

"It should be possible," Makara said. He hesitated, then spoke, still getting used to someone who would listen and not scoff at the dreams of a fourth son. "It is the firebird that concerns me."

"How so?" she asked, snuggling her warmth into his chest.

"Pulse weapons render the firebird far less effective, if not nullifying it," Makara replied.

"Doesn't *Aquitaine* have a weapon they call the Bubble Gun?" she pressed. "All that space forward on both *Urumchi* and *Viking* supposedly was a single, terrible weapon system that I seem to recall acted much like a firebird, only faster. Could we reverse engineer something like that to make the firebird act more like an oversized titan bolt?"

Makara flinched. She felt it, but that was okay. He didn't need to keep secrets from her.

"Direct-fire a firebird, instead of using it as a psychological tool?" he gasped.

"Worse, what if we could somehow flip a switch just before firing it, to give you two firing modes?" she asked with the most evil grin he thought he'd ever seen. "Keep *Ewin* honest, and let us saturate him with shrikes if he gets close or fires heavier missiles at us. Plus either punch him in the face with a condor or let it attack him like a mastiff."

"The Shogun has tasked us with inventing the future of *Dalou*," Makara said. "Us. I can see that we need to consider founding a university dedicated to sciences at *Urwel*, as well as a school for diplomats."

"Is that possible?" she gasped in turn.

"Even Komyo have planetary-scale budgets, dear one," he smiled down at her. "Colonists will need schools, towns, and other things. *Aquitaine* has what they call a Land Grant University model, where the state gives land, and the school is expected to train a significant number of men and women for military service. If we used the *Aquitaine* model exactly, we would of course train women. Not many would come, at least initially, but some."

"Oh, Makara, you have no idea," she laughed.

"No?"

"Noble ladies will not come, no," she agreed. "I was not born of a House. I had to become a bureaucrat and rise on my own merits, to the point that the Shogun tasked me with investigating a dangerous radical with curious ties to alien fleets."

They both laughed at that.

"But if we open the door to daughters of the middle classes…" she mused. "Women who might otherwise only have a hope of being married to a distaff branch of a minor house, that their grandchildren might move up."

"Warrior women in training?" he asked.

"Captains of *Morninghawk* warships, my dread Lord," she grinned wickedly. "Worse, we might invite *Aditi* and *Aquitaine* women to train us."

He paused, seeing the shape of the thing she was describing.

"Are you okay?" Samnang asked, suddenly concerned.

"Fine," he replied automatically. "If we are shaping the future of *Dalou*, of course the others will wish to see what form it will take. Perhaps even have a hand in shaping it, because those two already treat women as equals, while the rest of us poor barbarians have yet to learn. Could we entice *Yaumgan* to help?"

It was her turn to shiver. Kosnett had forged a strange if powerful connection, both through *Li Jing* and Captain Xue, as well as *Zhang Guolao* and Captain Lin, who had struck Makara as far too young to be in command of one of the Eight Immortals of the *Yaumgan* fleet.

"We can try," Samnang whispered. "What is the worst thing they could do? Refuse?"

"No, dearest," Makara joined her in shivering. "They might accept."

FIFTY-FOUR

Phil studied the big projection from his chair opposite Harinder. The flag staff was all on duty here, like a battle was imminent, but Phil knew better. Everyone wanted to see how the newcomers settled.

The Escort *Forktail*, commanded by Captain Tahn Sugawara, was a lighter ship than *Morninghawk*, but one designed for the *Ewin* frontier. Instead of one Falcon and four lighter shrikes as firebirds, *Forktail* lost two shrikes for an extra Main Gun and a pair of Point Guns. More effective against missiles and better shielding.

Storm Petrel was another squadron flagship like *Wraithruin*. Condor on the bow, falcons and shrikes on the engine pylons. Space inside for Ambassadors, in this case Lady Kugosu and a small personal staff.

Phil found it interesting that they'd chosen that particular ship. It had more of a reputation as a pretty ship than a junkyard dog. Education for important young men, evidenced by the fact that Crown Prince Shingo was aboard as a Trainee Officer. What *Aquitaine* would have called a Cornet on the way to becoming a proper Centurion back home.

Still, Phil had a whole squadron of warships around him,

even if he was currently down to only four of his corvettes. *Aranyani*, *Li Jing*, and *Juvayni* were there. Phil suspected that they might mutiny if he ordered any of them not to join him in sailing into *Ewin Principality* space and seeing if everyone wanted to behave.

As with *Dalou* and *Ellariel*, few outsiders had been allowed to visit any *Ewin* worlds. Phil supposed that he would have to go to *Ewinhome* eventually, but *Jacoby* came first. Let *Aquitaine* settle a rebel Baron and see what the King of *Ewin* had to say about it.

Eventually, *Ewin* would have to give up using missiles as a primary weapon. They were secondary for *Gloran*, and *Aditi* only sparingly used them. *Dalou* and *Yaumgan* not at all.

Pulse weaponry from *Aquitaine* would eliminate such things as threats, unless someone found a copy of Lady Moirrey's *Mischief* file, the early stuff where she'd gone a little crazy with missiles and mines, until Yan Bedrov had put his foot down.

Expeditionary-class ships didn't need long logistics trains of missiles and primaries. They had beams in many sizes, so all that extra cargo space on the Fast Clippers could be dedicated to replacement parts that didn't wear out as fast.

And food.

There were no long sails in the Balhee Cluster.

Sailing those sorts of distances were what retired Command Centurion Tomas Kigali used to be known for.

Phil wondered if the old man would just show up at *Vilahana*, one of these days, having come direct from *Petron* or maybe *Trusski*. Something for the record books. Just to remind people that he was always the best.

"We ready?" Phil asked, glancing over at where Harinder was smiling at him.

She was used to him by now. Knew his moods and foibles. Starting a new adventure was always a time for introspection. Drawing a line in the sand.

Writing letters to Casey *zu* Weigand, *RAN retired*, telling her the things he'd seen. Things that didn't necessarily need to go into the official reports to First Lord back home. Petia Naoumov was many things, but a poet and artist didn't make the top ten.

"All ships are on circuit, on hold," Harinder replied with a wry grin.

Phil checked the plot again. Without *Viking* he had five cruisers and five escorts accompanying him on this next leg of the journey. He found the symmetry pleasing.

"All vessels, this is Kosnett, aboard *Urumchi*. I have the flag," he announced in a formal, heavy voice. Like they were poised at the start of the next chapter. The next story. "*Forktail*, come to zero-one-zero from your current heading and begin accelerating. All other vessels form up in three lines astern, with *Shadowbolt* trailing *Forktail* and *Urumchi* trailing *Shadowbolt*."

He paused and watched everyone start maneuvering. His corvettes were sharp, but they were among the best he'd been able to hire, and had trained together for years now. *Forktail* was a stranger, but handled his orders well, Captain Sugawara perhaps understanding that he would have the honor of leading, and that Lord Sugawara would be pleased. *Shadowbolt*, true to Striker Solo's demands, would lead the big ships into *Jacoby*'s harbor so Phil could *have a chat* with the locals.

The rest of the force were to ensure that Baron Russand listened. At least eventually.

First Centurion Philip S. Kosnett was still technically invading a foreign nation with a battle fleet sufficient to probably annihilate anything he encountered until he got to a major Squadron base. And if he went back to *Meerut* for *Viking*, his other two corvettes, and the bulk of the pirates, even the Central Squadron at *Ewinhome* might be in trouble.

Hopefully, everyone would understand that and behave. Duels like *Ewin* tended to fight, on the ground with slugthrowing pistols, were for amateurs and fools. *Aditi* was tugging at the reins to enter a new future. *Dalou* sluggishly accompanied them, but Makara Omarov had shared with Phil his fear and image of an avalanche, and how he was planning to spend the next ten years getting ahead of it and trying to build the kinds of political and social structures that could withstand such a thing.

Phil's latest messages home to Fleet HQ had asked for some folks from the Academy, to be seconded to *Urwel* to help create something modern here. They hadn't been at *Ellariel*-jo long enough, so Phil had also requested that the Shogun send a team of warriors and bodyguards with him, that Xochitl Dar could start training them in her ways, just as *Stunt Dude* and others would learn the ways of the blade from them.

The ships were coming into sailing formation. Three lines of two on a plane, with the four corvettes in a diamond around them, and *Forktail* out front. Harinder nodded. Heather's image did the same.

"All vessels, stand by to jump," Phil said. "We will rendezvous in two days at Forward Waypoint Marie. And then on to *Jacoby*. *Forktail*, as you bear."

Phil found himself looking forward to what he might accomplish at *Ewin*. *Dalou* had managed to hold it together so far in the face of everything.

Did he dare dream that they all might?

Be sure to read the next books in the First Centurion Phil Kosnett series!

Encounter at Vilahana
Consensus at Aditi
Hegemony at Dalou
Princes at Ewin

Available at your favorite retailers!

ABOUT THE AUTHOR

Blaze Ward writes science fiction in the Alexandria Station universe (Jessica Keller, The Science Officer, The Story Road, etc.) as well as several other science fiction universes, such as Star Dragon, the Dominion, and more. He also writes odd bits of high fantasy with swords and orcs. In addition, he is the Editor and Publisher of *Boundary Shock Quarterly Magazine*. You can find out more at his website www.blazeward.com, as well as Facebook, Goodreads, and other places.

Blaze's works are available as ebooks, paper, and audio, and can be found at a variety of online vendors. His newsletter comes out regularly, and you can also follow his blog on his website. He really enjoys interacting with fans, and looks forward to any and all questions—even ones about his books!

Never miss a release!
If you'd like to be notified of new releases, sign up for my newsletter.

http://www.blazeward.com/newsletter/

Buy More!
Did you know that you can buy directly from my website?

https://www.blazeward.com/shop/

Connect with Blaze!

Web: www.blazeward.com
Boundary Shock Quarterly (BSQ):
https://www.boundaryshockquarterly.com/

ABOUT KNOTTED ROAD PRESS

Knotted Road Press fiction specializes in dynamic writing set in mysterious, exotic locations.

Knotted Road Press non–fiction publishes autobiographies, business books, cookbooks, and how–to books with unique voices.

Knotted Road Press creates DRM–free ebooks as well as high–quality print books for readers around the world.

With authors in a variety of genres including literary, poetry, mystery, fantasy, and science fiction, Knotted Road Press has something for everyone.

Knotted Road Press
www.KnottedRoadPress.com